PRAISE
for the
RED HAND ADVENTURES

"O'Neill has an eye for detail, atmosphere, and action...this is a rousing period piece that ends on a cliffhanger."

—*Publishers Weekly*

"Whether intended for a YA or adult audience, this is a book the entire family can enjoy reading...The book reads like a Boy's Own adventure and is filled with action involving bandits, pirates and rebels, reminding the reader of such grand entertainments as Rudyard Kipling's *Kim*, Michael Chabon's *Gentlemen of the Road* and John Milius' *The Wind and the Lion*...Four Stars."

—Kenneth Salikof for *IndieReader*

"Debut author O'Neill incorporates a great deal of cultural and historical context in his story...and will make the readers feel as though they have traveled back in time and fallen into that world. An exciting, exotic tale...The cliffhanger ending all but demands that readers jump to the next installment of the series."

—*Kirkus Reviews*

"Block out the next few hours, because you won't want to put this book down!"

—Kevin Max, Founder and Editor, *1859 Oregon's Magazine*

The
RED HAND ADVENTURES

Rebels of the Kasbah
BOOK I

Wrath of the Caid
BOOK II

Legends of the Rif
BOOK III

MORE PRAISE
for the
RED HAND ADVENTURES

Selection for the National Battle of the Books Contest
(Rebels of the Kasbah)

Selected as a *Publisher's Weekly* indie select book
(Rebels of the Kasbah)

Silver Medal Winner for the Mom's Choice Award
(Rebels of the Kasbah)

Bronze Medal Winner for Best Book Series—Fiction
in the Moonbeam Children's Book Awards
(Red Hand Adventures)

Gold Medal Winner of the Independent
Book Publisher's Living Now Award
(Wrath of the Caid)

Black Ship

PUBLISHING

Adventure Novels with a Shot of Wry

EX LIBRIS

The
RED HAND ADVENTURES

BOOK I

Rebels of the Kasbah

JOE O'NEILL

Rebels of the Kasbah

COPYRIGHT © 2012 BY JOE O'NEILL
Cover Art and Design by Kristin Myrdahl
Graphic Design by Anna Fonnier
Edited by Sara Addicott
Copy Edited by Bedelia Walton
www.RedHandAdventures.com

Black Ship

PUBLISHING

ISBN 978-0-9851969-4-3

For my lovely wife Kristin, my late mother Kerry,
and all my friends and family

SPECIAL THANKS

To Kristin, for her tireless assistance and work designing the cover and creating the beautiful maps. Further thanks to my editor, Bedelia Walton, for her dedication and long hours working on the manuscript. In addition, I want to thank Terese Roeseler, Levi Roeseler, Trey Roeseler, Toto Van Son, Sarah Van Son, Nancy Fischer, Anna Fonnier, and Val Vanderpool for the help they provided on so many levels. Writing this book has been a wonderful experience, and I am grateful for the constant encouragement and support you have all given me. Thank you!

—Joe O'Neill

JOIN THE RED HAND!

The Red Hand isn't just about reading books,
but also having a sense of adventure,
being curious about the world, where we've been,
and how we've gotten here.

It's giving back to those less fortunate and
having a sense of justice in our everyday life.

At Red Hand we are constantly holding writing contests;
trivia contests; sponsoring sports teams
(such as soccer and others);
teaching new adventure skills, and much, much more.

In addition, you'll be privy to new books and
other cool stuff before the general public.

To join The Red Hand, please go to
www.RedHandAdventures.com

I will remember what I was, I am sick of rope and chains -
I will remember my old strength and all my forest affairs.
I will not sell my back to man for a bundle of sugar cane;
I will go out to my own kind, and the wood-folk in their lairs.
I will go out until the day, until the morning break -
Out to the wind's untainted kiss, the water's clean caress;
I will forget my ankle-ring and snap my picket stake.
I will revisit my lost love and playmates masterless!

—Rudyard Kipling
The Jungle Book

Do not be fooled by windows.
Even the good ones offer limited views.
Instead, see the world in its proper perspective.
Spin a globe and land where you will.
Discover a place. Remember a place you have never been.
People & places, future & past. Ideas. History. Customs. Borders. Mysteries.

It's good to wonder.

1 2 3 4 5 6 7 8 9 10 11 12 13 14 15 16 17

A B C D E F G H I J K L M N O P Q

ARCTIC OCEAN

EUROPE

ASIA

PACIFIC OCEAN

AFRICA

INDIAN OCEAN

ATLANTIC OCEAN

AUSTRALIA

ANTARCTIC OCEAN

C5. LONDON, ENG.	F13. JIANGSU
E6.5. OTTOMAN	F13. SHANGHAI
E3. MOROCCO	

TABLE OF CONTENTS

CAST OF CHARACTERS

Tariq (tah-reek): An orphan street kid in Tangier, Morocco

Fez: From a Berber tribe in Morocco

Aseem (ah-seem): From Africa

Margaret Owen: An English girl

Mister LaRoque (la-rohk): A shadowy French underground figure

Aji (ah-jee): Tariq's best friend on the streets of Tangier

Sanaa (sah-nah): A beautiful Moroccan assassin; part of the resistance

Malik (ma-leek): A respected tribal leader; part of the resistance

Zijuan (zee-wan): A gifted Chinese woman and sage martial artist; has an orphanage

Jawad (juh-wad): A slave and camel jockey; longs to be a leader in the Caid's kasbah

Charles Owen: From England, decorated colonel in the British army; father to Margaret and David

Louise Owen: From England, devoted wife to Charles; mother to Margaret and David

Captain Basil: An Algerian trade merchant turned rogue pirate

Lieutenant Dreyfuss: A corrupt lieutenant in the British navy

Caid Ali Tamzali: An evil warlord; feared ruler of the Rif Mountains in Morocco, the kasbah is his castle

Note: For definition in this series, a Caid (k+aid) is a warlord in Morocco who answers only to the Sultan, the sovereign ruler of Morocco. He controls his own territory, but pays taxes and owes all allegiance to the Sultan. However, a more common definition of a Caid is a Muslim or Berber chieftain, who may be a tribal chief, judge, or senior officer.

Rebels of the Kasbah

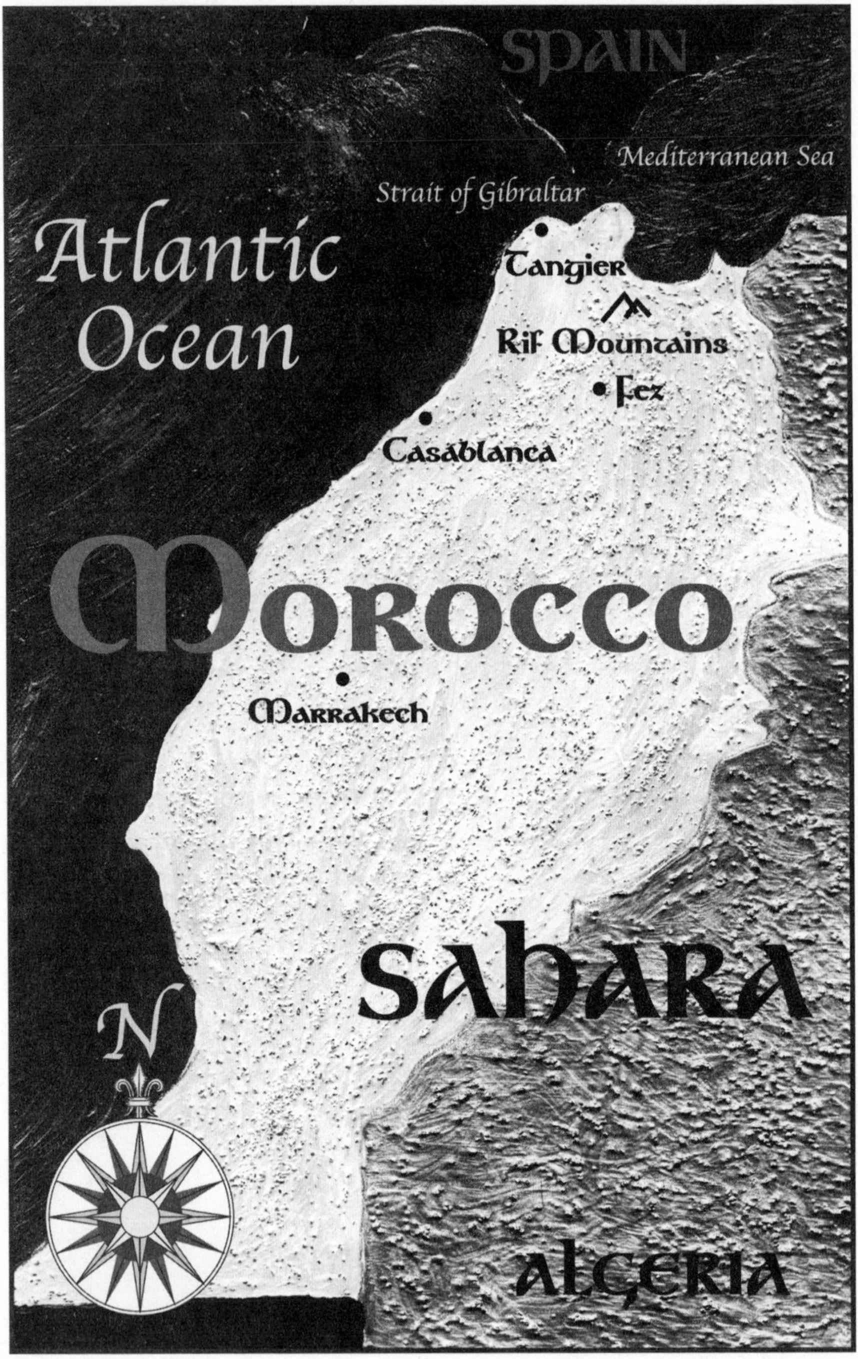
Spain
Mediterranean Sea
Strait of Gibraltar
Atlantic Ocean
Tangier
Rif Mountains
Fez
Casablanca
Morocco
Marrakech
Sahara
N
Algeria

CHAPTER
— *I* —

1912 MOROCCO

Morocco is located in northernmost Africa and separated from Europe by just fifteen miles of ocean called The Strait of Gibraltar. At the turn of the twentieth century, Morocco was a wild and lawless country ruled by tribal warlords, desperate bandits, marauding pirates, heartless politicians, and wandering nomads.

To complicate matters even further, England, France, and Germany—the whole of the European powers—sat watching Morocco like three cats eyeing a mouse, waiting for the opportune moment to pounce. Each country wanted the country as their own prize, and they were prepared to invade and attack at any moment.

Morocco in 1912 was a dangerous and desperate country. A country with an uncertain future on the brink of war.

CHAPTER
— 2 —

SLAVE AUCTION

The boy slowly opened his eyes. He wiggled his toes and fingers, and lifted his head. Overcome with dizziness, he set his head back down on what felt like straw. He was about twelve or thirteen years of age. His black hair fell halfway down his neck and seemed to have been cut with a rusty knife rather than the expert touch of a barber's hand. His skin was olive-colored and his face was lean and hungry. His eyes had a wild quality about them, and gave him the appearance of a boy who had known few peaceful nights. There was an indomitable fierceness about him.

"Be careful, my friend. You have had quite a blow," said an unfamiliar voice.

Suddenly, a face appeared over him. It was the face of a boy who looked to be about his own age. The boy's skin was midnight black and his hair was cut quite short, almost to the scalp. He was handsome, with a square and solid jaw and bright, inquisitive eyes. Already, muscles had formed around his shoulders and neck. He, too, had the look of a warrior.

"Where am I?" the boy asked.

"You are in a place that God cannot see. Because God would never let a place such as this exist," replied the black boy.

At that, the boy used all his energy to lift himself up, and sat leaning against a concrete wall. He noticed a stench—a foul mixture of rotten meat, urine, and feces. The room was completely dark, except for small windows on each wall where sunlight peeked in. Thick iron bars sealed the windows. The room was medium-to-large in size, perhaps thirty feet by thirty feet. Two wooden buckets had been placed in the middle of the floor, which was covered with straw. He saw other children sitting around the room, some looked to be younger than five years of age, but none seemed older than thirteen or fourteen. There was a mix of girls and boys in the room, a rarity in a Muslim culture. None of the children

3

cried. They sat huddled up with one another against the walls. The older ones comforted the young ones.

"Who are you?" asked the boy.

"My name is Aseem. I have been in this place for three days. You arrived about six hours ago." He knelt beside the boy. "That is a nasty welt on your head."

The boy felt his forehead and discovered a bump the size of an egg, about four inches above his right eye, along his hairline. His hand fell to his cheek, where he felt the residue of what must surely have been dried blood that had dripped down his face.

"I do not remember much. A man grabbed me from my bed. I tried to fight him. That is all I know."

"What is your name?" asked Aseem.

"My name is Tariq. I come from an orphanage in Tangier."

"An orphan? Many here are orphans. I am from a tribe a long way away."

"Were you kidnapped like me?"

"No. My father sold me to the local slave trader to settle a debt. It had been two dry seasons. My father is a farmer and there had not been enough crops. Being the youngest of seven, I was chosen."

"How could your father do such a thing?" asked Tariq.

"When the day came for me to leave, he looked at me with tears in his eyes and explained to me that in order to save my mother and my brothers and sisters, he had to make a sacrifice. It was the only time I have seen my father cry," said Aseem, who then shrugged. "So, I am resigned to my fate of being a slave."

"Is that what this is?"

"Yes. It is a slave pit. We are waiting to be sold."

"Sold to whom?" Tariq asked.

"I do not know."

Suddenly the door opened and a huge man entered. Standing maybe six-foot-three, about two hundred and fifty pounds, the man had large, muscular arms and carried a whip. His head was bald and a bushy black beard covered his square face. His eyes were dark and sinister-looking. Anger emanated from his very soul.

"Okay. When I point to you, you will go out this door, walk to the end of the hall, and wait for me. Do you understand?" he roared.

Suddenly, a girl of about thirteen years of age cried out. "Mister, please! This is a mistake! I'm not supposed to be here. I was at a hotel in Tangier." Her most distinguishing characteristics were her perfect English and her white skin. Every other child was of either African or Arab descent.

The man towered over her. "There is no mistake. Caucasian girls fetch the highest price. Ha!"

The girl burst into tears and, in a panic-filled moment, tried to run out the door. The man caught her with one hand and, in a single gesture, threw her against a stone wall, five feet away. She let out a shriek and curled into a ball. Her muffled cries echoed off the walls.

The man walked around the room and began pointing. One, two, three, four...until one after the other, the children got up and ran through the door and down the hallway. As the man came up to Tariq and Aseem, he pointed to them both. They rose and ran out of the room together, as instructed. Two other boys joined them. In line, all the children looked at one other. Everyone was between the ages of ten and thirteen, and all were obviously very scared. A few held hands. Although most were orphan boys who had been toughened by life on the streets, their fear was palpable. They waited like frightened innocents about to be executed.

"Okay. Walk out this door and do exactly as you are told," the man yelled at them.

The door opened, and the boys—all quite thin and dressed mostly in rags—walked through in a single-file line. The children entered a large, dirty, circular space, which was enclosed by stands of Arab men. There were dozens and dozens of these men, all dressed in traditional robes, smoking hookahs, chatting incessantly, eating figs and flatbread, and drinking mint tea. The boys were instructed to stand in the center of the ring.

A man in a black robe followed the children into the ring. All chatting lowered to a murmur as he commanded the crowd's attention.

"Gentlemen, I have for you a stock of exquisite slaves. These boys will ride and die for you. They are tough boys, of the right age and weight."

"Have them show us their spirit!" called out someone from the crowd.

"Yes! Put them to the test!" another cried.

"Okay, okay."

The man looked at the children. He had old, wrinkled brown skin and a long, skinny gray moustache. Bags sagged beneath his eyes.

"Slaves, when I say 'go' I want each of you to run to that rope right there and climb to the top. The first one to the top wins. The last one will get whipped. Do you understand?"

The children looked at him and then at a rope suspended from the ceiling. The rope hung directly to their right and was about thirty feet in height.

"Okay, then." And, with little time for the boys to ready themselves, the man's big voice commanded, "GO!"

Stunned, none of the children moved. Most of them just stared blankly at the man. A couple of them cried. A few were completely paralyzed with fear.

The large, muscled man who had led them into the ring was furious. "You heard him. Now, go!" And, with that, he cracked his whip, the tip of which hit a small boy on his back. The child let out a cry, terrifying all the other children. A second flick of the whip snapped over their heads. After that, slowly, the group of boys made their way to the rope and a few began to climb, cautiously.

"No! Faster!" the old, black-robed man shouted. "The first one to reach the top wins! This is a competition, you little idiots."

The boys quickly understood and soon began to claw at each other to get to the rope. The leader was yanked down to the sand. Another was taken down by his neck. The area around base of the rope turned into a melee of small limbs and bodies. The crowd yelled in appreciation of the struggle.

Tariq, still dizzy, wasn't making much progress. Boys kept tugging at him and pushing him down. He sensed defeat. But when he looked over to his right, he saw his new friend.

"Tariq," shouted Aseem, "if we work together, we can do this. Are you with me?"

Tariq felt a sudden surge of encouragement. "Yes!"

"Okay, follow me."

Aseem grabbed the boy next in line, who was trying to climb up, and yanked him down by his forearm. With his other arm, he grabbed Tariq's hand and guided him to the rope. Not letting go of Aseem's hand, Tariq placed his right foot on another smaller boy's head and thrust himself upon the rope. Once he had secured a place, Tariq pulled Aseem up. A couple of boys grabbed at Aseem's legs, but the firm grasp of Tariq's hand kept him from falling. He kicked at the boys below them until they let go.

The two boys, now about eight feet off the ground, began scaling the rope. It was a thick, knotted rope that burned their skin. Tariq let out a yelp when his lost his footing and skidded down; a long rope burn etched into his calf.

"Keep going, Tariq," encouraged Aseem. "We're almost there!"

The boys kept climbing until, about five feet from the top, Tariq felt a hand grab his foot. He looked down and saw a rough-looking boy with long brown hair, a dirty face, and murder in his eyes.

"Let go!" ordered Tariq.

"No!" the boy yelled back.

"Let go, or I'll kick you," warned Tariq.

"Go ahead!"

Tariq looked at the boy. He didn't want to kick him, but he understood that he must. Life at the orphanage had taught him well. When older boys had tried to steal his food, he learned he had to stand up to them even though they were usually bigger and stronger. If he hadn't done so, he would have been seen as a victim and a target for constant bullying. Tariq had been in many fights, even a few with a knife. Over time, he gained respect in the orphanage and even the older boys left him alone. He remembered the first law of the streets: *never, ever back down from anyone.*

Tariq took one last look at the boy and quickly performed a scissor kick. It was a move that he had perfected playing futbol (soccer). Shifting all of his weight to his opposite leg and letting it fly, his shin caught the boy squarely in the face, knocking him back and off the rope. The boy fell twenty feet to the sand, landing on his back with an audible "oomph." The wind knocked out of him, the boy gasped for air as panic filled his face.

"Did you see that?" asked one of the Arab buyers.

"That boy has spirit," said another, loudly, in agreement.

Aseem and Tariq continued to the top of the rope. As a gracious sign of team sportsmanship, Tariq allowed Aseem to touch the ceiling first. Aseem had helped him, and Tariq never forgot a friend.

They looked down at the other boys still climbing beneath them. A couple had given up or fallen and were now lying in the sand next to the boy Tariq had kicked off. Aseem and Tariq waited for the rest of the boys climbing the rope to reach them at the top, and then they all slowly returned to the bottom in a systematic order. The mayhem of the scramble up was now replaced with the civility of the descent.

The boys returned to a single-file line. Some were dirty, and most were scraped up, with scratches of blood etched into their skin. Tariq was breathing heavily.

"Okay, the bidding will commence," said the black-robed man, obviously the auctioneer. With this, he pointed to Aseem.

"How about this one? He was the winner, after all. A fine specimen, with natural agility."

"One thousand," a man yelled.

"Eleven hundred," followed another.

"I will pay one thousand five hundred."

"Sixteen hundred."

"Two thousand," a voice yelled out, above the shouted bids of the others.

"We have two thousand! Going once, going twice…sold to the family of Caid Ali Tamzali!"

The trade continued until, oddly, all the boys were sold except for Tariq. Some went for five hundred and others for quite a bit more. Those who had quit at the rope sold for less, while the stronger and more aggressive boys sold for much more.

Tariq stood by himself, obviously self-conscious and worried.

"Okay, we are now down to the last slave, who, if you'll recall, actually placed second. Who will start the bidding?"

"Fifteen hundred," shouted a voice.

"Sixteen hundred."

"Eighteen hundred."

"Two thousand."

"Two thousand two hundred," the initial bidding voice said.

"Two thousand two hundred going once, going twice…sold! Again, to the family of Caid Ali Tamzali," announced the man in the black robe.

As fate would have it, Aseem and Tariq had been sold to the same family. And because of their skill, they also fetched the highest prices of the night.

The two boys were shuffled off into a separate room. Once there, they were told to sit down by the large, bearded guard. All of the other boys who had been sold were also in the room, but seated at different benches. The guard placed shackles of steel chain around each boy's wrists and ankles. As the guard did so, the black-robed auctioneer entered the room, with the group of Arab buyers following behind him. One by one, they paid the auctioneer in cash and left with their new slaves. Finally, the auctioneer stopped in front of Aseem and Tariq.

"Okay, four thousand two hundred for the pair—a good deal. I think you've got the best jockeys in the crop," said the auctioneer.

"I should hope so, for the sum we paid," a fat and round man replied. He sweated profusely through his white scarf. Another man stood beside him. A tall, Caucasian man dressed in a western-style business suit.

The fat man handed an envelope to the auctioneer and another to the white man.

"This settles our business here," said the fat man.

The white man bowed his head slightly, and then quickly left the room. The auctioneer went along with the other Arabs and their slaves.

"Okay, you two. My name is Zahir. I am now your master and owner. Do as I say. Any disobedience or any attempt to escape will be met with my whip. Do you understand?" asked the sweaty, fat man named Zahir.

"Yes," both Aseem and Tariq replied.

"Good. Follow me," ordered Zahir.

The two boys slowly made their way behind Zahir, struggling with the weight of their new shackles and the awkwardness of walking with chains around their ankles. He took them outside to a wagon drawn by camels. He ordered them to sit in the back and tied them both to a rail on the side of the wagon.

"No funny business. There are three days of desert in any direction. Do not think of escaping—you would die and get eaten by the buzzards. Besides, where I'm taking you is like a fun playground. Okay?" Zahir laughed and walked away.

The boys looked at each other. The wagon was uncovered and the hot Saharan sun beat down on them. It was perhaps a hundred and ten degrees.

Tariq surveyed the surroundings. They were in some kind of caravan. Their wagon sat adjacent to the main building, which had held the slave auction. The building stood alone, with dozens of tents poking up around its perimeter. Tariq looked closer at the tents, and the people milling about and buying.

"This is some kind of black market. Look, that man over there is selling guns. Another over there is selling snakes."

"Do you see a way to escape?" asked Aseem.

"Perhaps, but getting out of these chains will take some doing. The lock looks easy enough to pick, if I had something to pick it with."

"You can pick locks?"

"On the streets of Tangier, one learns many useful tricks to survive."

Aseem watched Tariq as he tried and failed to wiggle out of his arm shackles. They were just too tight. Aseem surveyed the surrounding landscape and looked up at the mountains that lay directly before them.

"When I was taken from my village, they brought me here by wagon. I tried to track the distance in my head as we went along. I believe we headed south and then west, but I do not know this area."

Tariq nodded in agreement, and gave up trying to free his wrists.

"When I turned thirteen, my father had me live by myself in the mountains for seven days," said Aseem. "All he gave me was a knife for survival. He gave me one piece of advice, which was to always think before doing. In the wilderness, small mistakes can mean the difference between life and death. Not watching your footsteps and stepping on a loose rock can twist an ankle. Being frivolous with food and water can mean dehydration or hunger. The lesson was to always think before moving and to be aware of your surroundings."

"And, what do you think of our surroundings now?" Tariq asked.

"I think we are in a great deal of danger. I think we were purchased with the intention that we would die, and die quickly. I also think that you and I might have only one opportunity for escape, and we do not want to squander it. Any attempt to escape would only draw attention to ourselves, and would be punishable by death, so we must be sure that if we attempt it, we succeed."

"Why do you think we are in danger?" Tariq asked.

"That man in the black robe. He said that we will 'ride and die' for their pleasure. I am not sure what that means, but it cannot be good."

Tariq looked at Aseem and then at the sun overhead.

"I agree with you. The chances of escape are slim. We cannot hide and we cannot run. But I do not plan on dying for the amusement of these people."

"Neither do I," agreed Aseem.

"Okay, then. At our earliest opportunity, we will escape. I will look out for your back if you look out for mine." Tariq stuck out his hand as an offer of friendship.

"Tariq, I think that relying on each other is the only chance we have for survival. We have a saying in my tribe, 'The pack is always stronger than the lone wolf.'"

They shook hands and even managed a little smile.

The two boys sat in the wagon for two full hours under the hot sun. They barely spoke, but both managed to get in a fitful nap as flies buzzed around them. Tariq's lips felt chapped and dry. He was thirsty and very hungry. He could smell something delicious. As he looked about, his eyes came upon a tent; there, framed in the doorway, he could see some men eating lamb kabob and couscous. The aroma of the grilled meat filled the air, making his stomach pains even worse.

Finally, their new master, Zahir, came out of the building with two more slaves in tow—the white girl, who had earlier caused such a commotion, and a small, impish boy of about eleven or twelve. The boy wore round, tortoise-shell glasses. Zahir brought them to the back of the wagon, and shackled them in next to Aseem and Tariq. The two new slaves said nothing.

Zahir shouted to an older man, whom they hadn't yet noticed. "Shatam, cover this wagon, and get these slaves some food and water. I have to settle a few things. We leave in half an hour."

Old Shatam, obviously a slave himself, bowed slightly and went about covering the wagon with a light red fabric that, although thin, offered a great deal of shade. Next, he brought over a jug of water and a plate of hummus, pita bread, and dolmas. He said nothing to the children.

The four young captives began to eat and drink. All were famished and suffering from dehydration. There was really only enough food for two, and it was quickly devoured. They drank half the water and the three boys agreed it best to conserve and ration the rest for the journey ahead.

"What is your name?" Tariq asked the little boy.

"Fez."

"Where do you come from, Fez?"

"A small village. Our tribe was moving to a new location when we were ambushed by bandits. They killed my entire family. I was spared and sold to this place," he said softly, looking at the floor in the front of him.

"I am sorry, Fez. My name is Tariq and this is Aseem. We will look after you, okay?"

Fez didn't seem inspired by these words of kindness. He nodded solemnly and continued to stare at the ground.

"That man they call Zahir, he is the man who massacred my family and my people," Fez said sadly.

None of the other children knew what to say to this. They all looked at Fez with a mixture of fear, shock, and sorrow on their faces.

"He killed your family?" Tariq asked.

"Yes. In the mountains, he ambushed our entire village and slaughtered everyone but the children, who were spared only to be sold as slaves," Fez said, as a few tears ran down his cheeks. He was such a small boy, and so studious in his glasses, that watching him cry was painful for the other children.

The girl, who none of them knew, slid over and hugged Fez; he buried himself deep in her embrace. It was the first human contact he'd had since he'd watched Zahir butcher his mother and father. She patted his head and whispered to him that he would be okay.

Aseem turned to the girl. "What about you? What is your name?"

"I don't think she speaks Arabic," Tariq mentioned.

The girl's dried tears smudged the dirt that was now caked onto her face. Her dress, once probably quite nice, was ruined with dirt and looked as if she had been wearing it for days. Her blond hair fell halfway to her shoulders.

"I speak Arabic. I lived in Cairo as a child," she whispered.

The three boys stared at her, as none of them had ever seen a white girl before, and they weren't quite sure what to do.

"Where are you from?" Aseem asked.

The girl ignored his question.

"They said that white girls bring the highest price and the most pleasure in the harem. Do you know what that means?"

She hugged Fez one last time and, when he smiled up at her, she let him out of her embrace.

Aseem just looked at her, blankly.

"They said if I didn't do as I was told, they would hold a hot iron to my face and brand me for life. Then I would be ugly. An outcast."

Before she could say any more, Zahir appeared.

"Listen. We have one week's journey ahead of us. We stop every two hours to go to the toilet. You will eat once a day. If you try to escape, your hands will be tied and you will be forced to walk behind the wagon. Do you understand?" asked Zahir.

Everyone nodded slightly.

"Where are we going?" asked Tariq.

"You have been sold to Caid Ali Tamzali. You are his property now and will be for the rest of your miserable lives. For some of you, this may not be for more than a few weeks; for others, perhaps fifty years or more. Let go of any memory of your past life. It no longer exists. You are slaves now," he said and walked away.

The wagon began to move. It was the last in a caravan of seven wagons and various camels. Slowly, the caravan moved away from the trading post and into the Sahara desert. The children watched the building slowly retreat into the distance, until it was a just a speck on the horizon. They did not talk for a long time.

Finally, Aseem spoke up.

"You did not tell us your name," he noted, addressing the girl.

"My name is Margaret Owen. My family was vacationing here in Morocco from England. I grew up in London," she said softly.

"It is good to meet you, Margaret. Do not worry about what Zahir said. There is always a way out," assured Aseem.

"How?"

"I do not know at the moment. But I do know that I am not destined to be a slave and neither are you. You are much too pretty and proper. Tariq and I are already planning an escape."

"What escape?" she asked.

"We are working on a plan. Until we have one, please do not worry. Like I told little Fez over there—we will take care of you."

Margaret smiled at this kind gesture—a young boy promising to take care of her. Imagine! She didn't want to seem rude, but she had little faith that those two boys—both likely younger than she was—could do anything to help her escape. She didn't know what to think. Only two days ago, she had been in the comfort of her family in one of Morocco's finest hotels. Now, she was tied up in a wagon as a slave. She felt like crying, but she didn't seem to have any tears.

The sun began to fade in the distance, giving way to the stars and the heavens above. The temperature dropped considerably in the desert at night, so the four new friends huddled together in the wagon for warmth as they waited for morning.

CHAPTER
— 3 —

PIRATES

The *Dove* measured thirty-six feet in length, with fast, slick lines made for racing. She was built in 1904 and made completely of fir and teak. She cut through the Mediterranean Sea with veracity and the grace of a gull gliding along the wind.

Above, the skies were blue with just a hint of clouds on the horizon. The wind buzzed just short of twelve knots. It was, in other words, a perfect day—just meant to be spent out on the water in a sailboat.

At the helm stood Colonel Charles Owen, a tall and slender man with the posture of a career spent in the military, and a disposition that suggested a lifetime spent learning the nuances of leadership. Colonel Owen had been posted in Cairo, Bombay, and Singapore during his distinguished military career. He commanded the respect of men and had proved himself a valiant warrior and leader in the face of battle. On several occasions, he'd led his troops into battle against resistance fighters, always emerging victorious.

More than anything, however, Colonel Owen could be characterized as an adventurer. Born in London and educated in Switzerland, he was a master skier, mountaineer, and sailor. Above all else, he was an expert pilot. Although he was a more than capable seaman, his skill in an airplane was almost unmatched throughout England and Europe. He wasn't just an aviator; he worked with English engineers to make their planes fly higher and faster than any in the world.

In fact, he'd recently been a test pilot for the Blackburn Mercury. He'd crashed on the landing and, characteristically, came away unscathed. He recommended some engineering designs that he hoped would make the plane more sturdy and resistant to wind changes.

Charles felt content at the helm of his boat, *The Dove*, because he was enjoying his family's annual vacation. It was a tradition with the Owen family—his wife Louise, his son David, and his daughter Margaret—to sail to a new and exotic destination each year. Last year, they explored the southern coast of Spain, and the year before that, the French Riviera. While other families might take a steamboat, he preferred to 'earn' his vacation, also using the time to teach his wife and children a thing or two about survival. His son and daughter had both taken to seamanship and were now both capable sailors in their own right. The children led privileged lives, attending private schools, yet Charles felt they spent too much time with their mother and not enough with him. It was the reality of their lives, because he was constantly away on assignment, so Charles used these annual trips to try to instill some toughness in his children, if only for a few weeks each year.

He was excited to show them Morocco. As children, David and Margaret spent two years in Egypt, where they learned to speak fluent Arabic. This trip would be an excellent opportunity to continue their education.

"David, pull in the main sheet just a little, take out that bit of luff," he barked at his son.

Without hesitation, David pulled in the main sheet and tied it off. He was only eleven years old, but had already learned a hard lesson about what could happen when he disobeyed his father on a sailboat. Once, he was supposed to tie off the main boom, but had failed to tie a bowline knot as his father had instructed. The knot he tied could bare-ly be considered a knot at all—it couldn't have held a pair of shoelaces together. The knot immediately came undone, throwing the boom across the hull of the boat and almost decapitating his father. As punishment, David was forced to sand and varnish the entire deck. After three days' work, with sore fingers and an elbow that felt like it had a permanent knot, he had learned his lesson and now followed every order his father gave, without question.

"Do you see it?" his father asked, pointing just off the bow to port.

David put his hand over his eyes to block the sun. He scanned the horizon but saw nothing.

"No."

"Here, use this," his father said and handed him a monocular. David adjusted it until the horizon came into focus.

"Oh, there it is. How long before we're there?" David asked, having spotted the coast of Morocco.

"About an hour if this wind keeps up."

"Good, I think Margaret is going to kill me if she has to spend another day on this boat," David said, and his father smiled.

As if on cue, just then his daughter and wife emerged from the hold below, with a plate of brie cheese, fresh pears, figs, and English shortbread.

"You're right. I *am* going to kill you if I'm in this boat for another two hours."

"*I'm* going to kill someone if I don't get some of that cheese and pear. It smells delicious," Charles said.

Mrs. Owen made him a cracker sandwich and stuffed it in his mouth. Although he could be gone for as many as six months at a time, they maintained a very close and supportive relationship. Louise Owen treasured every second with her husband when he was with the family. The children felt a sense of comfort and security when he was home; when he was away, it always seemed like something was missing. Although they obviously loved their mother, having their father around instilled a certain confidence in them. He appeared never to worry and had an answer for everything. Above all, he was happy and cheerful, not withdrawn and distant like most fathers they knew. Perhaps it was because he was allowed to pursue his passions. Whatever the reason, Colonel Charles Owen always seemed to be content, almost as if a guardian angel was looking over his shoulder.

If the Owen family had been paying attention while eating their lunch, they would have noticed that a rather large sailing vessel had been following them off their stern for about twenty minutes. In the distance, it was only a white sail, but it was getting closer and closer by the minute. If they had spied it, the Owens probably would have assumed it to be one of the many merchant vessels sailing to and from the European mainland.

Unfortunately for them, they did not spot it, and it was the *Angelina Rouge*, a pirate ship that had been stalking and analyzing their movements.

"Looks like a family on a pleasure cruise," said First Mate Aquina.

"Any weapons onboard?" asked the captain.

"No. Just a family, it looks like. It's a small boat."

"What do you think the take will be?"

"Who knows? I'm guessing not much. The boat itself is probably the most valuable item."

"Well, it's been a slow month. Let's capture her and sail east toward the Ottoman Empire. I want you to captain the boat and take Millar and Cicero along with you."

"Yes Captain," Aquina said. He was a large Filipino man, maybe six-foot-two, and a former slave to a Belgian diamond merchant. His head was completely bald and a gold earring looped from his right ear. He had too many scars to count, most from knife fights, and a half-dozen tattoos across his back and chest. He had been a seafaring pirate for the past seven years, and held a scandalous reputation up and down the Mediterranean Coast. Aquina could have been the most feared pirate alive, but that distinction belonged to the other man on the *Angelina Rouge*, his captain—a man by the name of Basil.

Louise Owen was eating a pear and pouring some white wine for her husband when she spied the ship to the stern of *The Dove*. It was much closer than it had been just ten minutes prior. So close now, it was even possible to barely make out the outline of the crew on the deck. The pirate ship was running a second jib sail and making very quick time.

"Charles, did you see that ship?" she asked.

"What ship?"

"The ship directly behind us."

Charles looked around and spotted the ship for the first time. He was instantly suspicious. Most normal men might not have given it a second thought. But he was a man accustomed to worst-case scenarios and anything out of the ordinary caused him to feel a natural apprehension in his gut.

It was also strange for a ship to follow so closely.

"David, let me see that monocular."

His son passed him the monocular and then stood next to his father and mother, trying to make out the details of the neighboring vessel.

Charles spied approximately seven men, who were looking directly at him. Normally, the sight of seven men on a merchant vessel wouldn't arouse suspicion. But something about these men wasn't right. They weren't dressed right. Their postures suggested they were criminals, not seamen. All seven of them were looking at their boat; they were way too interested in him and his family than they would be if they were just planning to sail past them. He looked at their boat and knew he couldn't outrun them if they were interested in hostilities.

"David, pull in the main sheet," he instructed his son.

David dutifully pulled in the main sheet as tight as it could hold.

Charles decided to jibe at that moment, simply turning with the wind. If the other boat followed suit, he would immediately know their intentions—that they meant the Owen family harm. If they kept their course, he'd know they were in the clear.

"Everyone, prepare to jibe on the count of three," he yelled.

"Charles, what's wrong?" Louise asked, suddenly wary of her husband's tone.

"One, two, and three!" he barked, twisting the wheel, unleashing the main sheet as the boom swung overhead. Instantaneously, the boat was heading downwind, almost opposite their original course.

Charles looked behind him and, true to his suspicion, the other boat jibed as well.

"Charles, is it that boat? Is something the matter?" Louise asked, this time with more pronounced panic in her voice.

"Louise, go down and look in the blue chest next to our bed. At the very bottom, hidden in a pillowcase, is a shotgun and box of shells. Please bring them to me," he firmly requested.

"Charles..." she began to answer.

"Now!" he screamed.

Slowly, she went down the stairs. Both children were now looking at their father wide-eyed, with fear plastered on their faces. They had never seen this look in their father's eyes. A look of fear mixed with anger and, most of all, murder.

"Don't worry; everything is going to be all right," he said to them.

His wife ascended the stairs with the shotgun, and as she was about to reach the deck, he yelled to her.

"Keep it low and out of sight—place it right here next to me, along with the shells."

She did as she was told and then took up the monocular to have a look.

"Could they just be merchants?" she asked.

"No, not in these waters. There's a certain amount of protocol between sailors. Keep safe distances, signal your intentions. What are they doing now and how far are they behind us?"

"About five hundred feet and...Oh, my God! They've got guns, Charles. Four crewmembers have rifles."

"Okay, okay, let me think."

He looked around the boat and quickly looked back at their followers. They were making good time, but in ten or fifteen minutes, the ship would catch up with them. Charles couldn't fight them and expect to win. Not with seven of them, or possibly more, and he with only one shotgun and his family onboard. He couldn't outmaneuver them, either. Their boat was too fast, and they were most likely expert sailors with skills superior to his. There was only one other option, and he decided quickly, giving orders to his family.

"Louise, I want you to take David and Margaret below deck and put on dark colored clothing and life preservers. Also, take our travel documents and money and a change of clothes. Put them in the knapsack."

"Why?" she asked.

"You three are going overboard and swimming to shore," he answered.

"Are you crazy?"

"When you're ready, come back on deck, but only on your hands and knees so they can't see you. Then, come directly behind me and hide," he continued.

"Why?" she asked again.

"Please, just do it," he ordered.

She gathered the children and the three of them went below deck. Charles would have just one opportunity to execute his plan. If it worked, his family should be safe. It took some time for Margaret and Louise to change out of their burdensome boat attire into reasonable clothes for swimming. Louise followed her husband's instructions, putting all of their documents and a change of clothes into a cloth knapsack that she could strap onto her back. She also grabbed three cork life preservers.

Finally Louise, David, and Margaret crawled up from below and hid behind Charles. He looked ahead, but starting talking to them. If he was being watched, he wanted it to appear that his family was below deck.

"Okay, I'm going to tack and head back to sea. When they follow, at that instance all three of you will jump overboard. They should be so busy they won't see it. Once you're in the water, don't begin swimming right away. Wait a few moments until they've passed you. Then, swim for shore. Once on land, make your way to the Hotel Continental in Tangier. I will meet you there."

"Charles, we can't do this," Louise cried.

"Father, this is ridiculous. It's at least three or four miles to the beach. We'll never make it that far. And we can't leave you!" Margaret yelled.

"You'll make it. You have life preservers and the current will help. Don't worry about me. I'll be fine."

"Charles, look at me…please," Louise begged.

Hesitating, Charles finally looked around and tried to make it seem like he was looking at a sail. Finally, he met her eyes.

"I love you. Make it back to us," she said.

He nodded, and winked and smiled at her. There was no doubt of his love for her. He didn't need grand gestures to show it.

He turned back toward the bow.

"I'm going to tack now. Don't go until I say the word. We have to wait until they follow suit," he said, twisting the wheel, unleashing the main sheet, and bringing the sail to the port side.

He looked back at the other boat, but they did nothing.

"Why aren't they following?" Charles asked aloud.

"Perhaps they're not pirates after all," David said.

Just then, the suspicious boat did exactly as expected and followed with a tack. Charles knew that as the boat was turning, and the sails were coming about, the crew would be busy and distracted.

"Now!" Charles yelled.

The three went overboard as quickly as possible. The water was cold and the salt stung their eyes. They kept their heads down and didn't thrash their arms or legs. There was a bit of a chop in the waves, so they would be easily camouflaged.

The Dove sped ahead in the distance, getting smaller and smaller on the horizon. Charles became just a speck onboard. The pirate ship passed them after about ten minutes, but they were now much farther away, almost one hundred feet to the north.

The Owen family began swimming. The current was with them, but the chop made it a chore. The life jackets held their bodies up and made the swim much less arduous.

"Keep together; don't let each other out of your sight. The current should take us right in," Louise instructed them.

"Are there sharks out here?" David asked.

"David, shut up!" Margaret replied.

"Don't worry David, we'll be fine. Just swim as your father instructed, and tomorrow we'll all be together again," Louise said to her son. She was being stoic and strong, as a mother must be for her children. Inside, however, Louise was terribly frightened. Her husband was being chased by pirates, she was out at sea with her two children, and in two hours' time it would be dark. Not to mention the fact that there certainly *were* sharks in these waters and they usually started feeding around dusk.

The family swam for four hours, into the night. They were cold, exhausted, and scared when finally, their feet touched sand. They dragged their exhausted bodies ashore and all three collapsed on the beach.

"I've never been so happy to be on land in my life," Margaret said.

"Neither have I," David agreed.

"It's nice to hear you two agree on something," their mother said and all three laughed.

"What should we do now?" Margaret asked.

"Let's make a small shelter on the beach and then start out on the way to Tangier in the morning," Louise said.

"How far do you think it is?" David asked.

"Not far, perhaps ten or fifteen miles," Louise replied.

"I don't care how far it is, I'm just glad to be out of that ocean," Margaret said.

"C'mon," Louise instructed them.

They made their way up the beach to a tree line and walked about twenty feet inland. Bunches of palm trees crowded the beach, making for a perfect cover. Louise found an especially large one, sheltered from the wind.

"Let's camp here for the night. David, please dig a hole big enough for the three of us to sleep in. Margaret, please collect some large leaves that we can use as cover. I will collect firewood and put out the clothes to dry."

"What about dinner? I'm starving," David asked.

"I'll figure something out," Louise replied.

Within fifteen minutes, a camp had been prepared. Louise had found some citrus trees and gathered half a dozen oranges. She prepared a fire pit and placed dry twigs and leaves at the bottom. Then, she took two rocks together and began rubbing them back and forth. It took almost two full minutes, but at last a tiny spark flew from the rocks, igniting the pile of leaves and twigs, and immediately starting a small fire. Louise quickly applied more small pieces, then larger sticks, and finally some very large tree branches. Soon, a large, crackling fire was keeping the Owen family quite warm.

"Okay, strip down to your skivvies and place your wet clothes on these rocks."

"Dress down to my skivvies in front of you two?" David exclaimed.

"David, I'm your mother. I've seen you in your skivvies and much less. You'll be much happier out of those wet clothes," Louise instructed.

Everyone stripped down to their undergarments and laid the rest of their clothing on some rocks Louise had placed next to the fire. The fire was roaring now, and in half an hour, the clothes would be dry. Louise peeled the oranges and shared the pieces with her children. They happily sucked on and ate the oranges, letting the sweet juices swirl in their mouths.

"An orange has never tasted so good," Margaret said.

"These are delicious," Louise agreed.

The three had, in a matter of hours, come together to form a tightly-knit group. Danger will do that to people, even a family prone to bickering. There was no infighting and no whining—both Margaret and her younger brother David fully understood the seriousness of the situation they found themselves in. Six hours ago, they had been constantly arguing over the smallest things, but now they looked out for one another.

Above their heads, the Moroccan night was full of stars. It was quite dark now and extremely quiet. A faint wind could just barely be heard between the trees.

"Do you think Father is all right?" David finally asked.

It was a subject they had all been thinking about since they jumped off the boat, but no one had spoken of it.

"Your father is a veteran and a colonel in His Majesty's Service. I'm sure he can handle a few pirates," Louise told her son.

"I hope so," David said.

"Now let's fuel the fire and try to get some sleep. We've got a big day ahead of us tomorrow," Louise told her children. Louise placed several large branches and a rather big log on the fire. Margaret prepared their bed. The three of them snuggled into the sand and covered themselves with large palm branches. It wasn't especially cold, so the branches provided sufficient shelter.

"Mother, where did you learn to do all this? Start fires and all that?" Margaret asked.

"Your grandfather probably wished he had a boy instead of three girls, so he would take my sisters and me on camping expeditions in the Scottish Highlands every summer. That's probably why your father fell in love with me. On one of our first dates, I showed him some celestial navigation tricks my grandfather had taught me. I think your father quite liked the idea of a woman who was capable."

"Will you teach me?" Margaret asked.

"Of course."

"Good, I want to be capable."

"You are, Margaret. Now, try to get some sleep," Louise said.

Overall, a restless night was the best that could be expected. All three of them had fitful sleep, as the fire extinguished itself and the wind kicked up a bit. Margaret was awakened several times by the piercing wind and found it difficult to get warm and comfortable. At about three o'clock, her body finally surrendered and she gratefully slept for a few hours without interruption.

The next morning, Margaret awoke stiff and sore from sleeping on the hard ground. Sitting up, she thought she was dreaming. Had the previous day really happened? Was her father now out at sea? Had she and her mother and brother spent hours in the ocean and then camped out on a beach?

Wiping her eyes, Margaret realized she was not dreaming and, in fact, was very much awake. Looking out to sea, she was comforted by waves rolling up on the beach and the sun peeking out just over the horizon. There was something soothing—almost healing—about watching the ocean and the waves. She heard squawking behind her. Looking back and up into a tree, she saw that a group of monkeys had taken an interest in her family. There were six monkeys in all. They didn't make a tremendous racket; mostly, they stood on a tree branch picking at their fur, seeming to wonder who these new creatures were on their beach.

Margaret smiled at the monkeys and enjoyed watching them. Looking around, she noticed for the first time they were surrounded completely by water and jungle. There wasn't a boat or a person or a house in sight. The beach stretched for miles.

Staring at the ocean, she hoped to see *The Dove* somewhere on the horizon. Alas, all she spied were whitecaps and some hungry seagulls.

After a few moments, her mother came toward her, walking up the beach with some more oranges.

"Ready to leave now?" Louise asked.

"What time is it?" David asked, just waking up himself.

"I don't know, but let's get going. We can make the Hotel Continental by nightfall if we hurry."

The three gathered themselves. David could feel hunger pangs in his stomach but said nothing. He nibbled on an orange and handed a few pieces to Margaret.

"At least we won't get scurvy," he joked.

She smiled and nodded in agreement.

"Okay, I've found a path. Let's go," Louise told them.

They made their way off the beach to a path between an ever-increasing dense jungle of palm trees, almond groves, and several other species of trees and plants unfamiliar to Louise. After walking for half a mile, they came to a dirt road. It stretched out parallel to the ocean.

"Hopefully, if we walk west, we should run into a more major road that will lead to Tangier," she said.

They walked along the dirt road for a couple of hours and didn't see any sign of life except for wild sparrows and the occasional group of monkeys. They did manage to find a fig tree and ate a hearty breakfast of oranges and figs.

Finally, they came to a larger dirt road.

"I think this is probably used for travel. Hopefully someone will come soon," Louise promised.

After ten minutes, sure enough, a cart being pulled by two mules ambled down the path and stopped near the Owen family. A Moroccan family sat in front—a mother, father, and two young boys. Undoubtedly, this was the first time they had ever seen white people in their lives.

"We need to go to Tangier," Louise said, trying to slow down her words.

"Tangier?" the man asked.

"Yes, Tangier!" Louise repeated.

Although both the Owen children spoke fluent Arabic, they were rather bashful and allowed their mother to do the talking.

The Moroccan father didn't speak a word of English but motioned for them to climb in the back of the cart.

"Shukran, shukran!" all of them said, which means "thank you" in Arabic. They all climbed in. The cart was full of rugs and junk.

"I guess we caught them on market day," Margaret laughed.

"I guess so," Louise agreed.

The man looked behind him to ensure they were seated and safe. Then, he motioned for the mules to begin walking, and off they went on the dirt path.

After four hours, they entered the outskirts of Tangier. It was a small city compared to London. The buildings were much smaller and were made mostly of red mud and brick. The cart stopped, and the man motioned with his hands for them to hop out, that he had arrived at his destination.

"Thank you so much. Can I give you some money?" Louise motioned and started to pull out some bills from her money pouch. The man waved her off with the universal word for rejection.

"No, no," he said. He put his hands together and bowed slightly and smiled. Louise bowed in gratitude, and smiled back at him. Off the Moroccan family went, down a side alley in their cart full of junk.

The Owen family now found themselves standing in the middle of a suburban Tangier street with no idea where they were or how to find the Hotel Continental.

"Well, let's walk this way," Louise motioned.

They walked for several blocks, on streets lined with homes. Moroccans smiled at them, pointing at the ragtag-looking English family. Finally, they came to a more commercial district with shops and merchants. Pomegranates, lemons, and roasted almonds filled the air.

"My God, what is that smell? It smells so good," David said.

"David, don't blaspheme, and yes, it does smell good," Louise agreed.

At that moment a man appeared pulling a rickshaw—a two-wheeled cart designed for carrying passengers.

"Aye, aye. You go?" he asked, in broken English. He had a kind face with crow's feet stretching from the corners of his eyes. He was missing a front tooth and wore a traditional Moroccan djellabah. Only his was dirty and looked like it hadn't been washed in a week.

"Hotel Continental?" Louise asked.

"Yes, yes. We go." He smiled and helped each of them into the rickshaw. In a matter of seconds, he was off running through the cobbled and dirt streets on his bare feet. All around them, people pointed at the white people and laughed. They passed through streets filled with vendors, restaurants, and hookah cafes. An exotic array of spices, coffee, tea, lamb, beef, vegetables, and tobacco wafted through the air. All manner of colors and sights filled the streets, overwhelming the Owen family. They sat in silence, taking in the new world around them.

After twenty minutes the driver pulled up to the lobby of the Hotel Continental. Brand new, the hotel had been built in the Colonial style, and its magnificent white architecture stretched out along the ocean. Ten-foot stained glass windows of red, blue, and green shone beside the oversized oak doors to the entrance of the hotel. Two bellmen stood statuesque beside the doors, dressed in immaculate white suits with cream-colored turbans. The bellmen immediately came to the rickshaw and helped the Owen family to the sidewalk.

"Are you a visitor of the Hotel Continental?" one of them asked, in perfect English.

"Yes, we wish to check in," Louise answered.

"Excellent. Do you have any bags?" he asked.

"No. Our bags were lost."

"Yes, madame. Please follow me to the concierge."

"I need to make some change to pay our driver," she explained.

The man motioned to the other bellman and he quickly paid the rickshaw driver, who smiled, waved, and ran away.

"It is taken care of, madame. Please, come this way."

Louise and her children followed the bellman through the hotel's doors into the lobby. It was spectacular. The floors were covered with exquisitely detailed Moroccan tile. The ceilings were at least forty feet high. Tile also decorated each of the walls, and lovely Moroccan chairs and sofas were positioned elegantly around the lobby. Guests, mostly European, sat at the chairs and sofas smoking cigarettes and drinking tea. Hotel workers darted about, waiting on guests, moving luggage, and performing a variety of errands. Ceiling fans buzzed overhead. Smells of tobacco, melon, lemon, and the finest European perfume scented the air.

The family walked directly to the concierge, who was a smallish man, maybe five-foot-four, with a thin black moustache dressed immaculately in a black suit and tie.

"Hello, madame, how may I be of assistance?" he asked.

"Has a Mr. Charles Owen checked in?" Louise asked.

The concierge checked his register.

"No, nobody by that name. Might he be under another name?" he inquired.

"No, no other names. Do you have a room for us?"

"Certainly, madame. It is our off-season right now. We have a beautiful suite with an ocean view for only 150 dirhams."

"That's fine. I only have English pounds. Will that be acceptable?"

"Quite acceptable," he replied.

"I would like to leave a message for Mr. Owen, if he should contact the hotel. Please tell him that his family is safe and we are awaiting his arrival."

"Of course, madame. How many nights would you like to stay?"

"Three for now, but that may be extended."

"No problem at all, madame. Here is your key. You are in room 211, just up the stairs."

"Thank you."

If she hadn't been exhausted and scared, Louise might have noticed the subtle eye movements the concierge made to an unidentified gentleman in the back corner of the lobby—a tall, thin, and elegantly-dressed Frenchman who sat drinking tea, smoking a cigarette, and pretending to read a newspaper. He was watching the concierge out of the corner of his eye and saw the nod in his direction.

The man was unmistakable.

It was Mister LaRoque.

The family opened the door to their room and found a large suite with two bedrooms, a living room, a terrace overlooking the ocean, and an oversized bathroom, complete with a large bathtub. The view from the suite was remarkable, with wide ocean views as far as the eye could see.

"I'm going to take a bath!" Margaret said.

"I'm ordering room service. I want an omelet, chocolate cake, lamb kabob, baklava, fried mushrooms, and roast mutton. Mother, is that okay?" David asked.

"It's fine David. Why don't you go down to the kitchen and place the order?" asked their mother.

"Actually, I'll do it. David, why don't you take the first bath? You'll be quicker than Mother or me," Margaret insisted.

"Do I have to?" David asked.

"That's a good idea, Margaret. Yes, David, you do. You smell just like you've been in the ocean and then spent the night lying in the dirt. It's quite high time for a bath for all of us," his mother told him.

"Oh, all right, then."

Margaret took the menu from her brother and scanned it. "I'll get us a feast, don't worry. I think everyone could use a good bath and a meal," she told them before closing the door.

David went in the bathroom and closed the door. Soon, hot water was pouring from the faucet into the bathtub.

Louise Owen sat on the terrace overlooking the ocean. She was happy to be in a hotel room. Happy to be out of harm's way. Happy that her children were safe. But Charles hadn't yet checked in, and she knew that couldn't be good. Theoretically, he should have been at the hotel last night if he had managed to elude the pirates. If he hadn't, the pirates may have captured him, thrown him overboard, or killed him. But, in her heart, she didn't feel her husband was dead. During all those years he spent away at war, she always knew he would come back safe. She couldn't explain it; maybe it was a woman's intuition. She had learned to live with the worry and the dread and to accept fate. If her husband was meant to die, there was nothing she or anyone else could do about it. Still, she watched the water in hopes that the sails of *The Dove* would parade in front of her, with Charles at the helm—her husband coming back to his family.

Margaret made her way down to the lobby and approached the concierge.

"Excuse me, how do I order some room service?" she asked.

"Do you see that hallway? Go down that hallway, turn left, and go to the last door on your left. You may order room service at that door," the concierge instructed.

"Okay. Thank you," she said and walked away.

Walking down the hallway, she barely noticed how long it was and how out of the way it seemed. In fact, it was completely separated from the rest of the hotel. She followed the hallway, turned left as directed, and walked down another equally long hallway. It was very quiet, and seemed odd to her that room service would be in such a remote place.

She came to the last door on her left and knocked.

No answer.

She knocked again, to no answer. Slowly she opened the door.

"Hello?" she called.

Before she could hear a reply, she felt her mouth covered with a cloth and an arm wrap tightly around her neck. She tried to scream, but nothing came from her mouth. Quickly, her vision faded into darkness as she blacked out.

She would remember nothing.

CHAPTER
— 4 —

THE JOURNEY TO THE KASBAH

Margaret stared at the ground. She wanted to cry and missed her home and family. In the past seventy-two hours, she'd jumped from a boat, hitched her way to a foreign hotel, been abducted, and ultimately sold into slavery. She remembered the look on her mother's face in the hotel room, and the sound of her brother's voice. How she missed them.

"Do not worry. You will be back with your family," Tariq said.

"I know. I just miss them," she answered.

Aseem looked at Tariq.

"We are starting to climb a little. I can make out hillsides outside and mountains in the distance. We are now going east a little."

"How far do you think we have traveled?" Margaret asked.

"Conservatively, I think maybe fifty miles."

At that point, the wagon stopped. Zahir appeared at the back and opened up the tarp.

"Slaves, we are going into bandit territory. We may need to stop and hide. If any of you try to escape, we will kill all the remaining slaves. Do you understand?"

All four nodded their head in agreement.

"Okay. Do exactly as I say when I say it. If we run into trouble, we will have to act quickly."

With that, he closed the tarp and the wagon started up again.

"What does that mean? Bandit territory?" little Fez asked.

"Morocco is a poor country. In the mountains, the tribes rule the countryside. Usually, they pay off someone for safe passage. That was the custom with my tribe," Aseem said.

"You heard what he said. If any of us try to escape then he will kill the rest," Margaret reminded them.

"He could be bluffing. Otherwise, it just means we will have to escape together," Tariq reassured her.

"I'm scared of escaping," Fez said.

"We stand a much better chance of survival on our own than as captives with these people. Don't worry Fez, we will find a way out."

"I already know how to escape," Fez said.

"What?"

"Picking these locks is easy. Have you not noticed we are the last wagon train in line? We could easily slip out the back and escape into the countryside. The timing was not right in the desert. There would have been no place to hide, and water and food would have been scarce. This is perfect territory to hide in. We could easily disappear into the hills and valleys."

They all looked at Fez in amazement. The entire ride he hadn't said a word, and now his hands were unshackled and he had already formulated an escape plan?

"How did you pick that lock?" Aseem asked.

"It was easy. I had a bicycle back home and often had to adjust the chain. The connectors weren't much bigger than this lock hole. I learned how to disable and take apart the chain in seconds using a small nail. I always keep it on me."

"So, we have a mechanical genius in our midst. Fez, you may come in very handy," Tariq said and smiled.

"Can you undo all of our locks?" Margaret asked.

"Yes, no problem, but…" Fez hesitated.

"What is it?" Aseem asked.

"We only have one chance at this. If Zahir finds out I can pick the locks, he may do something very, very drastic. He might kill me, or all of us."

"I agree," said Tariq. "We must be absolutely sure that we can escape. One chance is all we have."

"Okay then, tonight it is," said Aseem. "We don't know how much farther we have to go before we reach our destination. Tonight may be our only opportunity."

Everyone nodded in agreement. The escape had to happen tonight.

After dark, it was colder than usual. The wagons were circled around a giant fire in the middle. The caravan had stopped in a long valley that stretched for miles. It had been a treacherous journey. At one point, one of the wagons almost slid down an embankment, which surely would have destroyed it, along with everyone and everything inside.

As expected, the four prisoners were kept chained to the outside wagon apart from the others. No one could sleep in anticipation of the escape plan, so they silently waited for a few hours until they were sure the rest of the camp was fast asleep. During that time, Fez silently and quickly unlocked everyone's shackles. They had managed to hide a little food from dinner, as they didn't know what to expect in the mountains or how easy it would be to find food. No matter the consequences, they all knew an escape would be better than remaining in slavery.

"Are you all ready?" Tariq whispered.

"Yes," everyone replied.

Slowly Tariq made his way out of the wagon. He crawled on his belly and stayed in the shadows. The others followed directly behind him. All of the camels and mules were fast asleep in the center of the camp. One camel stirred a bit, but nothing too unusual happened as they passed by. They crawled about twenty feet to a nearby rock and hid behind it.

"So far, so good," Margaret whispered.

They were about to crawl away when Aseem noticed something in the distance.

"Hold on," he told the others.

Aseem looked in the direction where he had seen movement and waited. Sure enough, after a few seconds, he saw the unmistakable outline of a person moving through the brush, about sixty feet away. The glint of a dagger reflected in the moonlight.

"We have a problem," he whispered.

"What?" Tariq asked.

"We are being attacked. I see shadows moving in the darkness."

"Bandits?" Margaret asked.

"Yes," Aseem said.

"What should we do?"

Aseem thought before answering.

"If I'm not mistaken, this is Tajakant territory. Their tribe is very wary of any outsiders. If you are not Tajakant, then you are considered an enemy. They will not hesitate to kill us if we are captured."

"Is there another way?" Tariq asked.

"No. The only way for us to escape is to pass through this valley for a few hundred yards. They are coming directly towards us. We cannot escape this way or we will be caught."

"What should we do?" Fez asked.

"We go back to the wagon and alert the others."

"What?" Margaret exclaimed.

"This will not be our only opportunity for escape. We will live another day."

"Are you sure?" Tariq asked.

"Yes. We must move quickly back to the wagon and alert the others."

"Okay, then. I trust you," Tariq said.

Reluctantly, they moved silently and slowly back to the wagon under the cover of shadows and darkness. They didn't seem to be spotted by the intruders. Once inside, all of them shackled themselves in.

"What now?" Margaret asked.

"Now, we yell and wake up everyone," Aseem said.

At once, the four started yelling and screaming.

"Bandits!" they yelled.

"Help us! We are being attacked!"

"Intruders!"

Quickly, the camp filled with life. There was much shouting and hollering as the camp prepared for battle. They heard yelling from outside the camp and then the sound of gunfire.

"Can you see what is happening?" Aseem asked.

"Just barely; Zahir has a rifle and a pistol, and is hiding behind a rock with another man. They are firing into the night. I don't see much else," Margaret said.

They heard more gunshots, and the sound of a man groaning. Just then, a man burst into the back of the wagon. His head and face were covered by a turban and mask. He was dressed completely in black and had a large, foot-long dagger in his hand. He was looking for blood.

"Aaaargghhh!" Fez screamed.

The man lifted his dagger and was about to stab Aseem when he suddenly fell forward and slumped in the wagon. Blood poured out of his head—a bullet had struck him in the back of the skull. Zahir appeared just behind him with a pistol. Quickly, he jumped in the wagon and peeked out from behind the tarp.

"We are being attacked," he said, stating the obvious.

"We know, we're the ones that alerted everyone," Tariq said.

"What?" he asked, looking at them, before focusing his attention outside once more. "We killed three of them. Hopefully they won't return. I am going back outside," he said, jumping out of the wagon.

The dead bandit lay in the middle of the wagon, blood pouring from his head. Margaret stared at the dead man's eyes. She had never seen a corpse before, not even at a funeral. Life drained from the man's face and his skin took on a ghostly white color. His eyes remained open.

"I wish someone would remove him."

Tariq moved up and searched the dead man's pockets. He found a small flint and tin for making fires but nothing else. He thought about taking the man's dagger but stopped.

"Zahir will notice if his dagger is missing," he said aloud.

Then, he thought of checking the man's ankles. Sure enough, the dead man had a small knife sheathed and hidden on his right ankle. Tariq hid the knife and tin in a loose floorboard in the wagon.

"Nice work!" Aseem said. Tariq winked at him.

After ten minutes, the battle seemed to be over. Just moments before, they'd heard intermittent gunfire and shouting. Now, it was completely quiet and still. Zahir opened up the tarp and dragged the corpse out the back of the wagon. As Tariq had suspected he would, Zahir picked up and sheathed the man's dagger before looking at the captives.

"We are going to break camp and travel by night. The group that attacked us was small, but they may come back with reinforcements. All of you stand up," he ordered.

Dutifully, the four stood up, and Zahir searched their clothes for weapons. Fez took the nail he'd used to pick the locks from his pocket and dropped it on the floor as Zahir was searching Aseem—a sly move that went unnoticed by Zahir.

"Just making sure you didn't swipe anything from this bandit. I wouldn't put it past thieves like you. How did you know we were being attacked?"

The four looked at each other before Margaret spoke up.

"I couldn't sleep and was looking at the stars outside. I saw movements in the mountains. That's all."

He looked at her closely and studied her eyes and voice. Satisfied with her answer, he ensured all the shackles were tight.

"Okay, then. Let's move."

The caravan moved slowly through the night. Two workers led the way, lighting the path by torch. Although it was only one mile to the end of the valley, the journey took the rest of the night. The four captives sat in the back of the wagon, unable to sleep. They worried about further bandit attacks or the wagon falling off a ledge, sending them to perish on the rocks below. Eventually, by the early hours of the morning, all four settled into a fitful sleep.

By nine o'clock the next morning, the desert was hot and the sun mercilessly beat down on the wagon train.

"I didn't know the desert could get this hot," Tariq said.

"Neither did I. It must be one hundred and twenty degrees," Aseem agreed.

"How do those camels manage in this heat with all that fur?" Margaret asked.

"I don't know. I would die if I had a fur coat on right now," Fez answered. They all laughed at the idea of little Fez with a fur coat.

"Aseem, do you think you can track our trail?" Margaret asked.

"I have been. From studying the distance we've traveled, our changes in direction, and the stars at night, I have made a map in my head."

"How did you learn to do all that?"

"I was taught by my brother."

"I can't believe you don't hate your father for selling you off," Tariq stated.

"Do you want to know my dream?" asked Aseem.

"What is it?"

"To one day return to my village a successful man. To look my father in the eye and show him that I am more of a man than he is," he said softly.

"You will do it, Aseem. We'll help you."

"Thank you. I think most of us have a home to return to."

"I don't," Tariq answered. "I never knew my father or mother. For years, my only home was anywhere I could put my head at night. Sometimes an orphanage, or a stairway, or maybe some grass in a park."

"How did you survive all those years by yourself?" Margaret asked.

"I'm a street rat. My friends are my family. We look out for one another. We feed one another. We learn how to survive. I had never known a good adult until three years ago, when a woman rescued me. Her name is Zijuan. She is my mother. She taught me to read and write. But she also taught me the difference between right and wrong, and made me believe that although I am an orphan, I still have a purpose in this world and I am capable of making it a better place."

"She sounds like a wonderful woman," Margaret said.

"She is. I hope to see her again someday."

"You will."

"What about you, Margaret?" Aseem asked.

"In the past three days, I have realized how wonderful my family is and how good my life was. Hearing your stories, I know have nothing to complain about. I just want to go home. I hope that someday all of you could meet my family. I think you would like them."

"I would like that. You're the first white girl I've ever known. You're not so bad," Tariq said.

"You're not so bad either, Tariq."

The caravan rumbled along in the heat of the day. The desert can reach one hundred and thirty degrees in afternoon. At that temperature, a man can die of heat exhaustion in just one hour under the sun. It is considered the harshest environment on the earth.

"My goodness, I am thirsty. I thought we were supposed to get water every couple of hours. We haven't received any since morning," Margaret said.

"I know. They seem to have forgotten about us," Fez agreed.

"Perhaps we are being punished," Aseem said.

"For what?" Tariq asked.

Aseem shrugged his shoulders and continued to stare at the wagon floor. All of them were quite hungry, but it was the thirst that tortured them the most. Their throats itched and felt scratchy and swollen. Their eyes were dry, and their energy was depleted. After a while, they lacked the energy to speak and could barely sit up.

Finally, the caravan stopped. Zahir appeared at the back of the wagon with a bucket and ladle.

"Everyone gets two ladles and no more," he said and lifted a full ladle to Fez's mouth. He gulped it down and another. He went to Aseem and then Margaret and finally to Tariq.

"Sir, it must be a hundred and twenty degrees outside," Fez said. "How are we expected to survive riding in a hot wagon, through the desert, with only two gulps of water per day?"

"The bandits shot two of our barrels of water. So, we are rationing. Slaves are the last to drink. If you die, then you die. It is in Allah's hands now," he said, closing the tarp behind him as he left.

They just looked at each other...

The next day, impossibly, was hotter than the previous one. The four of them lay sweltering in the wagon, as flies buzzed around their sweaty bodies. Each of them suffered from various stages of heat exhaustion. Little Fez's head throbbed with migraine headaches. Margaret could barely swallow, her throat was so swollen. Aseem had started to hallucinate from dehydration. Tariq, perhaps the strongest, merely slept in fitful sleeps. The wagon crept along slowly, as if its destination could never be attained.

At the end of the day, they finally stopped. Zahir appeared as usual with the bucket of water. Margaret could barely place the ladle to her chapped lips; the water, although warmer than room temperature, was the sweetest nectar she had ever tasted. Each took their turn, not wasting any energy on talking.

"One more day, perhaps two, and we will make our destination," Zahir said as he closed the tarp.

"I can't make another day. I'll die," Margaret said.

"Just try to sleep, and don't move. Conserve your energy. You will make it," Tariq reassured her.

That night the four slept a deep sleep, their pangs of hunger and thirst finally giving way to complete exhaustion. Each dreamt vividly and wildly, their subconscious minds living out their most fearful nightmares or vivid daydreams. Deep in the night, the wind kicked up a wicked screech, awakening all of them. The flaps on the wagons blew and shook and finally one of them came loose and blew into the wagon, allowing sand and wind to swirl inside.

"Try to get it back up!" Aseem yelled with urgency.

Tariq took the cloth and tried to replace it, but the wind was just too strong. With what little strength he had, he made one last attempt to replace the missing piece of the tarp. Finally, he gave up in exhaustion.

The four huddled together in the wagon, exposed to the howling wind and blinding sand. They sheltered their faces and hid under the cover. The wind continued to kick up even stronger, and they felt the wagon rocking and shaking until it finally tipped over on one side. The four ended up on top of one another, covered in sand.

The captives leaned against the inside of the overturned wagon. They were now actually more protected than they were before, as the wagon provided a barrier to the wind. No one spoke. They simply tried to protect themselves, their eyes itching and blinded by the sandstorm.

Tariq lowered his chin into his chest, shielded his eyes from the sand, and looked out across the other wagons. Three others had also toppled over. People ran everywhere, blinded by the sand. Clothes and rags and curtains flew about. There was no order, only chaos.

Just then, Tariq spied the food wagon. It had toppled over. He saw what he was sure was a jug of water and a pile of spilled fruit, and nobody seemed to have noticed.

"Fez, undo my leg shackles," he said.

"Why?"

"Because, I am going to get us water."

Fez slowly lifted his nail from its hiding place, and in a matter of minutes had freed his friend. Once released from the shackles, Tariq checked to make sure nobody was watching him, and then quickly made his way across the camp to the overturned food wagon. Sand flew everywhere, so much so that it was impossible for Tariq to see beyond three feet in front of his face. He didn't worry too much about being recognized. If anyone saw him, he would have looked like anyone else in the caravan trying to find shelter.

When he reached the food cart, he fell to his knees, gathered the water jug and quickly grabbed some figs and nuts, stuffing them in his pockets. He made his way back to his friends, throwing his body down behind the wagon, exhausted from the experience.

Tariq took a long, long drink of water, then passed the jug to Fez, who took an equally long drink. The four of them passed the jug back and forth five times until it was completely empty. Tariq then threw the jug as far as he could, away from them to avoid suspicion. Next, he shared his take of food. They each managed to stuff their mouths with food—slowly chewing, they enjoyed the sweet tastes, and felt their bellies receive temporary relief.

Their recovery felt instantaneous. Finally nourished, their body temperatures returned to normal. Their headaches subsided, and their bellies felt warm. Although the sandstorm continued through the night, they had been fed and their thirst had been quenched. Sand, compared to starvation and dehydration, was a mere nuisance.

By the rise of the sun, the sandstorm had subsided and the sun slid slowly up over the horizon. There was nothing to see except miles of rolling dunes and sand. The camp slowly came to life, as people shook the sand from their clothes, hair and bodies. Zahir walked from wagon to wagon, assessing the damage and yelling orders to each camp member.

Finally, he came to the slave wagon. He unlocked everyone's leg shackles.

"You will help right the wagons, clean the sand, and collect anything thrown about from the storm," he ordered them.

Dutifully, they went to each wagon and assisted in turning it over. The wagons were mostly just rickety carts with some wires strung over the top, used for draping cloth for shade. All the wagons were two-wheeled and each looked as if it could fall completely apart at any moment. The wood was rotten with worm holes and splintered from the sun.

The young slaves went through each wagon, brushing out the sand, which sometimes required a shovel, it was so deep. They fixed the overhead wires and assisted in hooking them up to the mules. Although it was a nasty sandstorm, the mules were unaffected, as they had been kept huddled in a tent for safety. In the desert, a mule was a lifeline, and it was critical they be protected.

Old Shatam, who fed everyone every day, had joined in cleaning the wagons. He reached out and gave a piece of lamb to Tariq.

"Hide this and share it with your friends," he said.

"Thank you," Tariq said and without so much as flicker, the meat was hidden in his clothes.

"Zahir is the most evil man I know. Do *not* upset him. You do not want to find out what he is capable of," Old Shatam warned Tariq.

"How long have you been with him?"

"With him? Not long. He is new and wants everyone to fear him. I have been with Caid Ali Tamzali for over thirty years, since I was a boy your age."

Tariq looked at him and calculated the man's age in his head. Although he would be only about forty-three, he looked closer to sixty. His skin was weathered and brown. He had scars up and down his back from repeated whippings. Tariq looked at him and became very sad. Was this his fate, to be a slave for the rest of his life? Would he surrender after time and just relent to being a servant? Would he grovel at Zahir's feet and beg for scrap pieces of meat?

"We should arrive at the kasbah tomorrow. At the slaves' quarters, do not trust anyone. Do not tell anyone of your secrets or plans. Zahir has spies everywhere and gives privileges in exchange for information. A girl was planning an escape two weeks ago and Zahir discovered her plan. As an example to the rest, she was dragged through town on a horse until her naked skin was rubbed raw with sores and bruises. After that, he had the other slaves stone her to death."

"My God!"

"Pray to your God, but I do not think He hears our prayers," Old Shatam said.

"Thank you," Tariq said, and walked away.

In two hours, the caravan had made repairs and was back on the trail. They moved faster now, as they were out of the valleys and in the open desert. Obviously, Zahir wanted to return to the kasbah without any further delays.

In the wagon, the four looked and felt considerably better than the previous day.

"I talked with Old Shatam. He gave me some lamb to share," Tariq said, and divvied up the lamb into four quarters, handing one to each of his friends.

They all chewed and savored the delicious kabob, allowing the juices and spices to linger on their tongues.

"Shatam also said to trust no one at the kasbah. We must not speak of our plans to anyone."

"We must only rely on ourselves," Aseem said. "We must make a pact—that no matter what, we will always look out for each other. Together, we can survive."

"Tariq already saved me once. I wouldn't have made it without that water last night," Margaret agreed.

"It was nothing. You would have done the same for me," Tariq replied and smiled at her.

"I agree. If we trust and rely on each other, we can find a way to escape."

"We must make a blood oath. Fez, please hand me your nail," Tariq requested.

Fez did as he was told. Tariq took the nail and punctured the skin on his right palm; blood dripped down onto his wrist. He handed the nail to Fez, Aseem, and Margaret, and in turn they each did the same. When every palm had been bloodied, they swore a blood oath, smearing each other's blood together on their palms.

"We are blood now, inseparable by life or death," Aseem said and smiled.

"I've never taken a blood oath before. Girls normally don't do that sort of thing," Margaret replied, with almost a giggle.

"What do girls do?" Aseem asked.

"Hmmm. Mostly, we might steal each other's clothes."

They all laughed and, for once, they felt good.

Unfortunately, it was a fleeting feeling. Later that morning, the caravan stopped and Zahir appeared at their wagon as usual.

"In a few hours, we will enter the kasbah. Do not look the Caid in the eyes. Do as you are told—always. Any disobedience and you will be whipped. Displease me more than once and you will be stoned to death. Do you understand?"

Each of them nodded their heads.

"Good. Now, you—I want the others to see something," he said as he unshackled Tariq's legs. Tariq followed Zahir out of the wagon, unsure about what he had done.

"Stand against the wagon, facing your friends," Zahir ordered.

Tariq did as he was told and leaned against the wagon; he looked directly at the other three.

Zahir took out his whip and slowly paced around behind Tariq.

"So, you think you can steal water from me, and I would not notice? You think you can steal just because of a sandstorm?" he screamed.

"No...I..." Tariq stammered.

The whip came down hard and fast on Tariq's exposed back; he cringed and screamed in agony.

"How did you get free?" Zahir asked.

"I don't know, the wagon turned over and I just saw the water."

The whip came down again, Tariq screamed even louder. He felt blood slowly trickle down his back.

"Why did you shackle yourself again once you were free?" Zahir inquired.

"I didn't want to escape, I just wanted to get a little water. We were dying. What good are the slaves you purchased if we are dead?" he asked.

Zahir stopped and stared at Tariq. He had made a good point, and this confused Zahir. Normally, slaves didn't show much independent thought. Tariq's response made sense. It would displease the Caid if he showed up with four dead slaves. The Caid might even take the losses out of his wages.

"Never let me see you steal again. And, if I see you out of your shackles without my permission, I will kill you. Do you understand?"

"Yes."

"Good. Now, let this be a reminder," Zahir said, took a step back, and threw all of his body weight into the whip.

The leather screamed through the air and snapped on Tariq's back. Blood splattered everywhere, some even sprayed on Fez, who was a full three feet away. Tariq whined with agony and sank to his knees.

Zahir picked up Tariq, threw him in the wagon and tied his shackles.

Coiling his whip, he stared at all the slaves. He looked to be the personification of evil, with steam rising off his bald head, sweat dripping down his black moustache, and his eyes devoid of any emotion. Finished with his display of dominance, he smirked and walked away.

Tariq passed out in the wagon; the pain from the whipping was too much for him to bear. The caravan started up minutes later. In the distance, the kasbah roof could just barely be seen over the sand dunes.

They would arrive by noon.

CHAPTER
— 5 —

THE STORY OF TARIQ

Three Years Earlier

Tariq, just ten years old, awoke with the early sunrise, as he did every morning. He, along with a pack of a dozen or so other orphans, slept beneath a dock on the Tangier waterfront. They used their bodies as pillows and huddled together for warmth, perhaps covering themselves with a garbage bag or worn blanket found in a scrap heap.

Despite his young age, he was the undeclared leader of this particular band of urchins. Just two days prior, he repelled a rival gang's attempt to take over their spot under the dock. At an early age, Tariq learned the secrets of combat—most importantly, the need to take out the leaders of any enemy as early as possible. Although the rival boy was three years older, six inches taller, and thirty pounds heavier, Tariq had hit him upside the shoulder with a maggot-ridden wooden board. The boy dropped to the sand and started crying. His friends, scared by the sight of their bawling leader, fled into the city.

Such was the life of a street orphan in Tangier. Every day was a constant struggle for survival—whether digging in trash for a piece of stale bread, running from the corrupt Tangier police, or fending off rival foes.

"Let's go!" Tariq said to his best friend Aji.

Aji was Tariq's age and had been an orphan since the age of five, when his mother had died in a wagon accident. His father was a drunk and a very mean man. He beat his son repeatedly, until Aji ran away to the streets. There he met Tariq and fell in with his group of orphans. They had been fast and best friends since that first day. Tariq, never having known his own parents, felt a soft spot for any child joining the orphan fraternity.

Aji wiped the sand from his eyes, stood up, and ran to catch up to Tariq. His stomach, as usual, was empty and grumbling.

They made their way on the dock to one of the many fishing boats preparing for the day's catch. The fishermen, with their sinewy muscles and bronze skins, went about preparing the boat for launch by coiling rope, tightening lines, studying the weather for possible storms, sharpening gaff hooks, and most importantly, preparing bait. Mostly, this last chore consisted of taking live sardines, hooking them on the line, or throwing them into a water bucket for future use. Sometimes they split the guts for chum.

Tariq and Aji silently kneeled about ten feet from a boat with a particularly nice captain. The laws of begging were understood by all parties. The boys never made a sound, never pleaded their hunger, and the sailors never acknowledged their presence. They simply went about preparing the boat, without so much as looking up at the two boys. After twenty minutes, when the boat was ready for the voyage, a sailor might casually flip the sardine guts and a few whole sardines in the direction of the boys. The boys would silently pick up the scrap fish and run down the dock. Never a word was spoken; it was just a quiet understanding between a working man and a couple of boys trying to survive.

Today, the crew prepared the boat as usual, even going so far as to cast off the lines, allowing the boat to drift a few feet from the dock. Just when it looked like Tariq and Aji would go hungry, the captain tossed the sardine guts and a haul of ten sardines to the boys. This time he gave them a slight wink. The boys quickly grabbed the fish, waved to the captain, and divided their breakfast.

Tariq hungrily consumed half of the guts and then sucked on the raw sardines. They were salty, so salty, but the protein made his stomach growl a little less.

They walked back up the dock and into the city streets of Tangier. The city was just coming to life. Merchants swept the sidewalks in front of their stores. Cafés brewed coffee, and mothers sent their children off to school. It was a world that did not belong to Tariq and Aji. They were merely outsiders to normal society. As society's rejects, they had developed not only an affinity for survival, but also a distrust of anyone in the mainstream. Each day was a different, degrading experience, to the point that they no longer noticed the frowns and sneers from bystanders. They barely acknowledged the shoves and profanities from annoyed merchants when they begged for food. Such was the life of a street orphan.

Tariq's stomach still whined with emptiness.

"Aji, since today is your birthday, I have a special surprise for you. We're going to eat like kings!" Tariq proclaimed.

"How?"

"You know the Hotel Continental? Each Sunday, they prepare a buffet fit for the fattest of monarchs. Eggs from the biggest hens, bacon as thick as your thumb, pancakes, lamb roti, cakes, and rice."

"How are we going to get in there? They won't even let us in the door."

"Not the front door. But they have a patio in back where all the rich Europeans eat. All we need to do is to hide in the bushes—we'll watch and wait until someone with a particularly big plate of food leaves it for just a second. And then we pounce!"

"It sounds like a good plan," Aji agreed.

"Of course it is. But we can only do it one time, because the hotel guards will catch on. So we need to make it count."

"Let's go!"

The two boys quickly ran down the alleys and side streets and in ten minutes were standing outside the Hotel Continental. Two doormen stood at the front door, guarding the entrance. Tariq and Aji nonchalantly hid behind a large potted plant and then crawled on their bellies to the side of the building, just out of the view of the doormen. The side of the building was on a sea cliff. They walked down the cliff and began climbing the scaffolding that supported the underside of the rear deck. Up above, on the deck, Europeans ate at tables under large white umbrellas. Shrubs and planters lined the perimeter of the deck, to prevent the hotel guests from catching a glimpse of the unseemly buildings of downtown Morocco. These barriers were a perfect cover for the two boys.

They climbed ten, fifteen, twenty, and finally thirty-five feet up the wooden scaffolding. Like monkeys climbing trees, they scaled upwards in only a matter of minutes. Soon, both were hidden in a shrub on the deck. Only four feet away, a German couple had just sat down with two heaping plates of breakfast. The food was piled high and wide on both plates.

"Ah, this looks wonderful," said the husband, a rotund older German man with a bald head, handlebar moustache, and generous midsection.

"The crab Benedict looks delightful. Too bad no strudel," said his wife, an equally portly woman with blond hair and rosy cheeks.

"Hmmm," the husband said, eagerly chewing his food.

The boys watched the couple finish their plates and drink two cups of coffee. The man belched before loosening his belt a notch and pushing himself away from the table.

"I'm going for seconds," he proclaimed.

"I'm going to the ladies' room," said his wife. "Please bring me back some French toast, scrambled eggs, and some pieces of cantaloupe. I'm trying to watch my figure."

Her husband nodded in approval and returned to the buffet line, filling his plate equally as high as the first time. He made a second plate for his wife, returned to the table, and sat down. He had just started to eat when he spied some fresh doughnuts being dipped in hot oil and topped with chocolate, raspberry jam, or powdered sugar. He quickly stood up and made his way to the doughnut stand, leaving the two full plates on the table.

Tariq looked around; the deck was only a third full and most people were too concerned with their own food or company to notice an innocent shrub moving around. With the dexterity of a cat and the quickness of a hummingbird, he reached out and grabbed the two plates of food, bringing them back behind the foliage, safely hidden from view. Tariq and Aji moved a couple of shrubs down and away from the Germans, watching for their return.

The man came back to his seat with three doughnuts and prepared to settle into a second course, when he noticed his plates had gone missing. He looked around, looked at the shrub, looked behind him, and even looked under the table. A waiter walked to his table.

"Excuse me sir, is there a problem?" asked the waiter.

"I had two full plates of food right here and now they are gone. Did you clear them?"

"No sir. Perhaps one of the other waiters cleared your table."

"But I was only gone for a second."

"I'm sorry, sir. It's a full buffet, please help yourself."

"Fine. But darn it, I was looking forward to that food. Now I have to walk up again. Oh, never mind," he said, and began swearing in German under his breath.

Tariq and Aji smiled and sat on the edge of the deck, their feet suspended a hundred feet above the ocean below. They were safely camouflaged from the hotel patrons and could eat their breakfast in silence. They stared at the ocean and happily lapped up the sausages and pancakes, hash browns, crepes, and smoked salmon. They hadn't eaten this well in over a month. Although they were happy their bellies were finally full, they were also a bit sad being around the rich European families, with their fine cotton shirts and new leather loafers. Being around families always made Tariq feel sad inside. He knew he would never have one of his own.

"Tariq, what do you think will happen to us when we grow older?" Aji asked.

"I don't know. I'd like to be a fisherman."

"I talked with that woman at the soap market — you know, the fat lady who wears a red wig? She said that orphans like us either end up dead or in jail by the time we're twenty."

"Sheesh, who cares? Do you know how old twenty is? It's like forever from now," Tariq said.

"I guess you're right."

Aji hesitated; then continued.

"It's just that I get sad sometimes. I miss my mother and I wish my father wanted me."

"I know."

"Sometimes I wonder if I could go back to my father."

"He would just beat you more."

Aji sat in silence at this.

"Don't you want a family, Tariq?"

Tariq thought about this for a moment.

"I don't know. Sometimes I dream about having a mother and father. Or, that my real mother will find me. But I don't really think about it much."

"We're kind of like brothers, Tariq."

"That's right, my brother Aji. I'll never leave you, Aji."

"I'll never leave you, either, Tariq. Together to the end!"

"Happy Birthday, my friend."

They finished their plates and set them on the deck. Completely satisfied, they carefully made their way down the scaffolding, crept past the doorman, and were soon wandering the streets of Tangier. They visited all their familiar haunts. Most days, their time consisted solely of finding food and begging for coins. Now, with their bellies full, they found themselves feeling much more content and almost carefree. For one day, they felt like typical boys. They played cricket and hide-and-seek, and even did a little fishing, although neither of them caught anything. Aji found a five-dirham coin, so they were able to buy couscous for dinner.

The sun was setting and the two sat in a park and watched the soft glow of red and yellow. In the distance, Muslims made their call to Mecca and prayers rang out across the city.

"Tariq, this was my best birthday ever," Aji said.

"No problem, Aji," Tariq replied and smiled.

When the sun had finally set, they left the park and began the journey back to their usual spot underneath the dock. The day had been so good, they wanted to extend it. They sang and laughed and told jokes. In their absent-mindedness, they lost their way. Soon, they were in a part of town that could be considered enemy territory. The ghettos—or medinas—of Tangier were no different from the poorest parts of any other major city. City blocks became properties of gangs. Turf was established. To enter a foreign gang's territory was to risk life and limb.

Tariq stopped mid-step.

"Aji, do you know where we are?" he asked.

Aji looked around.

"Muhammad."

Tariq nodded in agreement.

Muhammad El Hadji was fifteen years old and the most feared boy in the orphan underground. He had not yet graduated to adulthood and the full rank of criminal, but that was only a matter of time. He had been orphaned at five years old when his parents were killed by a corrupt police chief. Muhammad took to the streets and was a hellion from the start. At age ten, he killed another boy over a lost wager. At twelve, he was already extorting money from local merchants. At one point, he had attempted to move in on the gambling racket in his neighborhood, but that proved too big of a move for a boy of his age. The local gangsters beat him within an inch of his life and broke both of his thumbs. Since then, he had resigned himself to terrorizing orphans and committing petty theft, but his reputation was still that of a ruthless thug.

Tariq and his friends were considered too small of fish to be bothered by Muhammad. One of them might catch a beating from him once in a while, but that was it. There were so many orphans in Tangier that for Muhammad to try to control all of them would be like trying to catch schools of fish with a glass jar. At first, they were everywhere, and then, nowhere. Tariq and his friends slipped in and out of the shadows, remaining safely anonymous.

Still, they didn't like the idea of being in Muhammad's territory after dark. He might take it as a slight to his authority.

Both boys began to walk faster and to look around nervously. Their chatter and joking stopped. Block after block, they moved stealthily and silently, hoping to avoid any detection or suspicion. They were three blocks from a local police station. Although the police could be even more of a headache than Muhammad, at the moment the boys felt maybe they could provide them with some amount of safety.

But that's when Tariq saw them.

Just ahead, three boys were leaning against a wall, their silhouettes barely visible in the darkness. They were staring at Tariq and Aji, watching their every move.

"Walk forward. Don't look them in the eye. If they get in our way, let me do the talking," Tariq instructed Aji.

The two boys continued to walk, staring straight ahead. Tariq and Aji were about ten feet from the neighborhood boys when the three of them emerged from the shadows and blocked their path.

"Eh, what do we have here? Rats? What are you rats doing in our neighborhood?" one of them asked.

"Nothing. Just walking," Tariq answered.

"Just walking? Rats don't walk; they scamper and hide in gutters. Why aren't you in a gutter, rat?"

"We're not rats."

"I say you're a rat. You're less than a rat."

"We were just walking," Tariq answered, trying to remain calm.

At that point, another taller boy joined the three. He had shaggy black hair and peach fuzz above his lip. In his right ear, a gold earring.

It was Muhammad.

"What do we have here?" he asked.

"Some rats in our territory," the other boy told him.

"Don't you know this is our neighborhood, rats? I'm sick of rats in this city. You look so ugly. You smell. Don't you have a home?" Muhammad asked disgustingly.

"Don't you?" Aji said.

"What did you say to me, rat?" Muhammad said, and pushed Aji.

Suddenly, the four boys surrounded Aji and Tariq, who now stood back to back. Although they were much smaller than the other boys—and petrified—they did not show fear.

Tariq understood the law of the street. He knew could not show fear. He could not back down. To do so would brand him a coward. Once identified as such, he would be subject to constant beatings and ridicule. It was better to stand up for himself, endure a beating and show honor.

He didn't see the first blow. It came from his left. It wasn't such a hard punch; it surprised him, more than anything. He bent his knees and lunged straight into the belly of Muhammad. Surprised, Muhammad was knocked back a foot, but easily kept his balance and threw Tariq to the ground. He brought his right foot up and kicked Tariq square in the cheek. Tariq struggled to his feet but Muhammad easily threw him down again.

"What are you doing, rat? Trying to tackle me? Are you crazy?" Muhammad yelled, with a look of hatred and murder in his black eyes. He seemed to go crazy. It seemed as if a lifetime of suppressed rage rose up and shot out of him like a fire hydrant.

"Let's teach these rats a lesson. Hold this rat down," Muhammad instructed two of the boys, who then held Tariq down by his hands and feet.

The other boy put Aji in a chokehold. Muhammad began hitting Aji relentlessly.

"No," Tariq yelled.

Aji managed to break free and kicked Muhammad in the groin. Muhammad fell to his knees in pain. Aji broke away and tried to run but was tackled by the other boy.

Muhammad, with murder in his eyes, grabbed a stick and brought it down hard on Aji's temple.

Aji dropped to the ground, listless and limp.

Dead.

"NO!" Tariq yelled.

Muhammad was slumped over, out of breath. He turned Aji over onto his back. Blood spilled down from the back of his head onto the city streets. His eyes, still open, stared back at Muhammad. Muhammad kicked him to ensure he was dead. Aji's lifeless body did not move.

Muhammad stared at Tariq.

"You're next!" Muhammad spat. Walking to Tariq, Muhammad raised the stick high over his head, about to bring it down on Tariq's skull.

Tariq prepared for the blow. He looked at his best friend's dead body in the street. He saw his life behind him. He prepared to die. Closing his eyes, he said a small prayer.

Until it stopped.

Inexplicably. Miraculously. The blow did not come.

Tariq looked up and saw that Muhammad had been knocked to the ground. A shadowy figure—a stranger—moved swiftly and fast, knocking down the two boys holding Tariq. The mysterious stranger wheeled around and struck Muhammad again, this time with a blow to the head.

Muhammad staggered and took off running down the alley. His underlings joined him and they all soon sprinted away.

Tariq lay on the ground. Blood streamed down his cheek, mixed with salty tears. He started crying uncontrollably—a combination of adrenaline, shock, and grief at witnessing his best friend's murder.

The stranger went to Aji's body, lifted it up carefully, and spoke to Tariq.

"Let us go and bury your friend," the voice said. It was a feminine voice, soft and melodic.

Tariq wiped his tears and followed the stranger, who carried Aji's body. They loaded it in the back of a small wagon led by a donkey. The stranger covered Aji's body with a rug and motioned for Tariq to get in the cab next to her. Tariq looked at Aji one last time and saw the medallion of a black panther hanging from his neck by a leather strap. Aji had believed the medallion was good luck, and it was his only real possession. Tariq removed the medallion from around Aji's neck, put it in his pocket, and joined the lady.

Quickly, she drew in the reins, and the donkey began trotting up the city street.

Tariq looked at her. She wasn't a Moroccan, or even an Arab woman. She looked different. Yes, she had black hair like an Arab, but her skin wasn't as dark, and her eyes were different. Skinnier, somehow. She wasn't young, but she wasn't old, either. Her attire was entirely black, even her shawl. Normally, Muslim women only wore black when they were in mourning.

"My name is Zijuan," she said.

Tariq said nothing.

"I am sorry for your loss. We will bury your friend tonight. He did not deserve to die this way," she said.

"It was his birthday," Tariq muttered.

Zijuan looked at Tariq. She had seen so much tragedy in Tangier. So many young lives wasted. So much potential squandered. She wished that burying this boy would be an exception. The fact was, every week she buried another orphan. Some due to malnutrition, others to disease, but most of them died violently, killed by the police or rival gangs.

They continued for a mile out of town, away from any housing developments. The moon was full and illuminated the dark path in front of them. They came to a small cemetery, its entrance marked with a large olive tree. The graves were marked with stones and numbered about one hundred.

Zijuan took a shovel from the back of the carriage and began digging. At first, Tariq watched her. But after a few minutes, he got out of the cart and went to her.

"Let me. It's my job. He was my friend," he said.

She stopped, stared at him, and handed him the shovel. He began to dig, one scoop at a time, until he was covered in dirt and had dug a hole deep enough for Aji's body.

"Come with me," she said.

Together, they wrapped Aji's body in the rug, careful to tuck in the sides, and together they lifted the body and brought it to the grave. The body was heavy, heavier than Tariq thought a starving young boy could weigh. They gently lowered his body in the hole.

"What was his name?" Zijuan asked.

"Aji," Tariq said.

"Put your hands together and let us say a prayer for your friend," Zijuan instructed.

Zijuan lowered her head, put her hands together in front of her chest, and began to silently pray. Tariq did nothing. He did not pray. He just stared at his friend's body—wrapped in a knotty old rug, lying in a makeshift grave. He felt numb.

When she finished her prayer, Zijuan started filling the hole with dirt. Tariq stood next to her, dirty and bloodied.

"You did not pray," she said.

"I don't believe in God anymore."

"God did not kill your friend."

"But God let it happen."

"I think God sent me to protect you," she said.

"But you didn't protect Aji."

"I know you are hurting inside. But you must say a prayer for your friend."

"What should I say?"

"What would you want him to hear?"

Tariq thought for a moment. Zijuan stopped shoveling and waited for him.

"God, here is my friend, Aji. Today was his birthday. We went to the Hotel Continental and ate a very good breakfast. Aji's favorite food was moussaka. His favorite game was cricket. He was my best friend. Please look out for him. I will miss him very much."

"That was an excellent prayer," she said and began shoveling again.

In spite of everything, Tariq felt much better having said goodbye to his friend.

Zijuan finished shoveling the dirt and packed it tightly.

"Find some stones to place on the grave," she instructed Tariq.

Tariq took some time and gathered the ten best stones he could find. Together, they made a little sculpture on top of his grave. Zijuan took a piece of paper from the carriage, lit it, and placed it next to the stones. She pulled a pomegranate from her pocket and placed it on the grave as well. She said some words silently.

Tariq stood in silence watching Zijuan.

Then Zijuan motioned for Tariq to sit down.

"Tell me about yourself," Zijuan asked.

Tariq shrugged his shoulders and looked at the ground.

"Who were those boys that killed your friend and were about to kill you?"

Tariq said nothing.

"I imagine you're an orphan without a family or home?"

Again, Tariq said nothing.

Zijuan gently placed her index finger under his chin and brought his eyes to meet hers.

"Tariq, I run an orphanage. I would like for you to join our family. You will have a home and food and, most importantly, an education."

"Why?" he asked.

"Why what?"

"Why are you helping me? Nobody ever helps me."

"Oh, Tariq, you poor little boy. I help you because I know your pain. But you need to know that life doesn't have to be this way."

"I don't care."

"Come with me. I can provide you with a home," said Zijuan.

"It's my fault he's dead."

"What?"

"I'm the one that kept him out late for his birthday. It was my idea to steal food from the hotel. If it weren't for me, Aji would still be alive."

"Tariq, I want you to listen to me. Never allow yourself to become a victim. There will be many, many people who will try to keep you down. They will spit on you, call you a dirty orphan, and treat you as a second-class citizen. Do not give into being a victim and do not ever give in to guilt. It was never your fault for trying to show your friend a good birthday. It is solely the fault of those other boys that your friend died. Do you understand me?"

"Yes."

"Good. Let's take you to your new home."

Zijuan and Tariq rode silently in the carriage. Tariq suddenly felt an overwhelming sense of fatigue. After a few minutes, he drifted into a deep sleep.

Tariq awoke the next morning. He had slept in her guest room on a bed just below a window. It was the first time he had slept in a real bed in over three months. What awoke him was the smell of cooked rice, eggs, and vegetables. The smells were wonderful, and a smile formed on his face. On a chair next to his bed was a brand new outfit of brown pants, a nice red shirt, and goat-leather sandals.

"Tariq, I was just about to wake you. Please take a bath. I've prepared one for you in the lavatory. Afterwards, please put those clothes on," said Zijuan's voice from another room.

Tariq tiptoed to the lavatory and sure enough, a bath was waiting for him; steam from the hot water rose up and covered the mirror.

Slowly, he put his toes, then his foot, then his leg, and finally his entire body in the bath. A bar of soap lay to one side. He took the bar and thoroughly cleaned himself. A bath was considered a luxury. Some of the other orphanages had baths and he loved to just sit and soak. Most of the time, he had to wash himself in the river with the sewage and the cold water. He took his time, and after thirty minutes he emerged from the bath, toweled himself off, and put on the new clothes. They felt very good and were brand new. They were probably made from Egyptian cotton of the finest quality. He looked at himself in the mirror, and saw that he looked like a regular schoolboy.

He walked into Zijuan's living room, which sat between the kitchen and the door to her bedroom. Outside was a small deck with a small table and two wooden chairs.

"My goodness, I thought you might be in that bath all morning. Here, let me prepare some eggs for you. Go ahead and sit outside."

He did as he was told. The terrace room was on the second story. Below him lay a large courtyard with a fountain and a statue of a fat man. The courtyard was very nice, blanketed completely in grass and surrounded by tall bamboo for privacy.

Zijuan brought a plate of three eggs over-easy, an extra-large helping of rice, and a pile of vegetables and placed it in front of Tariq. He began devouring the food.

Zijuan laughed watching him eat at such speed. The food scarcely touched his lips. She was accustomed to starving orphans, and they all ate the same way: as if the plate of food might disappear if they didn't finish it in a minute's time.

"Tariq, this is your first lesson. You must slow down when you eat. When you eat slowly, the food has time to digest, and it will stay in your stomach longer. Chew your food—seven chews and then swallow."

Tariq did as he was told, slowing down and counting each chew.

"Now, hold the fork like this, not with your entire fist but with just your thumb and your index and middle fingers," she instructed him.

Tariq held the fork as he was instructed, and it felt quite awkward. But a hot meal was worth a little awkwardness.

"When you're finished we will burn your clothes," Zijuan said.

"Why?" he asked, with a full mouth.

"Because it is bad luck to keep clothes from a funeral. It attracts demons."

Zijuan watched him as a mother watches a child. She had seen and cared for too many orphans, yet she still felt such compassion for these children who had endured such a hard life.

Tariq stopped chewing and looked at her.

"What happens when we die?" he asked.

"Are you worried about your friend?"

"All I can think about are memories of him. Just yesterday, we were laughing together and sitting over the ocean. Now he is gone and I don't know where."

Zijuan brushed his hair and brought him in close for a hug.

"Each religion believes something different."

"What do you believe?" he asked.

"I am a Buddhist. I believe in reincarnation."

"What does that mean?"

"It means that your friend's spirit will be reborn in someone or something else. That this is just one of many lives we live—and with each life we learn."

He sat for a moment, deep in thought.

"I miss him so much."

"I know, Tariq," she said. Before she could continue, Tariq began to cry uncontrollably, hugging her tightly. His tears soaked her robe. For once, he finally felt safe. As an orphan, he had learned to suppress fear and grief, and he hadn't cried in years. In the presence of Zijuan, he felt safe enough to let himself become vulnerable.

When he finished crying, Zijuan wiped his tears.

"Tariq, there's something we must do. We must go to Aji's grave each day for the next thirty days to mourn. During this time, I want you to think about your life."

"My life?"

"You have a choice, Tariq. You can live a righteous life and honor your friend Aji, or you can live a life of wickedness, where his life will have meant nothing to you."

Tariq played with Aji's medallion that he now wore around his neck. He thought about those words, "You can live a righteous life." He had never given much thought to the idea of good or evil. Until now, his entire life had been focused on one thing—survival.

He made a pledge at that moment to honor his friend and his brother. He would find a way to make a difference in this life, and would leave the world a better place for having lived in it. He didn't know how, but he had a feeling Zijuan would show him the way. Already, she was teaching him, and he was a willing student.

Three Years Later—The Day of Tariq's Kidnapping

Zijuan awoke to the children screaming in the wee hours of the morning. Quickly, she put her robe on and went downstairs.

The children were frantically running and pointing.

"What happened?" she asked.

"Tariq is gone!" one of them screamed.

"What?"

"A man appeared at the window. He came in, hit Tariq and dragged him off."

"When?" she asked.

"Just a few moments ago."

Zijuan ran outside, followed by a few of the children.

"Tariq!" she yelled.

She ran from block to block yelling his name. Neighbors came out and joined the search. For an hour she ran up and down the city streets yelling for Tariq, but they never found him that night. She returned to the orphanage to tend to the scared children. Bolting the window above Tariq's bed, she put the children back to bed and stayed with them in their dormitory for the rest of the night. The youngest ones cried, while the older ones lay traumatized. She told them bedtime stories, but how do you console a child that has witnessed one of their friends being abducted right in front of them? Would they ever be able to sleep in that room again? Would they ever be the same?

The next morning she gathered all the children together.

"I understand how scary last night was for you. I have decided to move all of your beds upstairs, and I will live downstairs. We will also bolt all the windows at night," she explained

"What about Tariq?" one asked.

"I will work with the local police to find Tariq."

"They won't care about an orphan."

"You are not orphans. Orphans are children without families. All of you have a family. If the local police do not find Tariq, then I will find him myself."

"How will you do that?"

"I have my ways."

That day Zijuan went to the local police precinct. She waited for half the day before talking to a junior officer who seemed more interested in his coffee than helping her find Tariq. He took her name and told her he would stop by the next day. He never showed.

The next day, Zijuan went to the offices of Yasouf Malouda. Actually, it wasn't an office at all, but a tucked away restaurant with a very limited clientele.

Yasouf Malouda was the local gangster overlord that presided over her neighborhood. Since the police were either corrupt or incompetent, the citizenry paid local mafia to keep them safe. For over three years now, Zijuan had been paying Yasouf to protect her orphans. This protection meant that the local gangs weren't allowed to recruit them. The slave owners were forbidden from taking any children to be sold in the slave markets. It was a very expensive arrangement, and it took all of Zijuan's resources to make the weekly payments. But, in her mind, it was worth every penny. Without this protection, her orphanage would be open to every thief, drug runner, and pimp within a mile radius.

She had never, in three years, asked Yasouf for so much as a favor in return. But that was about to change.

A thug greeted her at the restaurant door and recognized her from the neighborhood. Usually, it took weeks to get an audience with Yasouf. However, considering the circumstances, she simply had to have his immediate attention.

Zijuan walked to a large back room with tables and cushions, rather than chairs, along each wall. There were about ten people in the room but only one was seated. A few stood chatting and sipping lime juice, and three others watched the entrance to the room.

Zijuan sat down on a pillow opposite Yasouf. Zijuan was not Moroccan; however, she garnered much respect in the neighborhood for running an honest orphanage.

"Zijuan, I am Yasouf; please, what will you have to drink?" he asked.

"I would just like some water, thank you."

A waiter bowed slightly and disappeared.

Zijuan had paid this man every week for three years, yet she had never once met him. He was in his mid-fifties, with a big belly, and wore a traditional Moroccan tunic. His face was tan and jowls rolled over his cheeks. Sweat dripped down his neck and he continually fanned himself with a small paper fan in his left hand. His eyes were gentle, more so than Zijuan expected, and he seemed to be trustworthy.

"I understand one of your orphans has disappeared?" he asked.

"Yasouf Malouda, in three years I have never asked you for anything and have paid my protection money each week. I am asking you now. I must find this boy."

The gangster poured himself a cup of mint tea and breathed a heavy sigh. Like most Moroccans, he preferred extremely sweet tea and placed four spoonfuls of sugar in his cup before stirring. The waiter returned with a cold cup of water, placed it at Zijuan's side, and disappeared.

"I know everything that happens in this neighborhood. I knew your orphan was missing an hour after it happened. Let me assure you, my people had nothing to do with it."

"But you know who did?"

"Yes, but, it's complicated."

"I'm listening."

"Since the French have taken an interest in our country, the rules have changed. It used to be that there was a certain amount of order. Five years ago, I would have your boy back to you and the people responsible would be lying in a ditch with their throats cut. But now..."

"So the French have something to do with it?"

"Not the French, but a Frenchman. His name is Mr. LaRoque. He is a dubious character, who has invaded every space of the Moroccan underground. He controls the black market—opium, prostitution, and the trading of human beings as slaves. Mr. LaRoque has the protection of some higher-ups in the French military. As long as he has military protection, it is impossible to get to him."

"So he does whatever he wants?"

"Let's just say there's a very difficult truce in place. He plays in our little playground and we let him, as long as he doesn't kick too much sand."

"That's it? This LaRoque steals my boy and there's nothing you can do? Perhaps I should be paying my protection money to the French military?"

Yasouf did not like this line of thinking or the tone of her voice.

"I would recommend that you watch your anger with me. Even I have limits of what I will abide from a woman. And yes, you must pay me protection. The French military doesn't care about your little orphanage. Without my protection, every criminal from here to Casablanca would be preying on your orphans."

"I'm sorry; I did not mean any disrespect. Tariq is a very special boy to me. Imagine if you lost a son, how would you feel?" she pleaded.

Yasouf thought about this for a moment before continuing.

"Your boy was sold at a slave auction yesterday, I've learned, to none other than Caid Ali Tamzali, who has a kasbah about a five or six days' ride out of town, on the outskirts of the Rif Mountains. Your orphan was probably purchased to become a camel jockey."

"What?"

67

"Young boys are prized to ride camels. They are small, relatively inexpensive to purchase as slaves, and it is a very dangerous business. Most die within a month or two."

"How do you know this?"

"I have my sources."

As she stood up to leave, he stopped her with his hand.

"Madame, please do not take Ali Tamzali lightly. He is as ruthless as they come. He reports directly to the Sultan; he is not a man to be trifled with."

"Thank you for your concern, but I will take care of this."

She walked out. She knew where Tariq had gone and who had taken him. The problem was there was no possible way she could leave the orphanage for more than a day or two, let alone two full weeks. She had to find another way to help Tariq.

She knew of some resistance fighters in the Rif Mountains. A long time ago, before she had started the orphanage, Zijuan had been a different kind of woman—a soldier who traveled the plains of the Sahara fighting alongside nomads and various tribes. She still had contacts from back then, and she hoped one of them could help her.

She quickly made her way back to the orphanage. There wasn't a moment to waste.

CHAPTER
— *6* —

LESSONS OF A CAMEL JOCKEY

A kasbah is a combination of castle, palace, and living quarters. It is a kind of city in the desert, completely self-contained and self-sufficient. Like castles in Europe, most kasbahs were strategically placed on high ground or built adjacent to a mountainside to prevent enemy attack.

The Kasbah of Caid Ali Tamzali was more impressive than most. The buildings and walls were made of red clay, which allowed them to blend seamlessly into the desert. Regal flags flew from almost every rooftop, providing an element of whimsy not experienced at most other kasbahs. It sat in a tiny oasis, complete with a well and several palm trees. Just three miles to the west was the entrance to some smaller hills and a valley that stretched for many miles. Ride northeast for three or four hours and the Rif Mountains presented their majestic beauty.

The location of this kasbah was no accident. Invaders from the adjacent mountain range would need to cross open desert to reach it, making a surprise attack nearly impossible. The gully from the oasis provided protection from the desert winds, as did the kasbah walls. It did, however, have one weakness: a solitary, lonely hillside riddled with prickly pear cactus. That weakness could provide cover for a sneak attack—not from a large army, but from a small band of fifty or so soldiers.

The caravan moved, as slowly as a slug, across the desert and finally arrived at the kasbah gates. Two guards came out from behind the gate, greeted Zahir, and did a cursory check of the wagons. Satisfied, they allowed the caravan to enter the kasbah grounds.

Inside, the kasbah was transformed—the red clay exterior giving way to a magnificent display of colors, gardens, architecture, statues, fountains, artwork, and beautiful Moroccan mosaics that adorned nearly every wall, and even the floor. Smells of jasmine and palm oil wafted through the air. Giraffes, monkeys, hyenas, lions, zebras, and other

69

beasts circled in cages or roamed freely. Kasbah patrons in the traditional Arabic attire of dishdasha, fancy Saudi agals, and informal shawls walked and chatted throughout the grounds. Parrots and toucans squeaked from branches. Kasbah performers juggled and swallowed fire. Arabic women, dressed in niqabs and burqas, walked together in sets of three or four. Their faces and bodies completely covered from head to toe, it was their eyes outlined with black kohl that scanned their surroundings like a panther stalking its prey.

The caravan dispersed and the captives' wagon was taken to the furthest building from the gate. A guard appeared at the back of the wagon and grunted for them to follow him. They obediently climbed out and followed the guard to a set of two doors.

"You three will follow me," he said, pointing to the boys as he walked through the door on the left.

An old woman appeared in rags and grabbed Margaret by her wrist hard, forcing her to walk through the door on the right. Margaret looked back at her friends and felt very alone. Tariq caught her glance, gave her a little smile, and nodded his head before disappearing into the doorway. That small gesture gave Margaret a measure of hope.

The guard took the three boys down a long hallway to an area where another guard was seated at a desk. He took down their names, ages, height, and weight. Then, he unshackled their leg irons and proceeded to open a door behind him.

The boys followed the guard through the door into a large room. Cell bars lined both sides of the room. All along the bars, the boys saw dozens of small hands and legs, and pairs of tiny eyes—the faces of young boys, dirty and squalid.

At the far end of the room the boys saw a door with a huge lock. To get to the door, the three newcomers had to walk through the room, flanked by all the jailed orphans yelling at them.

"Look at the new boys. So skinny and weak!"

"You better not come in here. We'll get you if you come in here."

"Do not sleep tonight. We'll get you once you fall asleep."

At once the chamber grew loud with shrill and shrieking voices. Boys laughed and hollered at the new slaves.

"Enough!" the guard yelled and the room fell quiet.

He unlocked the door and threw the boys in with the rest before locking the door behind him and walking out. At once, Tariq, Aseem, and Fez were surrounded.

"You better not win anything or you're through!" one yelled.

Another boy pushed Aseem, who pushed him back. A couple of others tried to tackle Tariq, but he hit one of them in the mouth, knocking him away. Fez was pushed to the ground, but he quickly got up. In a few seconds, all three of their backs were pressed against a stone wall. Over twenty boys had them surrounded, yelling and pushing at them. Finally, the boys stopped and one stepped forward.

"My name is Jawad. I am the leader in this place. You do as I say and you will get along," he instructed them.

Jawad was about as tall as Tariq, but with dirty hair and mere rags for clothes.

"What is that medallion around your neck?" Jawad asked Tariq.

Tariq said nothing.

"I asked you a question. You want trouble? What is that?" Jawad asked.

Again, Tariq said nothing. He held onto the medallion owned by Aji and stared back at the boy.

"When I ask you a question, you answer me!" Jawad yelled and shoved Tariq. Tariq shoved him back, but soon eight other boys had joined in and Tariq was pushed to the ground. They began kicking him and hitting at his head. Tariq balled himself up in a fetal position but was still kicked and punched badly.

Aseem and Fez joined in, but they were outnumbered. It was a scrum. The hard, wet dungeon floor scraped and battered their knees. When it looked hopeless, as if these other boys might beat them to death, a loud "screeechhh" sucked all the energy from the room. At once all the boys stopped and looked up.

The three boys had not noticed it when they arrived, but a monkey sat on a perch above the door—a small monkey with brown fur and white whiskers.

He screeched again and the boys cleared away.

Aseem, Fez, and Tariq stood up as well. They made their way to the corner of the cell, and soon Jawad came up to them.

"That is a little game we play with the new boys to see who is tough. If you don't fight back, you'll never make it. Welcome to your new home," he said and shook each of their hands.

The boys looked at each other in amazement, still smarting from their wounds and scrapes.

"That is nothing. Wait until you race. If one accident doesn't kill you, you'll wish it had. And there is no mercy. I once had to race three races in a day with a broken wrist. They do not care."

"Camel races?" Tariq asked.

"Of course. I am the finest camel racer in all of Morocco. The Caid himself asked to see me after one of my races."

"How long have you been racing?"

"Over two years, longer than any racer in history, I am told. I have been in over 300 races."

"That is impressive," Aseem exclaimed.

"Thank you," said Jawad.

"What about the monkey?" Fez asked.

"That is Ocho. He is, well, kind of like a guard. He picks out who will race, who will eat, who will get time outdoors."

"You're kidding?"

"No, he is a very smart monkey. What are your names?" Jawad asked.

"I am Aseem."

"I am Tariq."

"I am Fez."

"Fez, like the city?"

"Yes. My father always wanted to visit Fez but never had the opportunity, so he named me Fez."

"Ha, that's funny. Okay, let me tell you the rules," Jawad started.

"First, I am sure you met Zahir. He is the most evil guard in the kasbah. He will kill you for no reason at all. So steer clear of him.

"Second, you will receive no training, so you must listen to someone in the group for your first few races. It is all part of the wagering, racing the new boys who have no training. But if you don't do well you will get whipped. If you continually don't do well..."

"What?" Tariq interrupted.

"A boy once came in last for three straight races, and we never saw him again.

"Third. Do not steal. If you have a quarrel with someone, talk to me. We are slaves, but we are not animals.

"And the last rule is," Jawad continued, "don't upset the monkey. If he points you out, the guards will beat you and put you in solitary. It is a horrible place. A box barely big enough to squat in with a hole in the ground. By midafternoon, it is so hot you could pass out."

A guard came in with a large plate of food and set it next to Ocho. The plate was filled with mounds of beef, bananas, and even a few pieces of baklava. All the boys gathered around him with their hands raised, waving and jumping for his attention. Ocho nonchalantly played with the food and then pointed at a boy.

Everyone stopped and stared at the boy. On cue, he started pantomiming a monkey, walking on all fours, making monkey noises, and jumping up and down.

Not completely satisfied with the performance, Ocho tossed him a banana. The boy took it and greedily started eating it.

Ocho pointed to another boy. This boy, however, gave a much more spirited performance, vigorously jumping up and down.

Excited, Ocho jumped up and down and then threw the boy a huge piece of meat.

"Ahhh," said the other boys, in appreciation.

Ocho then pointed at Aseem.

All the boys stopped at looked at Aseem. He did nothing.

"Act like a monkey—that's the only way you'll get food," one whispered to Aseem.

"I'm not acting like a monkey."

Ocho screamed at Aseem, but Aseem refused. Ocho screamed louder but still Aseem did not move. The monkey began pacing back and forth and screaming.

"If you don't do it, soon the guards will come in and you'll get beaten," another whispered.

"Just do it, Aseem. It's just a stupid monkey," Tariq instructed him.

Slowly, Aseem began to simulate a monkey in a very lazy attempt. Ocho still shrieked at him. Aseem became more and more animated; he hooted like a monkey and even banged against the cages. Soon, it was a very comical performance. At one point Aseem lifted his arm, smelled his armpit, and fell over backwards in mock disbelief.

Ocho loved that, and threw Aseem a piece of baklava.

"I would have preferred a piece of meat," Aseem said and walked away.

After ten minutes, all the boys had given their performance. Aseem was joined by Tariq and Fez. Fez had garnered a nice piece of lamb while Tariq managed a banana. Together, they shared their meal.

Soon, all the boys were asleep. The dungeon was extremely dark with only two small windows for light to creep in. Aseem, Fez, and Tariq used one another as pillows and managed a restful sleep. Without sandstorms or chains or bandits to worry about, their tiny bodies collapsed from exhaustion.

"Squaawwkkkkk!" screamed Ocho.

Slowly, the orphans woke up and moved about. Tariq was extremely sore. The ground was hard and had stiffened his back and neck, but it was the whippings he had endured at the hands of Zahir that caused his entire body to feel like one massive welt. Blood had soaked through his clothes, and purple bruises formed where the leather had met his bare skin. He walked gingerly, and pain shot through his thighs with every step.

"Squaawwkkkkk!"

With that, a guard came down and unlocked the door.

"Okay you slaves. Get up and out there!" he yelled.

The boys exited the cells and ascended the stairs to the dungeon doors. The shock of the bright sunlight forced them to shade their eyes. Tariq, Aseem, and Fez followed the other boys outside. Fez took care to place his glasses in a safe place. He would be racing blind, but he'd rather take that chance than risk breaking his precious glasses.

"What is happening?" Aseem asked.

"We're practicing today," one answered.

The boys were quickly shuffled to a food line. An old servant, with a rice concoction of fig, raisin, and goat, loaded two ladlesful into the outstretched hands of each orphan. No plate or silverware allowed. The boys gobbled the mixture, and most of them didn't spill a single grain of rice.

The operation was swift and orderly, and in five minutes all had eaten and were being shuffled to a different area that included the stable. Most of the boys went directly to a camel and began preparing it for a ride. Jawad took the three new boys, had each grab a bridle and saddle, and told them to follow him.

"You will need to place these bits in their noses. I will help you," Jawad said. He showed them how to clamp the bit to the interior of each camel's nostrils and then place the reins around its neck. He slowly exhibited the proper technique, then made each boy do it themselves to show they understood.

He spoke to each camel with a quiet, soothing voice and then placed a blanket on its back and tied it down underneath its belly. He performed this task four times and again ordered each boy to do it without instruction.

When the camel was prepared to ride, Jawad had it sit down and await the rider. He used the Arabic word for sit—"iijilis." Slowly, each camel sat on its knees in turn. Then, Jawad showed each rider how to mount the camel, grip the reins, and how to give a variety of commands for stopping, trotting, and galloping to full speed.

"The reins are everything, as is your confidence. If the camel feels you are afraid, he will not listen to you. Be strong and confident in the saddle. Grip the reins firmly, but gently, it doesn't require much movement from you to get the camel to obey your command. Never hit a camel or treat it poorly. Their lives are more prized than one hundred of ours. Always treat it with respect."

Each boy mounted his camel and waited for Jawad.

"Okay, follow me. Loosen up the reins and use the word 'kef' to make it stand," he ordered.

Each boy did as he was told. Slowly, each camel rose except for Fez's. His stubbornly sat.

"Oh, you're on Old Kasseef. He's stubborn. Pull on his reins a little harder and use your knees a bit."

Fez did as he was told and suddenly the camel rose to his feet.

"Now, say the word 'macha,' loosen your grip on the reins, and kick in your heels a bit."

"Macha, macha!" each boy yelled.

"Not so loud. Camels are quite smart and inquisitive, just say it normally," Jawad instructed.

The camels began to walk, following one another out the gate.

"Camels are pack animals, so they will always want to stick together. The best way to punish a camel is by separating it from its pack."

For twenty minutes, Jawad walked with them, barked out instructions, and improved their form. Satisfied, he prepared them for the next step.

"Good, good, now we're going to get them to run. Loosen up on the reins even more, stand up, and yell 'jara' in a more excited voice."

Each boy did as he was told; it was quite scary being on such a tall animal and telling it to run. But none of their camels ran.

"No, you're all too afraid. Say it quickly, and gently kick your heels. Not too strong. You must let him know you want to run," he yelled, and had his own camel running in a matter of seconds.

"This is madness. If I fall I'm going to die!" Aseem yelled.

"I guess we have to learn sometime," Fez countered.

Fez dug his heels in a little more, stood up, and yelled "jara." His camel began to trot and then, at more urging, fell into a quick pace with little Fez bouncing on top.

"I'm going to die!!" Fez screamed as he galloped past Tariq and Aseem.

Tariq and Aseem looked at one another, shrugged their shoulders, dug their heels in, and yelled to their camels. It didn't take long before they were also at a full gallop, racing after Fez.

Camels can run at a speed of up to forty miles an hour. Because the rider sits six feet or so off the ground, it takes time to adjust to the camel's movement. Each one is different—some camels are jittery, while others offer quite a smooth ride. The boys continued to practice for the entire day, learning how to control a frightened camel, allow it to eat, stand up in the saddle to race, and take off its saddle and bridle.

Tariq was having the most trouble. His wounds were aching and his entire body was sore. The pain made focusing and concentrating very difficult. At one point, he thought he would pass out. He simply kept trying to hang on and to push the animal to run faster. He found himself going in fits and starts. The camel would run, but only for a few feet, and then it would jog or stop entirely.

Each boy had fallen two times but never seriously. They hadn't ridden their camels very fast or hard, still scared by the prospect of going so fast on such a tall animal. The other boys were much faster and able to control their camels with greater efficiency and dexterity than the three beginners. By the end of the day, the boys were dirty and sweaty and tired from racing under the hot desert sun.

"You only have three days to prepare for the next race. You must get faster. If you're that slow in a race, you will each get whipped for sure," Jawad scolded them.

"We're trying," Tariq replied, annoyed.

"No, you cannot try, you must do. These camel races are very serious to the Caid and to the sheiks. It is a matter of their honor. If you are racing their colors and you do not do well, some of them may just kill you to show their ferocity to the others. You must learn to go fast."

Aseem just nodded and said nothing. It was hard enough learning how to ride a camel for the first time; how were they expected to race and compete against boys so much more experienced?

For the next three days it was the same routine: rise early, prepare the camels, and then ride them all day. As the days passed, the boys slowly grew more and more comfortable with galloping at full speed and could even saddle and unsaddle their camels by themselves. They were still not as fast as the other boys, but they were getting much better.

The night before the race none of the boys could sleep.

"I heard a boy died in the last race," Fez said.

"I heard that too. And another boy's legs were crushed," Aseem added.

"Just try to hold on and try not to finish last. At this time, we must just survive; there's no way we can beat Jawad and some of the other boys," Tariq agreed.

"I'm scared," Fez confessed.

"I'm scared, too," Tariq admitted.

"I don't want to die, Tariq," Fez said.

"Just hold on tightly and move with the camel like we were taught."

"I miss my parents, Tariq. I miss my family. I don't know if I can do this," Fez said and began crying.

"Fez, listen to me," Tariq explained. "I know the pain you are feeling. But you are not alone—you are never alone! Aseem and Margaret and I will look after you. You will be fine, that is my promise."

"Okay," Fez said, his tears slowing.

"Besides," Tariq continued, "you're the best camel rider of all of us. I can barely stay on the thing, and Aseem looks like he can barely sit on it."

"I can't sit on it because my bum is so sore. I haven't been able to sit down for three days!" Aseem said and Fez started laughing.

"See there? Just treat the race like a big game and you won't be afraid. Don't think about falling, only think about going faster and winning," Tariq said.

"Okay, thank you, Tariq," Fez said and smiled.

"It is my pleasure, Fez, my little brother."

All three boys settled back into bed, each with their own thoughts. Tariq lay awake. He had to be strong for little Fez, but inside he was just as scared. He could scarcely stay on the camel himself—and that was only running at half speed. What happened when the camel ran at full speed in a pack of others? He had seen some of the scars on the other boys. One had a scar running all the way down the back of his leg from a fall during a race. He was told that the boy still had to race with a broken leg, and it almost killed him. In just three days, two boys had gone to the nurse after nasty falls.

Over the past three days, Margaret had endured a much different kind of prison.

First, she was forced to bathe for two straight hours before putting on a long flowing kaftan brightly colored in red and yellow. Then, she was shuffled into a windowless room with only some pillows to sit upon. After a few moments, an older woman took her through a hallway and into a kitchen. The woman said nothing to Margaret, and didn't so much as make eye contact or smile in the least.

In the kitchen, there were about thirteen or fourteen girls, all around Margaret's age. Each stopped their work and stared at the Caucasian girl, some whispered to one another, but no one spoke a word loud enough to be heard. Each of them performed a specific task. Some peeled potatoes, others chopped onions, and the rest went about cleaning and scrubbing.

The older woman had Margaret sit at a table next to another girl. The girl was a few years younger than Margaret, perhaps ten years old. She managed to give Margaret a bit of a smile. Margaret smiled back and felt relieved that at least someone was friendly. The younger girl was scrubbing vegetables with a loofah made of dried sea sponge. The older woman gave Margaret a similar loofah and pointed at her to follow the younger girl in scrubbing.

Hundreds of potatoes, turnips, carrots, and other vegetables were mounded on the table in front of them. Each girl would take a vegetable, dip the sponge in water, and scrub vigorously until all the dirt was removed. Margaret followed the example of the younger girl and began scrubbing and washing alongside her, tossing the scrubbed vegetables into the designated bucket.

Nobody said a word or gave Margaret any kind of instruction. Some of the girls continually peeked at her, curious about her white skin.

Margaret scrubbed vegetables for the rest of the day. After a few hours, her fingers became soft, then started to ache and split. Her fingers were tired and hurt, but she dared not complain. She was scared, yet the scrubbing was somehow peaceful. It provided her with something to do rather than sit and worry.

After another hour, a different older woman came to the kitchen. All the girls stopped their work and followed the woman. Margaret joined the formation at the end of the line.

The girls were led through a series of hallways and finally reached a large door with two sentries on either side. The sentries opened the door and the girls were ushered through. They walked into a magnificent room about forty feet high and half the size of a football field. The floor, ceiling, walls, and pillars were made of the finest Italian marble. Jasmine incense and myrrh created a beautiful aroma. Massive vases of peacock feathers were everywhere.

The room was littered with pools and fountains. Many of the girls dipped their toes in the fountains and others lazily slept on the many pillows and couches. On the ceiling and walls were enormous stained glass windows of every color and image, allowing sunlight to fill the room but preventing the harem from being seen by outside eyes.

Once inside, the older woman allowed the girls to wander freely. The other girls quickly dispersed. Margaret walked over to an empty wall and sat on a pillow. She felt more alone than ever. She missed Tariq, Fez, and Aseem and wondered if she would she ever see them again.

Margaret started to cry softly. She missed her parents. She missed her home.

A very fat girl called Fatima saw her crying. She went up to Margaret and stood over her.

"Why are you crying?" she yelled at Margaret.

Margaret said nothing, balling up her knees tightly to her chest.

"You think you're better than the rest of us because you're white?" Fatima scolded her.

"No," Margaret muttered.

Fatima grabbed Margaret by the hair and stared her straight in the eyes. Margaret trembled with terror.

"Listen little girl, you do exactly as you're told, you understand?" Fatima scowled at her.

"Yesss," Margaret stammered out.

"You get in my way and you won't live a week, you understand?"

"Yes."

"Good, now go get me some tea and then fan me with a feather," Fatima ordered.

Margaret did as she was told.

Fatima was squalid and obese, with rolls of fat dripping down her body. She was constantly sweating and eating. Her face was pudgy and caked with mounds of garish makeup—like a grotesque clown. A black moustache formed around her upper lip.

Fatima was not necessarily desired by the Caid or anyone else within the kasbah, but she held considerable power within the harem because she was bigger and fatter than the other girls. She was a bully and forced the younger, skinnier girls to perform tasks for her. As she was unattractive and unwanted, this was her way to get back at the more attractive girls. Yes, they may be desirable, but they were forced to become her servants. From the outside, life in a harem might seem ideal, even dreamy. The reality was quite different.

Within the harem there was a very strict hierarchy. New girls were treated harshly and forced to serve the other, more senior, members. This might include scrubbing their backs as they bathed, painting their toes, fetching them food and water, washing their laundry, or spending countless hours brushing their long, thick hair. But it was the verbal abuse that was the most difficult. The older members ridiculed and mocked the new girls in an effort to tame them into servitude. Ungrateful or rebellious slave girls could expect a good beating from the older members of the harem. At times, they might even take a piece of wire, hold it to a flame until it was red hot, and then singe the bottom of a slave's foot—holding it in place until the girl screamed with agony. This torture left a scar to remind the rebellious girl of her place in the harem.

Margaret spent her first days within the harem scrubbing vegetables and waiting hand and foot on fat Fatima. None of the girls talked with her or comforted her. Some made eye contact and a few smiled, but that was all. No one was friendly.

It was as if someone had given the other girls specific orders to ignore her.

The sun appeared over the mountains, signaling Ocho to wake the orphans. The group quickly assembled and marched outside. Instead of their traditional handful of rice, the slaves were urged to sit down at a table. Covering the table were crepes with jam, figs, juice, and pastilla, a flaky pastry filled with roasted pigeon. The boys inhaled the delicious breakfast. Tariq learned this feast was customary prior to a race, as the Caid and the sheiks wanted their riders full and strong.

Next, more changes were in order. The boys were shuffled off to a bathhouse. Inside, twenty tubs full of warm water lay in rows. The boys were each given fifteen minutes to wash themselves.

"I could get used to this," Fez said.

"This is very nice," Aseem agreed while washing his hair with lemon-scented soap.

A servant entered the bathhouse carrying a long stick with jockey uniforms hung from beginning to end. A guard went to each boy, measured up his size, and placed a uniform next to his tub. After all the uniforms had been distributed, the guard ordered the boys to dress and meet him outside. The boys dressed, with the help of Jawad, and lined up single file outside the bathhouse.

"Okay. You follow me, single file, and never look anyone in the crowd in the eyes. Do you understand?" the guard asked.

"Yes, sir!" they replied in unison.

The camel jockeys marched in unison to the stables. At the stables, they randomly selected a camel and were ordered to form a single-file line. Aseem struggled to control his camel, while Fez and Tariq seemed to have complete command over theirs.

"What's the problem? Why won't he obey me?" Aseem asked in a worried tone.

"His name is Kino. He's the fastest camel in the stable but also the most wild. You must be very firm and control him with strength," Jawad told him.

Aseem pulled on the reins more tightly and squeezed his thighs in hard. This helped to control Kino a little, but he was still quite spirited.

The jockeys marched the length of the kasbah, and its inhabitants came out to greet and cheer them. People threw flowers and rice at the boys and beat drums. Many waved red flags, while others danced and clapped their hands. Women yelped and screamed and men chanted. The boys felt like heroes walking through the crowd. For the first time since their capture, all three boys smiled.

They exited the kasbah gates into an entire village of tents that had been erected during the night. Under the tents, sheiks and warlords from various tribes basked and bargained, surrounded by their slaves and harems. The sheiks were easy to spot—their robes were overflowing with pageantry, and they walked with an air of entitlement and superiority. Under the biggest tent sat a man on a gigantic throne made of oak. The man was fat, with tanned skin, a black goatee, and rosy cheeks. He ate grapes slowly as he watched the camels emerge from the kasbah.

"That is Caid Ali Tamzali," Jawad whispered.

The three boys couldn't help but look sideways at the Caid. He was seated front and center, and his eyes blazed through them—hotter than the Saharan sun.

In the back, although they could not see her, Margaret Owen sat watching them. They would not have recognized her. She was wearing entirely Arab garb, and her face was completely covered.

The boys were ordered to stop their camels and to form a single line in front of the tents.

"His Excellency Caid Ali Tamzali is proud to present today's race, fifteen miles through the desert and back. We will now choose the riders' colors." Zahir appeared with a large basket.

"Each of us will be given a scarf and that is the sheik we will ride for," Jawad explained.

Zahir reached into the basket and handed each rider a ball wrapped in paper. Each boy took off the paper and placed the scarf around his neck and shoulders. The scarves had bright colors and represented the houses and kasbahs of the various sheiks and the Caid.

Fez was given a yellow and black scarf which represented the house of Sheik Hasim Asoof.

Aseem's was a blue and maroon scarf honoring the house of Sheik Ali El Babel.

Finally, Tariq's package revealed a scarf colored red and white—the scarf of Caid Ali Tamzali.

"You better ride fast. The Caid does not like to lose when he is hosting a race," Jawad whispered.

Tariq placed the scarf around his shoulders and steadied his camel. He stared out into the desert, where the orange sun was just coming complete on the horizon. A stiff breeze at his neck, his heart pounded in his throat.

The riders were now in single file waiting at the starting line. They would ride for seven and a half miles into the desert, circle a flag marker at the half-way point, and then race back. Guards on horseback and camels patrolled the route to ensure no one escaped.

Right before the start, several guards came to each rider. With brine rope, the guards tied each boy's ankles to his saddle and his wrists to the bridle. The ropes were supposed to help riders stay on galloping camels, because the reality was, if a rider did fall off he would almost certainly be dragged to his death.

Once all the riders were tied in, the Caid stood at his chair with a rifle, held it high, and fired. Almost every man in the crowd also held a rifle high and commenced firing after the Caid's first shot. The desert suddenly became an echo of gunfire and explosions, and the camels lurched forward in response to the noise. Off they went, racing into the desert.

The camels seemed to understand that this was a real race and began to run harder and faster than they had during practice days. Tariq felt the rope dig in and begin to burn his skin. Aseem bounced up and down and struggled to maintain control. Little Fez, the lightest of the group, was having the easiest time.

For the first mile, all the racers stayed in a tight pack, but then the more experienced riders began to increase their leads. Jawad went to the front followed by two others. Fez was in fourth, while Aseem and Tariq were at the end of the pack, almost last. Only one other boy was behind them.

After a few more miles, the pain from the rope was excruciating for Tariq. With the camel's every step, he felt it dig in, and soon his wrists were covered in blood. He tried to loosen the rope, but it was tied too tightly. All his struggling made him go slower, and soon he was in last place and unable to keep up with the pack. He grimaced with pain and ground his teeth together. He couldn't see how he would make it back.

Aseem slowed down.

"Are you okay, Tariq?" he yelled.

"The rope is burning my skin. Every time the camel goes fast, it digs in deeper."

"Try leaning forward more to take tension off the rope," Aseem suggested.

Tariq tried this technique and it helped a little. He was able to go faster, but the two still lagged far behind the group.

"The Caid will kill me if I finish last," Tariq worried.

"Don't worry, I will finish last," Aseem reassured him.

The group gained more and more distance on them until the last camel in front of them was no bigger than a tiny dot on the horizon. Aseem and Tariq rode as fast as they could, but the pain was too much for Tariq. He had to slow down every thirty seconds. Blood continued to drip down from his wrists, drenching his hands.

Up in front of the pack, Jawad separated himself from the other boys. He was fifty feet ahead of the closest rider. In the distance, he could see the tents and urged on his camel. The animal lunged faster, and Jawad increased his lead with each passing minute. He rode on until he crossed the finish line first. Everyone shouted and whooped and hollered. More gunfire erupted in the air. Women came and threw flowers on him. Sheik

Raz Khamin greeted him personally, first by taking his dagger to the ropes that bound Jawad's ankles and wrists, and then by helping him off the camel and escorting him to his tent. There was always a considerable amount of wagering on each camel race, and Sheik Khamin had won a small fortune for finishing first. He kissed Jawad on both cheeks and ordered his senior servant to prepare a feast for Jawad. As a slave, Jawad would not be allowed to sit at the Sheik's table, but would eat his feast with the other camel riders in the servants' quarters.

Jawad smiled broadly, and thanked the Sheik for his generosity.

The other riders trickled across the finish line. Fez finished fourth, extremely well for a new rider. The second- and third-place riders were greeted almost as enthusiastically as Jawad had been. Their sheiks had won wagers as well. Slowly, the entire pack crossed the finish line, with the exception of two—Aseem and Tariq.

Caid Ali Tamzali sat angrily waiting for Tariq to arrive. Zahir stood at his side. No rider for the Caid had ever finished this poorly. With each passing second, the Caid became more embarrassed and angry. Zahir could feel his master's temper rising to a boil. Zahir would take care of it.

By the time Aseem and Tariq crossed the finish line, Tariq was in so much pain he could scarcely remain seated on his camel. His ankles and wrists had been scraped raw, and blood and skin dripped down his feet and hands. His face was white, and he felt he might faint from the pain. He leaned forward on his camel and draped his body over its back.

Zahir came from the Caid's chair, unsheathed his dagger, and cut Tariq loose. He dragged him by his outstretched arm through the sand. Tariq moaned in pain, but Zahir paid him no mind. He dragged Tariq past the tents, back into the kasbah, and past the silenced onlookers. Zahir would make an example of Tariq for anyone else who dared to embarrass Caid Ali Tamzali.

Next to the slaves' quarters, Tariq was tied up, with his hands stretched over his head and his bare back facing Zahir. Zahir took out a leather whip with silver lacings at the tip.

"What kind of riding was that? You have embarrassed the Caid. You have embarrassed this house!" he yelled, and brought the whip down on Tariq's bare back. Tariq yelped in pain as he felt blood begin to drip down his back.

"You ignorant, pathetic little slave. We treat you well and this is how you repay the Caid?" he screamed and brought the whip down again. Tariq screamed in agony.

Zahir whipped him twice more, and by this point Tariq could barely keep from passing out. Zahir put down his whip, walked behind him, and grabbed him by the neck.

"Do you know how much money you cost the Caid today? Do you know how much money you cost me? I should kill you right now and be done with it. The only thing that has saved you is the fact that this was your first race. If you ever race that slow again, I will slit your throat and feed your dead body to the hyenas."

Tariq moaned again, his vision blurry with pain. Zahir untied his wrists and led him to a metal box about three feet by three feet with just a few holes punched on top for air. He threw Tariq inside the box.

"Stay here for a couple of days and think about how to go faster," Zahir sneered, and locked Tariq in the box.

Once inside, Tariq immediately passed out. The box was too small for him to lie down flat, so he had to curl up in a fetal position. His back was sore and raw, and his entire body throbbed with pain.

He did not cry. He would not give them that satisfaction.

Tariq started to dream, and as he drifted off, he dreamt of Zijuan. He saw her face and her smile and he knew she was thinking of him. He remembered something she once said to him.

"Tariq, you already have two strikes against you. You are poor and an orphan. You must be stronger and smarter than the others. You must turn your circumstance into a positive one. You must use your suffering to create strength. You have already tasted how hard life can be. Nothing can hurt you now, so you have the freedom to be fearless."

Tariq lay in the box all day, drifting in and out of consciousness. It was unbearably hot and his sweat mixed with his blood. At dusk, he finally fell into a deep sleep.

During the night, Tariq heard the lock rattle and the door swing open. He felt soft and tender hands lift his body out of the box. He was disoriented—it was very dark outside, and he had been sleeping very deeply. He felt the soft hands sit him down in the sand.

"Is your name Tariq?" a female voice asked.

"Yes," he answered. He looked up and saw a beautiful woman, dressed as a belly dancer, kneeling in front of him. She had a bucket of water and some food with her. She began rubbing a warm cloth on Tariq's wounds.

"I've put some healing herbs in this water. It will help your wounds. Here, I've brought you some orange and lamb. Please eat it, you will need your strength," she said.

Tariq slowly ate the slices of orange. He had eaten nothing since breakfast and had barely noticed due to the pain in his body. The juices invigorated him and he sat up a little.

"Who are you?" he asked.

"Your friend Zijuan has asked for me to look out for you."

"Zijuan? How do you know…?"

"I don't have time to explain. You are in very serious danger. I am going to help you escape."

"Escape?"

"Yes. The plan is being put together as we speak. It will happen very soon, so be prepared."

"Who are you?"

"I am a dancer in the Caid's harem."

"One thing, I have a friend. She is a white girl. Her name is Margaret Owen. We must bring her and two other friends."

"One of your friends is the black boy that rode with you?"

"Yes, his name is Aseem."

"He was also beaten for finishing last. I will try to get you and your two friends out, but it will be very difficult to get Margaret away. She is being saved as a gift for the Caid's son. He is returning soon from the wars in the north."

"No, we must bring her. I promised," he said, looking the woman in the eyes.

"Okay, I will see what I can do."

"What is your name?"

"Do not worry about my name for now. Just wait for my signal. Now, don't let anyone know you ate, or there will be questions."

"One last question, when will we escape?"

"Soon. Very soon."

CHAPTER
— 7 —

THE STORY OF FEZ

The Rif Mountains have more tribes than can easily be counted. Different dialects, customs, languages, and cultures separate the tribes, as if they were completely different countries. Although many people speak Arabic or Berber, there are literally dozens of local languages and dialects.

Mehdi Akoujan was the leader of a tiny mountain tribe whose history and roots went back centuries. His particular tribe had settled in the Rif Mountains, which were located within the realm of Caid Ali Tamzali. The Caid ruled these areas with an iron fist, often raiding local tribes—killing the adults and enslaving the children.

Only thirty-five years old, Mehdi was tremendously young for a chieftain—the youngest anyone could remember. He was extremely handsome, with a thin face, slight black beard and bright, inquisitive eyes. His posture was perfect. Although born in the mountains, he had an air of nobility about him. Ever since he was a teenager, men had followed him; leadership came as natural to him as swimming does to a fish.

Mehdi had reached an uncomfortable, but necessary, truce with one of the Caid's henchmen. Each quarter, Mehdi offered the man a bribe, usually consisting of animal pelts, spices, and food crops. In return, Mehdi and his tribe were spared from the onslaught of the Caid's army. Payment arrangements like this one had gone on for thousands of years with various sheiks and caids. Ali Tamzali was simply the latest.

He sat around a campfire with the other tribal leaders drinking mint tea and smoking a hookah. The sweet melon tobacco helped him think.

"Ali Tamzali has aligned himself with the French like a tick with a dog. If we oppose him, we will make an enemy of him, as well as the French army," Nur Akoujan said.

"If we align ourselves with Ali, then we risk alienating ourselves from the other tribes who oppose Ali and the French," countered Allal Acchaari.

Nur and Allal were the second and third in command, respectively, behind Mehdi. They were both wise men in different ways. Nur was younger and more adventurous, while Allal was older and more conservative.

This was the debate at hand. Many of the local indigenous tribes had begun banding together to fight Ali and the French occupation of Morocco. This was very unusual. Century-old feuds prevented many tribes from even talking with one another. Tiny wars and flare-ups were common as tribes struggled to retain their territories. It was because of this chaos among neighboring tribes that Ali Tamzali was able to consolidate power.

"What do we have to gain by opposing Ali, and what do we have to lose? If we oppose him, we risk being annihilated by a superior army. If we side with him, we risk being wiped out by the other tribes," Mehdi reasoned.

The men in the group sighed and nodded their heads. It was not an easy situation. Mehdi had to decide which allegiance he would show—neutrality was not an option. Risk was unavoidable. As a leader, he needed to decide who he thought would win the war, and what he stood to gain and to lose.

"Ali has had our people in his chains for years. We give him everything we have and barely survive. Another bad winter and we'll starve for sure," Allal stated.

"Ali has not been so unkind to us," Nur responded. "It could be much worse. Many, many tribes have been massacred at his hands. We have our lives. We have our tribe."

"Ali will not protect us from the other tribes," Allal said, growing a little impatient with the conversation. "He just wants his payment. If we don't align with them, we will be at war one way or another."

Mehdi knew this to be true. Ali would not really protect them; he was only interested in the protection gifts and bribes. Mehdi lived alongside the other tribes, traded with them, and shared the same mountain paths. It was more than convenience—they were in many ways the same people. Together they endured the harsh winters and brutally hot summers. They all depended upon hunting and goat herding to survive. They shared many of the same customs and culture. To betray these tribes in favor of the Caid would be akin to betraying a brother.

"I think we must align ourselves with the tribes and prepare for a war with Ali and the French," he finally said.

The group was silent. For weeks, even months, this had been the main topic of conversation within his village. Everyone knew that a decision was coming, yet Mehdi had remained entirely neutral on the subject. A smart leader, he knew he needed to gather his facts before making a decision. He also had to determine where his people stood on the matter. By a vast majority, most of them wanted to side with the other tribes. The only elder tribesman who wanted to side with Ali was Nur.

"If the tribes can indeed unite, Ali will not easily wage war," Mehdi continued. "The other tribes and the Moroccan government are already fighting the French. If they prevail, any tribes that allied themselves with the French and Ali will be extinguished."

"Do you think the French will lose?" Nur asked.

"For centuries, outsiders have tried to control Morocco. They have tried to change our religion, our language, our dress, even our songs and dances. But in the end, they all leave, in one way or another. The French will be no different."

"It's settled then," Allal proclaimed.

"Yes. We are now at war with Ali Tamzali," Mehdi proclaimed, arose, and left the campfire. The group was solemn. They understood what the forces of Ali Tamzali were capable of. They also understood that they would be shown no mercy.

Mehdi walked back to his tent, where his wife Salma and his only son Fez were busy preparing dinner. Children had not come easy to him and Salma. After many years of trying, they finally had a boy. Their child had been born premature and sickly. Many thought he wouldn't survive for a month in the harsh mountains. Mehdi of course wanted a great name for his son, but the boy had fallen in love with a little fez cap when he was just a baby. He would sleep in it and play with it for hours, so that's how they came to name their boy Fez. Mehdi never admitted that, for fear of embarrassing his son, so he made up a story about wanting to visit Fez, the city. In truth, he disliked cities. They were noisy and busy and extremely impersonal. He liked his mountains and the desert and being with his people. Fez was born with poor eyesight, a huge detriment in the mountains. Glasses were not common in his tribe, but Mehdi had found an eye doctor at a gypsy camp and traded a small ransom for Fez's tortoise-shell glasses. Fez treasured those glasses above all else, and was always so careful with them to ensure they were never broken.

Fez left the tent to fetch some water, leaving his parents alone.

"How did it go?" she asked.

"We are at war with the French and with Caid Ali Tamzali. We have decided to align with the other tribes."

This was not altogether good news in the tent. For five years, there had been relative peace in their tribe. Yes, they had to pay Ali, but there was always someone to pay—if it had not been him, they would have been forced to pay some other warlord. Salma had lost a brother and her father in the last war. And too many boys from her tribe had lost their lives too soon.

"How will it start?" she asked.

"The snow is melting. In two or three weeks a garrison from the Caid's army will come to collect payment. He won't get any."

"Then what?"

"We hide and we move and we fight, as always."

That was their way. Their tribe was a group of guerrilla fighters. They hid in the mountains and attacked in small numbers. It was a hard life for a woman and a child. They were forever on the move.

Fez came back to the tent with a bucket of fresh spring water.

"And how are you today, my son?" he asked.

"Excellent, Father. I am learning how to navigate by the stars," he replied.

"That is good; very, very good."

"I also made something for you." Fez handed his father a steel can with a string attached.

"Put this to your ear," said Fez, before walking out of the tent.

His father did as he was told, and he soon heard Fez's faint voice in the can. He talked back into it, and Fez replied. After a few moments, Fez came back into the tent.

"That is remarkable. How did you think of that?" his father asked.

"It just came to me," Fez replied nonchalantly.

Fez's father had known for years that his son's ability lay with his wits and not his fists. He had always been smaller than the other boys. Fez was not a coward, but athletic prowess did not come naturally to him. This did not bother his father, who believed it was better to have brains than brawn. A sharp mind could prevent wars—or win them. His father understood that times were changing in the world, and for the tribes. There were mechanized horses and flying machines and things completely beyond his understanding. The next leader of their tribe would need an understanding of these new things. He would need to be inquisitive and smart.

His son was growing into a very smart boy.

The next morning the tribe packed up their tents and began the trek to higher ground. This was the first step in preparing for war. Positioning themselves on higher ground meant it would be much more difficult for the French and the Caid's armies to find them. It also provided new terrain and new hiding spots. There was one other important strategic advantage to higher ground—they would be closer to neighboring tribes in the event of an attack.

The Rif Mountains receive more rainfall than any other area in Morocco. At lower elevations, the mountainsides are covered with Atlas cedar, cork oak, Holm oak, and Moroccan fir trees. Up higher, the trees are much sparser, but the area is still covered by maquis, or scrub brush. In the winter, snow blankets the ground. Many lakes and rivers lay in the Rif Mountains.

All tribes in the area use an established set of trails that wind throughout the mountainside. Sometimes, these trails are easily followed. Other times, they are extremely difficult to find and only a seasoned tribe member knows of their existence.

Members of Mehdi's small tribe rode up a mountain pass on mules, while some walked alongside carrying huge makeshift backpacks made of a strong cotton fabric. The chill from the mountain air stung their skin and they pulled furs and blankets over their shoulders. Although they were still dressed in the long, flowing robes of traditional Berber djellabahs, the furs and blankets provided added warmth. The pass they traveled was surrounded by vertical ridges on either side, and in some areas was so tight that the tribe was forced to stay in single file.

"Fez, when is the best time of year for hunting?" Mehdi asked his son.

"Spring, when the babies are born. The herd is increased."

"Good, and which animals are the best to kill?"

"The old ones, and then the males. Never kill a female or a baby."

"Excellent. Where and when is it best to hunt?"

"Near watering holes or narrow mountain passes like this one. The best time is early morning when animals are feeding or drinking. It also provides a full day for skinning."

"Very good!" Mehdi praised his son.

"Fez?" his mother asked.

"Yes, Mother."

"Who rules our tribe?"

"A tribal council of five men. Each selected for bravery or intelligence. However, the village elders also have a great deal of influence over tribal matters."

"And how do we treat elders?" she asked.

"With the utmost respect, for they have seen more life than any of us and can help guide the way."

"Very good."

This was how their travels generally proceeded. His father and mother would continually quiz him on matters of the tribe, hunting, farming, and trading in an effort to pass on the ways of their tribe and to teach him how to survive in such a harsh environment. Life could be very short in the Rif Mountains, so adulthood came at an early age. It was expected that most girls would marry at thirteen and begin raising families. The average lifespan of a male was around thirty-three years of age. However, their tribe didn't track age in the same way as Westerners. In fact, they scarcely had a concept of time but tracked life more by the passing of the seasons. Due to the hot sun and harsh climate, most members seemed much older than their actual age. Fez's father was, indeed, only thirty-five but seemed much older. Also, in their tribe, unlike many Muslim cultures, the women were valued and cherished. They were expected to hunt and fight alongside the men. In return, they were given much respect and standing within the tribe. In spite of these advances, however, women were still not permitted to sit on the tribal council.

As they continued walking and talking, Mehdi suddenly felt a tingle on his skin. He was a warrior and a hunter, and had personally killed eight men in battle. His sixth sense, an animal sense, almost always warned him when trouble was near.

"Stop!" he ordered.

The caravan behind him stopped. He walked forward on the trail. Something was different. Something wasn't right. He stared up at the canyon walls, realizing this would be the perfect place for an ambush. The enemy would have the advantage of higher ground, the area was barren and there was scarce cover, and both ends of the trail could easily be blocked.

"Something isn't right," he said to the others.

"I don't hear anything," someone said in the rear.

"Shssshhhh," he scolded. "Move out. Quickly and silently. Now!" he whispered.

The entire caravan, as if a switch was turned on, began to run as silently as a cat on a rooftop through the canyon. Living in the wilderness had taught them, as if second nature, to scramble up mountainsides without tripping over as much as a stone.

The first shot rang out and almost took off Mehdi's ear.

"They are firing, take cover on either side, shoot at the mountain ledges," he ordered.

The entire tribe split into two groups, one along each cavern side. Both men and women unsheathed bows and arrows, and a few had rifles.

Bullets ricocheted off the mountain walls, which were made of mud and clay, sending splinters of rock falling down upon the group. Both men and women returned fire, although the enemy was entrenched, deep within the mountainside.

"I am going up. Stay with Fez!" he ordered his wife.

"No Mehdi, it is too dangerous!" she yelled back.

"Stay here!" he screamed, looked her in the eyes, and started running.

He ran off into the gully ahead, a few bullets narrowly missing his body. He ran for a hundred yards through a hail of gunfire, and managed to find safety behind a large boulder. A ledge stretched upwards to his right. Without thinking and without hesitation, he charged up the ledge, both silently and swiftly, as if a ghost were skipping along the mountain edge with a twelve-inch dagger in his hand.

The first bandit, hunched down like a coward behind a rock, didn't even know Mehdi was there. Mehdi put his hand over the man's mouth and thrust his dagger into his neck. In seconds, the man was dead. Mehdi grabbed his rifle and ammunition, reloaded, and scanned the edge. A bullet ricocheted off the rock in front of him. He quickly analyzed the direction of the bullet and saw another bandit barely visible behind a rock in the distance. With just one shot, the man's turban burst into a cloud of torn fabric, hair, and blood.

The ledge led to a clearing about thirty feet in, which is where the majority of the bandits were holed up. Mehdi hoped there wouldn't be too many of them. Usually bandits attacked in small groups, hoping the element of surprise and position would provide the needed advantage over their prey.

Another bandit, clothed all in black, came running towards Mehdi in a suicidal charge.

Mehdi dropped him with one shot.

Now he had evened the battle. The bandits no longer had the advantage of positioning, and Mehdi's tribe no longer had to fight on two fronts. He could sit here and pick them off or make a charge into the clearing. The only problem was, he didn't know their numbers. Three or four would be no problem. Much more than that, he might be outnumbered.

He reloaded again, pondering the best strategy, when he felt the knife at his throat.

"If you move so much as an inch, I will spill your blood all over these rocks," the voice said.

Mehdi instinctively dropped the rifle and put his hands behind his neck. He hadn't expected this. Usually bandits are fairly rudimentary in their battle plans and limited in number. He was sure he could have bargained with them or shot his way out of the ambush.

He felt his hands being tied and was forced to stand up. He was thrust around to meet his attacker.

It wasn't a bandit at all. It was Zahir, Ali Tamzali's garrison.

"Walk with me, Mehdi, and don't do anything stupid," he growled.

Four other soldiers were with Zahir. They each walked behind Mehdi with rifles ready at hand. Soon the group was back at the caravan.

"I have Mehdi, your leader. Do not fire. We have you surrounded. You all know who I am!" Zahir yelled.

This was no ordinary attack by common bandits. This was a well-planned ambush. Zahir had been expecting them.

Zahir and Mehdi and the group walked in front of the hidden caravan. There wasn't a heart that was not racing. Zahir was a monster in their region. He slaughtered entire tribes for the smallest grievance. He now had them surrounded and their leader bound at knifepoint.

As second in command, Nur stood up without putting down his weapon. He could easily see Zahir, Mehdi, and the guards directly in front of him.

Just then, over one hundred soldiers, each armed with rifles, showed themselves on the ridge above and pointed their weapons directly at the caravan.

"You see my friends, you are surrounded. So please place down your weapons and let us talk in peace," Zahir said.

Nur looked up at the numbers of soldiers. They were, indeed, surrounded and vastly outnumbered. To fight would be suicide. He threw down his bow and arrow and raised his hands.

"What do you want, Zahir?" Mehdi asked.

"We had an agreement that is now broken."

Mehdi said nothing. He was busy calculating the situation and his next move. He was tied up and surrounded but not without options.

"Imagine my surprise when one of my scouts noticed your tribe packing up and moving so early in the season. If it had not been for our sheer luck, you might have escaped into the mountains," Zahir laughed. "Of course, as always, I am much too smart for you, Mehdi. You should know that by now."

"What do you want?"

"Nothing I cannot take."

"We have furs and spices and anything else you want."

"Oh, I will take them all, and much, much more."

Fez looked at his father one last time. He looked at his mother and saw a tear in her eyes. He was too young to understand what was happening. Too young to understand that true evil did exist in the world.

He looked at his father. His father stared right through him and, clearly, Fez saw him mouth these words: "Avenge us."

And then,

"I love you, my son."

Some acts in the world defy reason. There is no reason for death and wars and genocide. Only God has such answers. Only God knows such reasons. That night, Fez lost both his family and his tribe. He, along with the other children, was tied up and chained to be sold at a slave auction. He would never see his mother and father again. He would never see his tribe again. He was now an eleven-year-old boy alone in the world. All the adults in his tribe had been massacred, save one.

Nur rode away with the army, side by side with Zahir.

"You will be my chief scout in this region, Nur. I want to know the whereabouts of every tribe, and I want them slaughtered like dogs. You know these mountain ranges better than anyone," Zahir told him.

"I will need at least fifty men," Nur replied.

"You will get a hundred men, each able and armed with the latest French rifles. I want this area secured, do you understand?"

"Yes."

"When you return, you will have twenty slaves, a herd of camels, and your own little kingdom."

"That is the arrangement," Nur agreed.

"You did excellent work here. Welcome to the army of Caid Ali Tamzali."

"I am your humble servant," Nur said and bowed.

Nur had felt himself numbed with the battle. He didn't like slaughtering his people. It made him feel sick inside. The one thing that made it possible for him to carry out such unspeakable acts was that he didn't have any family. His wife had died during childbirth and both his parents were long dead. Their deaths had planted a kernel of anger in him and he had begun to feel that God was against him. This kernel of anger and hatred turned into a full blown mass of weeds in his soul when a woman he wanted for his new wife rejected him, and the tribe elected Mehdi as tribal chieftain rather than him. All these setbacks made this betrayal possible.

True, he was younger than Mehdi, but he was also the strongest one in the tribe and the best hunter. He was young, but so what? He rightfully deserved the title of Chieftain and he knew that better than anyone else.

As he rode away, looking back at his massacred people, he made himself feel nothing. To feel anything would be too much. He simply decided not to think about his actions and to look forward to his new power.

He failed to understand that every action has a consequence. An evil deed always manifests itself somewhere else.

What goes around, will indeed, come back around.

CHAPTER
— 8 —

THE PLAN

Tariq was thrown into the prison chambers, barely conscious, his body bruised and bloodied. Fez brought him over and placed him next to Aseem, who had also been badly beaten, but not nearly as severely as Tariq. Aseem's lower lip was swollen and scratched, and a huge knot had begun to form just above his right eye. He placed his arm around Tariq and allowed his head to rest on his shoulder.

Fez brought them both some water.

"They almost killed him," Fez whispered.

"Tariq couldn't help slowing down, his ropes were tied wrong and they cut into his skin," Aseem replied.

"There's no way he can ride in the next race. It's happening this week, to celebrate the homecoming of the Caid's son."

Jawad had witnessed Tariq being thrown into the chamber and came over to the three.

"He will have no choice. He has to race. Just pray he doesn't pick the Caid's colors again."

"Is there any way to get him out of racing?" Aseem asked.

"No. It doesn't matter what he looks like or how broken he is. Boys race with broken legs and wrists all the time. It simply affects the odds on the wagering."

"Jawad, I have a question," Fez started.

"Yes."

"You're the best jockey in our ranks. You win countless races. Why are you down here?"

"Two more races and I will join the light cavalry of the Caid," he explained.

"Really? You can win your freedom?"

"Yes, but it is not easy. Only a few have done it. I plan on being a sergeant in the cavalry," he said hopefully, and then walked away leaving the three alone.

Tariq was resting fitfully. Aseem placed Tariq's head on a soft mound of dirt and allowed him to drift into a deep sleep.

"Tell me about your family. You never speak of them," Aseem gently pressed.

"I cannot bring myself to," Fez answered.

"I understand. This all seems like a bad dream. No, a nightmare from which I'm hoping we eventually awaken."

"I don't believe my family is dead."

"But you said…"

"I know what I said, but I don't believe it. I just don't believe it. I'll hear my mother's voice in the morning or imagine myself walking at my father's side. I keep seeing their faces in my head. I keep hearing their voices. Do you know what my father's last words to me were?" he asked.

"No. What were they?"

"That he loved me. I know they are dead, but I just can't accept it. And I can't figure out how to avenge them. I'm only a kid, and I'm not very coordinated. I'm not a warrior like my father."

"Fez, you rode better than anyone in the race. Better than Tariq or I."

"It's because I am the lightest. It wasn't skill, really. I had a fast camel and I just hung on."

"Don't be so hard on yourself."

"You don't understand, Aseem. I should have done something—I should have helped them. It is all my fault," Fez said, and slowly began to cry.

"Fez, you are just a boy like all of us. There is nothing you could have done to protect your mother and father. Nothing. It is not your fault."

"What am I going to do, Aseem? You and Tariq and Margaret are all I've got in the world. My entire tribe is dead."

"We are all any of us has anymore. We will make it through this together. I promise."

"I have a way out," Tariq said, still groggy and light headed.

Both Aseem and Fez stared in amazement.

"We thought you were sleeping!" Aseem said.

"Trying to. Fez, we may have an escape plan."

"How?"

"Trust me. It will be all right."

"And what do we do once we get out? We're still all alone."

"We will be free."

"We're just kids."

"Not anymore, we're not. None of us is. I don't know how, exactly, and I don't care. I have to get out of this place."

"So do I."

"Tariq, promise me one thing?" Fez asked.

"What is it?"

"Promise me, no matter what, you won't leave me."

Tariq smiled.

"I'll never leave you Fez. Do not worry."

Fez smiled back and settled down to sleep, Except for his new friends, he was all alone in the world. Only three weeks previously, he witnessed the massacre of his entire tribe. He now found himself enslaved in a dungeon. But through it all, he was still alive and he still saw beauty in the world. Maybe if he had been an adult he would have let all these things dominate his thinking. Maybe if he had been older he would have been crushed by his situation. Being a child somehow made him more resilient. He still held out hope. He would always miss his mother and father, but his life would still go on. The world, in all its evil, remained an amazing place. After all, he had placed fourth in a camel race. It was the first time he'd ever done well in anything athletic in his life.

A few hours later, to his amazement, Tariq found himself sitting in a bed in the nurse's quarters. The nurse was tending to his wounds; she had bandaged his ankles and wrists where the rope had burned into his skin, and had fed him plenty of food and water. His spirits had been raised considerably. He was starting to fall asleep once more when the woman appeared again. At first he wasn't sure she had been real, he had been so delirious. But again, here she sat, next to his bed.

"You look a lot better," she said.

She was just as beautiful as before, but there was something wild about her. Her figure was slim and muscular, not good for an Arab woman. It generally meant she worked in the fields alongside the men. Her face was thin and dark, and her long brown hair fell just below her shoulders. It was her eyes, however, that captivated men's hearts. They were green, but they seemed to be on fire, piercing through anyone that met her gaze. Her beauty was her disguise. Men often underestimate a beautiful woman. They assume that she is incapable, playing and jousting for her affection without really asking themselves about her desires and her strengths. They think of a beautiful woman as a thing to be won. Her beauty masked something that was undeniably very dangerous.

"Did you get me into the nurse's quarters?" Tariq asked.

"Yes, I called in a favor from a guard. Now, please be quiet as I have our escape plan," she whispered to him.

"You do?"

"The day of the race, ride the route as usual. This time, however, there will be an ambush on the Caid's security. You will be met by some tribesmen. Ride with them and you will be safe."

"What about you? What about Margaret?"

"I have that planned. Once the Caid finds out what has happened, he will send fifty or more soldiers to track you. Margaret and I have a plan to escape during the chaos of the moment. Do not worry, your friend is safe and I am looking after her."

"Okay, I think I understand. Just ride as usual and we will meet the tribesmen."

"Yes, one more thing; you can tell absolutely nobody of this plan. Nobody! Ride with your friends, and they can escape along with you, but do not tell them of the plan. Do you understand?"

"Yes."

"Good, I must go. This is the last time you will talk to me. It is too dangerous to keep meeting."

"Just one thing, please, what is your name?" Tariq asked.

"I will tell you once you are free. Get well, Tariq. People are looking out for you."

She disappeared out of the tent and Tariq sat alone with his thought. *People were looking out for him.*

How marvelous. How amazing to know that his little life actually meant something to someone. He thought of Zijuan as he would a mother. He thought of his new friends and felt good, in spite of everything that had happened.

The next day Tariq practiced racing as usual. He was allowed to sleep in the hospital, but he still had to tend to his camel and train each day. Although he tried valiantly to ignore it, his wounds were such that bouncing up and down in the saddle caused considerable pain. Worse, the hot desert sun warmed his skin to such an extent that he sweated profusely and the salt itched and pained his wounds. His body, trying to heal itself, tired easily, so he was exhausted by the middle of the day. He was only riding half days and not allowed to see Fez and Aseem, as they went on longer rides in the desert. Mostly, he rode by himself with not much improvement.

"You look like a boulder that's been crushed under a hammer," Jawad rode up next to him. Jawad had stayed behind to assist in mending one of his camel's hooves.

"I feel like one," Tariq wearily replied.

"You must find a way to ride faster, Tariq. Ignore the pain. If you do not ride faster, the Caid will have you killed for sure."

Tariq liked Jawad, and he had certainly helped him become a better rider, but the way he talked of the Caid made it seem like he was already part of the Caid's army. It sometimes seemed as if Jawad enjoyed being a slave.

In a building not far away from the jockeys' chambers, the situation was quite different.

Margaret was miserable. She was not making any friends, and Fatima kept torturing her. Most days, she sat by herself and talked to no one. Just when she had lost all hope, a beautiful girl with fiery green eyes sat down next to her.

"You know a boy named Tariq?" she had asked.

"Yes!" Margaret answered enthusiastically.

"I have spoken with him. He was beaten unmercifully for losing the camel race. He is not in good health. He asked about you."

"Where is he? And where are Aseem and Fez?"

"Please keep your voice down. Anything said in this place will surely get back to Zahir. They are all in the slave dungeon. Aseem was beaten as well, but not as severely as Tariq."

"Who are you?"

"I am a friend, that's all you need to know for now. My name is Sanaa. How are you holding up?"

"I hate this place."

"As do I," Sanaa agreed.

"You know this little brat?" Fatima, witnessing the conversation, approached the two of them.

"Fatima, this is none of your business. Leave us alone," Sanaa quietly said.

"Everything that happens in this place is my business. Stop talking to the white girl!" Fatima yelled, loud enough to attract the attention of the other girls.

Sanaa stood up, faced two inches from Fatima's nose, and glared at her.

"Fatima, I'm giving you one chance to leave us...," Sanaa said.

"Or what?" Fatima interrupted her.

With that indiscretion, Sanaa whirled around in a three-sixty, elbows up, and hit Fatima square in the nose. The large woman was knocked down so quickly she scarcely had time to brace her fall. Blood squirted from her nose and her eyes quickly swelled up. In an instant, Sanaa was on top of her, forming a scissor with her legs, and squeezing Fatima's fat neck between her muscular calves.

"Fatima, do you not understand me? I said to leave us alone. Or do you require a broken neck to obey me?" Sanaa asked, seething between gritted teeth.

"Help me," Fatima barely whispered.

"Nobody in this place will help you, you know that. It's every girl for herself. Now, you and everyone else leave the white girl alone or you will deal with me."

Fatima's hippo-like face started to turn white and then purple. Her eyes bulged out of her sockets.

"Okay, okay," she relented.

Sanaa released her grip and Fatima gasped for air and crawled away. Deliberately, Sanaa sat back down next to Margaret.

"Sorry about that; sometimes lessons must be taught the hard way," Sanaa said matter-of-factly.

"My goodness, could you teach me to fight like that?" Margaret exclaimed.

"Perhaps, we shall see. We have more important things to discuss."

"Such as?"

"You, as a proper English girl, are a prize in the Caid's harem. You are being saved as a gift for the Caid's son. He is due to return on Saturday. After that, I doubt I can help you. You will be moved to different quarters away from me. He may even move you to an entirely different kasbah."

The color completely disappeared from Margaret's face. To date, nothing had happened to her. She had been thrown in this glorified prison and spent her days sitting on a pillow by herself, waiting on Fatima, and scrubbing vegetables. She understood the life awaiting her. She understood the consequences. She would be a slave to the Caid's son and would have no life of her own. She witnessed how the women had been treated by the Caid. They were looked at as little more than objects, easily replaceable and discarded like heaps of trash. She had personally watched as the Caid had slapped a girl and thrown her down some stairs, for the slightest of grievances.

"What is his son like?" Margaret slowly whispered.

"He is like his father, only even more ruthless, because he is trying to prove himself as a dictator. It will not be a good life for you," Sanaa said, with such practicality that it seemed she was discussing whether to drink coffee or tea.

"What am I going to do?"

"Your friend, Tariq, asked me to look out for you and I promised that I would. That gives us five days to escape this place," Sanaa whispered closer to Margaret's ear.

"Escape?" Margaret whispered back.

"On Saturday during the camel race. Do you think you can do it?"

"I'll do anything to leave this place."

"It will be very, very dangerous. It may come down to killing a man. Can you do that?" Sanaa asked, deliberately looking Margaret in the eyes.

Margaret looked at the floor and slowly nodded her head.

"A week ago I thought I could never kill anyone. But being trapped in here, and seeing the kind of man the Caid is, I could kill if I needed to."

"Have you ever fired a gun?" Sanaa asked.

"Yes, my father showed me how on some of our camping expeditions."

"Good, do not speak a word of this to anyone. Do you understand?" Sanaa asked.

"Yes, I understand."

"I will discuss our escape plan in more detail as Saturday approaches. Until then, act as if nothing is happening."

"There's nothing else to do. I'm bored out of my mind."

Another day passed, and Tariq's body was quickly healing—the benefits of youth! He was feeling much better and was eating a bowl of grapes in the nurse's quarters, which were empty, with the exception of one nurse in the corner. Tariq didn't notice him, but Zahir walked in and silently made his way next to Tariq's bed and sat down, startling Tariq.

"So, are you comfortable, my little friend? Getting everything you need?" Zahir asked.

Tariq said nothing and put down the bowl of grapes.

"I am glad you are so happy in this nice little hospital. You, being a new slave and all, should only have the best treatment. And finishing last in the camel race, we should get you your own room with only the finest linens!" Zahir said sarcastically.

Tariq lowered his eyes and said nothing. He detected the anger in Zahir's voice. His body tensed with fear.

"I should stick this dagger in your eye, carve out your eyeball, and then carve out the other one for finishing last. Give me one good reason why I should not."

Tariq's mind raced. What could he say that would make sense to Zahir?

"I came in last on purpose," he said.

"What?" Zahir asked, surprised by the response.

"I came in last in the camel race on purpose."

"Why?"

"To increase the odds on the next race. If everyone knew I was a bad rider and injured, the odds would go high in my favor."

Zahir lowered his dagger with a puzzled look on his face.

"Go on."

Suddenly, Tariq felt confident. He felt his street hustling ways returning.

"I had a deal with a guard. I was to lose the last race and then win this race. He will stand to make a fortune. The deal was that I help him and then I escape."

"What guard?"

"I don't know."

"What do you mean you don't know?"

"In the dungeon there's a little window next to where I sleep. After my first day of practice, it was obvious I could ride well. A voice approached me from outside and told me this plan. He said if I lost the first race badly, it would put the odds on me so high in the second that he would make a fortune."

Zahir stopped to consider this. It was a devious plan, and far too intricate for a child to concoct. If this was indeed the plan, then Zahir could make a fortune himself.

"How will you win the race?" Zahir questioned him.

"My only competition is Jawad. My plan was to bribe him to throw the race. It shouldn't be too hard. I may have to bribe one or two other riders as well."

"What if Jawad doesn't accept your bribe?"

"Then I have another plan to slow him down," Tariq explained.

"How?"

"Jawad is the only jockey allowed to ride in his own saddle every race. The rest of us must choose our saddles randomly. I will loosen his saddle strap to such an extent that it easily falls off. If that doesn't work, well, I will push him off his camel."

"You think you can do this?"

"If I lose, the guard already promised to kill me. I will win this race, do not doubt me."

"If you do not win, you will wish the guard got to you first," Zahir sneered at him.

"I understand. I am only a slave, doing what I am told."

Zahir's greedy mind started spinning. If the race was indeed fixed, he could wager and win a large fortune. In fact, he could wager against some of his rivals and weaken them—taking their money at the same time! After the race, he could easily dispose of this slave boy.

"Who else knows of this plan?" Zahir asked.

"Absolutely nobody, I promise. The guard made me swear to secrecy."

If nobody else knew of the plan but some lowly guard, then the fix would not reach the bigger bettors. Zahir could get fifteen-to-one, or even twenty-to-one odds. With his winnings, he could purchase several slaves for himself, a bigger house—perhaps even a stable of new stallions.

"Okay. I will let you ride. But Allah help you if you do not win. Do you understand me?" Zahir ordered.

"I will not lose. You can count on me. I am your humble servant," Tariq said in his most sincere voice, and bowed deeply as a sign of reverence.

"You may stay in this hospital and mend yourself," Zahir said. He wanted his rider strong for the race.

"Yes sir. Thank you, sir," Tariq answered and bowed again.

Zahir left the hospital with visions of gold and rubies in his head. Although he was Ali Tamzali's right hand man, he was never very good with finances. In fact, his poverty was a subject of ridicule among the court's inhabitants. In spite of his looting and pillaging, he was so poor he could only afford two wives. He possessed a terrible understanding of politics and, unknown to Tariq, was a habitual and unskilled gambler. As luck would have it, he had suffered huge losses in the past four races and this was his opportunity to win some of it back.

He quickly crossed through several tents until he came to a crimson and gold tent with a statue of a large boar out front. He was familiar with this tent; he had been to it many, many times. He briskly walked inside. Sitting at the far side was an especially obese man with a small moustache. A young boy fanned the back of the man's head with a fan made of ostrich feathers.

The man was Barbar, the bookmaker of the kasbah. Although there were equally as many bets amongst other participants, Barbar ran the only "legitimate" betting parlor in the kasbah.

"Zahir, my friend, to what do I owe this pleasure?" he asked.

"I would like to place a wager on this week's race," he said, sitting down.

"Of course you do. Which racer, and how much?" Barbar asked.

"Do you think Hari Kazim would bet against me?"

"Perhaps. What do you have in mind?"

"What are the odds on the boy who finished last in the past race?"

"Not nearly so good now that you almost beat him to death. Twenty-three-to-one," Barbar replied.

"Do you think Hari Kazim would accept a wager of ten thousand?"

Barbar stopped breathing and looked closely at Zahir. Did he know something? Zahir owed almost forty thousand in outstanding debts.

"That may be too rich for his blood. If I lowered the odds to sixteen-to-one, he might be willing to take the wager. Why so much on such an incapable jockey?" Barbar asked suspiciously.

Zahir had expected this line of reasoning and came prepared with an answer.

"I'll let you in on a secret," he said and lowered his voice.

"Yes?"

"That boy can really ride. I was wrong to beat him. It turns out, his ropes were too tight and he couldn't sit in the saddle properly. It was a fluke that he lost," Zahir explained.

This was his big secret? If it was anyone else Barbar wouldn't have believed them. But Zahir was no strategist. All brawn and no brains, with a penchant for easy money. He enjoyed a powerful position and assumed that power transferred to games of chance. His ego would not allow him to accept that he was a very poor gambler.

"That is interesting. I think Hari would be willing. Let me ask him and I will return tonight with an answer," Barbar said.

"Thank you Barbar. I will be at my tent tonight," Zahir stated and began to rise.

"Can I interest you in a cup of mint tea? Stay for a spell, my friend?" Barbar asked more out of politeness than anything. Nobody relished the company of Zahir.

"No, no, I must be going. I look forward to your answer," Zahir said, kissed Barbar on both cheeks, and exited his tent.

Gambling in the kasbah was very different from gambling in most places. Although side bets took place, almost everyone went through Barbar. The reasoning was simple. If you won a bet against a rival, Barbar would ensure that everyone knew of the winner, the loser, and amount won or lost. It was a matter of pride to win bets. He was more like a gossipy hairdresser than bookmaker.

Zahir walked out of the tent with a small smile on his lips. His future was set. He would win this race, cover his losses, and ridicule his biggest adversary in the process.

Hari Kazim sat in his tent nursing a splinter that had lodged itself into his toe. All day the pain throbbed and he could scarcely walk more than a few feet.

"Damn this eternal piece of wood. My house for a pair of tweezers!" he bellowed.

Barbar entered his tent, kissed him on both cheeks, and sat across from him.

"I don't come bearing tweezers, but I bring a wager from one of your rivals."

"Who?"

"The illustrious Zahir. He asks to bet against you specifically in this week's race."

"Oh Zahir, doesn't he already owe me twenty thousand? If he were not aligned with Ali Tamzali, his left hand would already be chopped off and fed to the jackals."

"A fine idea. But I think you'll find this wager an interesting one," Barbar said with a seductive grin.

"Go ahead."

"He wishes to wage ten thousand on the boy who finished last in the last race."

"The boy that raced our colors? I thought he was dead!"

"No, not dead, just beaten severely."

"What are the odds?"

"Sixteen-to-one, against of course," Barbar informed him.

"So Zahir wants to wager ten thousand on a jockey with only one race under his belt—in which he finished dead last—and was then beaten to within an inch of his life?" Hari asked.

"Precisely," Barbar agreed.

Hari sat in stunned silence, momentarily forgetting the throbbing in his toe.

"Does Zahir have some kind of mental retardation? Is he a simpleton and just hides it well? Or has he gone completely mad?"

"Perhaps, but he seems able enough."

"If it was anyone but Zahir, I would question the purity of such a wager. But Zahir? Only he would be stupid enough to believe in fairy tales and long shots. I'll gladly take his wager."

"I thought as much," Barbar said.

In the nurse's quarters, Tariq sat in his bed eating fresh figs and drinking lime juice. He would be allowed to skip training tomorrow thanks to

Zahir, and was even allowed to keep sleeping in the hospital until the day of the race. In fact, Zahir had instructed the nurse to give him extra attention and see that he received two rations of food every day. At this rate, Tariq might actually gain weight! The race was only three days away. The plan was simple enough, but he couldn't help but worry. Being a boy of the streets, he realized at an early age that the best laid plans rarely worked as desired.

If you want to make God laugh, tell him of your plans! Zijuan used to tell him.

The worst-case scenario Tariq could imagine was that Zahir would somehow figure out his entire plan was fake. Tariq knew he'd be found out if Zahir watched him on his camel and saw how poorly he rode. He must somehow continue to convince Zahir that he was an excellent rider.

The next three days would be the longest of his short life.

In the morning, Tariq made it down for practicing. He met Aseem and Fez in the stables.

"Well, don't you look much better? I guess that hospital stay did you some good," Fez laughed and greeted him.

"I agree. What are they feeding you?" Aseem asked.

"Much more than that monkey is feeding you," Tariq smiled and hugged them both.

"Seriously, you were just supposed to be up there for a day or two. It's been over four days. How did you manage that?" Aseem asked.

"I guess they like me. Or perhaps they feel bad for beating me so severely. They must get their money's worth for slaves, right?"

"Good point. Well, we've found Fez's calling. He's a natural rider and really improving. Even Jawad is impressed," Aseem said and slugged Fez on the arm. Fez, not accustomed to such praise, turned red with embarrassment.

Jawad nodded his head a little to acknowledge the compliment.

The training went horribly for Tariq. His skin was still sore and blistered from the last race. He could scarcely sit in the saddle. Tariq didn't know if Zahir was watching, but knew he would be suspicious if he saw Tariq in this condition. He needed an alibi for his poor riding.

In the meantime, both Aseem and Fez had improved quite a bit. Fez had gotten so good he could do a full sprint and stand on his toes in the stirrups. He'd developed his racing form, keeping his back straight and parallel to the camel's back. Little Fez had become a fine rider.

After the ride, Tariq undid the saddle as he was taught, fed the camel, and watered him down with a sponge. He was tired and his whole body still ached. As he walked back to the hospital, Tariq yearned to be able to lie down and sleep. But suddenly, somebody grabbed him by his shirt and threw him against a wall.

"I thought you said you could ride!" Zahir yelled at him.

"Who did you tell about our bet? Everyone was looking at me before practice," Tariq quickly explained.

"What do you mean?"

"Who did you tell? It was obvious that people knew something was up. I really had to ride poorly so they wouldn't suspect anything."

"You rode poorly on purpose?"

"What else was I going to do? If I rode well then everyone would be in on it. It was difficult riding that poorly. Every time I wanted to go fast, I had to pull on the reins to slow down."

Zahir let go of his shirt.

"I never thought of that."

"I also noticed that Jawad coasts in the beginning and counts on a late sprint to win most races. I can build up a huge lead in the beginning and he won't be able to catch me."

"You're sure of your plan?" Zahir asked.

"Please, do not worry. I know what is at stake. I was the best jockey in the Tangier Stakes. I will win by a wide margin. I am not worried."

Zahir stood back and studied Tariq. To a man in his right mind, with his wits about him, Tariq's little con would have been easy to see through. But when a man is in tremendous debt, he will believe almost anything. Zahir was quite a desperate man, willing to believe against all logic that Tariq was going to win the race.

"Okay then, get some rest tonight. The race is tomorrow. Do you want to stay in the hospital again? I can arrange that," Zahir asked him.

"No, others are already getting suspicious. We want them to be at ease for tomorrow. I will sleep in the slaves' quarters with the other riders."

"Okay. I will see you tomorrow. And, one more thing, little slave—if you do not win, I will not just beat you, I will make you suffer for ten years. Pain will be your constant friend. I will make it my life's mission to see you suffer. Do you understand?" Zahir asked, and Tariq felt a chill run through his body. He could see that Zahir was not joking. Tariq could almost feel the evil coursing through Zahir's veins.

Tariq stared at the fat rolls around Zahir's neck and the bushiness of his black beard and smelled the foul stench of his breath. Zahir's cheeks were puffed up and red, his eyes black as the devil. He towered over Tariq and made him feel so small.

"I know this, sir. Again, I am the best rider in the camp. Please do not worry. I will make you a very rich man," Tariq said in his most convincing voice.

"Very well, then," Zahir said and walked away.

Tariq let out a huge sigh of relief. He felt his little heart beating hard in his chest. He slowly walked back to the slaves' quarters, his legs shaky and his stomach queasy.

"It's good to have you back," Fez said.

"The hospital was very nice, but it got a little lonely. I even missed that stupid monkey," Tariq replied and smiled.

"Tariq, there is talk about you and Zahir. That you two have something going on," Aseem asked.

"Like what?"

"That he bet a lot of money that you would win."

"That's ridiculous, I can't even ride."

"I know, it doesn't make sense—but that's the rumor."

"I'll be lucky even to make it through the race tomorrow."

"That's what I'm worried about. You're still not fully healed. If you finish last again, I don't want to think about what will happen to you."

"Listen, at tomorrow's race, both of you stick close to me, no matter where I am."

"Why?" Fez asked.

"Just trust me. Stay close to me, no matter where I am in the race."

Aseem and Fez looked at each other, concern on their faces. Tariq was probably the worst rider in the field right now. He had missed so much practice and he was badly injured. If they all finished last, it would mean beatings, and perhaps death, for all of them.

"Tariq, I have not known you for very long, and I am scared to death of finishing last, and I fear we will. But if you say to stay with you, I will trust you," Aseem said.

"Are you planning an escape?" Fez questioned.

"Just trust me, and don't say anything to anyone. I am not saying there is an escape plan. I am merely saying to stay with me during the race. You are my friends. I would never do anything to harm you. I have my reasons for asking this of you."

"We put our lives in your hands, my friend. I will not question you," Aseem said.

"I will stay with you tomorrow, no matter what," Fez said and patted Tariq on the shoulder.

"Good. Thank you for trusting me. Get some sleep. Tomorrow will be a good day," Tariq replied, and each of them settled down to sleep, using one another as pillows.

In the harem quarters, Margaret was just drifting into sleep when she felt a knife at her throat. She opened her eyes and Fatima was on top of her.

"So, little white girl, where is your protection now? It's just you and me now, little girl. You disrespected me in front of the entire harem. You insulted my honor. In here, that is worthy of a death sentence," Fatima whispered.

Margaret felt paralyzed with terror. She couldn't breathe. She couldn't yell. Her arms ceased to follow her commandments. She thought of her parents and her brother and all the lovely times she had experienced in England. She thought of her young life, how short it had been, and how much more she wanted to do. She knew, at this moment, she was going to die. Looking up at Fatima, she saw darkness in her eyes—only evil and hatred. Any moment, she expected to feel the cold steel cut her throat and her life slip away as she slowly bled to death. She knew this wasn't a dream or a fantasy. Margaret had heard it was a common occurrence—only a week before Margaret had arrived at the harem, another girl had had her throat slit.

But that didn't happen.

Margaret looked up and saw a hand come from behind to cover Fatima's mouth—and then a dagger slit her throat. The figure with the dagger pulled Fatima off of Margaret. Bleeding from the wound in her neck, Fatima continued to struggle for a few moments until Margaret saw her go lifeless. Margaret sat back in horror, Fatima's blood dripping down her chest.

"Go wash yourself off," Sanaa whispered.

"What did you do?" Margaret asked.

"I did what was necessary. She was going to kill you."

Margaret looked at Fatima's dead body. The life had been drained out of it, as if Fatima's soul had simply disappeared and her body was discarded—like a crab abandons a shell.

"Do not be troubled by this, Margaret. She has *not* gone on to a better place. She was a very bad person. Now please wash yourself," Sanaa said firmly.

Margaret did as she was told. It was just after midnight, and the rest of the harem slept peacefully. Not one girl awoke from the commotion. Sanaa had been so skillful that barely a sound had been made. Quickly, Margaret washed the blood from her chest and from her shirt. Her hands shook violently and she wanted to cry. But she held her emotions firm and went back to sit next to Sanaa.

"We must cover and hide the body. Fatima is very senior in the harem. There will be an inquiry into her death, and naturally, I will be the main suspect," she explained as she wrapped Fatima's body in a rug. Margaret helped, barely, and in her state of shock was speechless as she moved Fatima's lifeless feet and covered them with the rug.

"You and I are in grave danger now. We are very low in the hierarchy of the harem. Either the Caid or the other girls will demand retribution." Sanaa continued to talk as she wrapped the body completely.

"Help me move it. There is a little crawl space over there, under some stairs. She may go undiscovered for a day or two."

"What happens to us when she is discovered?" Margaret asked.

"Likely, we will be stoned to death."

Sanaa led Margaret to a crawl space under the stairs leading to the roof. In the very back it was completely dark, and they shoved the rug into the shadows. It could not be seen from the hallway; even by leaning down and peering into the space it was next to impossible to see.

"Margaret, tomorrow is our escape. You must do as I say. With Fatima dead, there is no way either of us can stay here. Either we escape or we die. Do you understand?"

"Yes," Margaret replied softly.

"Tomorrow, when we are shuttled off to watch the races, you and I will divert ourselves from the group."

"How will we do that?"

"Leave that to me. Once we are away, we will need to do something dangerous. Have you ever ridden a camel?"

"No. But I am an equestrian rider back in England."

"Hopefully you will be fine. Riding a camel is not so different. We will have one chance, and that is all," Sanaa said, as they both returned to their sleeping quarters.

"I will do anything you ask. I just want to escape so I can return to my family."

"Be courageous, and you will. See it in your mind and it will be so," Sanaa said and, for the first time, seemed gentle.

Margaret tried to sleep, but her mind raced through the possibilities that lay ahead. If they were unsuccessful tomorrow, then she was a dead girl. All she knew was that any escape would be very dangerous, and Sanaa seemed very worried.

CHAPTER
— 9 —

A SPOILED CHILD

"Oh, Zahir is the most talented boy in his class. You should hear him play the nay. He could charm the prophet Muhammad himself. Zahir, come play your nay for our guests," Zahir's mother, Bula, asked.

Bula was hosting a tea party with six other women. Her husband, Orsoo, Zahir's father, was quite a successful rug merchant who sold to the highest government officials and sheiks. Bula was, to be blunt, a woman of girth. Her buttocks barely fit into her cane chair, which seemed to be struggling to keep from breaking at the joints. But in truth, it was the largeness of her personality and her imposing voice that made men's feet tremble in their sandals. She had a way of taking up all the space in the room—no matter the conversation, Bula twisted it around so that she was the main subject. Everyone within earshot was subjected to her point of view and her opinion—everything from how to slice an onion to foreign affairs with the King of France. However big her body and voice, it paled in comparison to the size of her narcissism. Although she was not, by any standards, an attractive woman, she fancied herself a raving beauty that captured men's attentions wherever she went. Lately, she had her eye on a banker, who trembled at the sight of her and hid during her many appearances at his bank. Her flirtatiousness was neither subtle nor inviting. The banker, a mild-mannered and meek married man, shriveled at her overt sexual suggestions and barely smiled at her attempts at charm.

Zahir, rotund himself for a boy of twelve, appeared magically for the ladies with his nay in hand. While these Arabic flutes are typically made of cane, Zahir's was made of teak by the finest craftsman in Casablanca and polished with palm oil. It was an instrument more fitting of a professional musician than a twelve-year-old boy.

The women all silenced themselves waiting for Zahir to play. He loved the attention—any attention—and gladly accommodated his mother's friends.

However, the musical talent his mother thought lived within him was rooted more in her wild fantasies than in truth. The fact was, Zahir was awful. Actually, "awful" is too kind. He was probably the worst nay player in the history of nay players.

He spit and spat and gargled his way through a popular song from the time. At least, it may have been an attempt at the song, but nobody could be sure. If he hit a correct note, it was purely by accident.

After the three-minute recital, most of the women looked ready to throw themselves off the balcony into the streets below to escape the immeasurable torture to which they had just been subjected. The women applauded politely as Zahir gave them a bow and ran away, thoroughly pleased with himself. Down the hallway he ran, to the study, looking for his father, a man equally as enormous as his wife.

"Zahir my son, come sit in your father's lap," his father commanded.

Zahir eagerly obliged. Sitting in his father's lap was one of his favorite pastimes, usually because it meant some sort of treat.

"What can you tell me of the earth my son?" his father asked him.

"I don't know," Zahir replied.

"The earth is Allah's creation and the domain of man. It is our duty to command all plants and wildlife that preside on it. We are its master and every living thing is our slave. Do you understand?" his father asked.

"Yes, Papa."

"Good, and what is the law of power?" his father asked.

"I don't know," Zahir again replied.

"Only the chosen few are permitted to rule. Only those born into royalty and a certain class of people have the necessary capacity to rule. Those chosen people have a responsibility to rule those beneath them with an iron fist. People only respect force. Do you understand?"

"Are we those people?" Zahir asked.

"Of course. That is why you are not allowed to play with the street urchins or the servants' children. They are not your equals. You must play only with the children of our friends and those at your school."

"I understand, Papa."

"Good. Here is a gold coin, my son. You are very wise and will some-day make an excellent leader."

Zahir took the gold coin, leaped off his father's lap, and ran to the streets below—never bothering to even say thank you.

Down below, Zahir walked confidently through his upper middle-class neighborhood. His family was not truly rich, as his father would have him believe, but they weren't far off. Zahir's father was a self-made man who had built up his wealth from nothing after having grown up in a poor neighborhood in Marrakesh. After Zahir's grandfather died at an early age after working sixteen hours every day as a rug maker to sup-port a family of seven, Zahir's grandmother (who was forbidden to work by Islamic law), was forced to move her large brood in with her own parents. This was not an uncommon situation for the time, and thank-fully, his grandparents were kind and looked after their grandchildren as their own.

Zahir's father hated his childhood. Although his mother was a kind woman, as were his grandparents, he could not tolerate the taunts of the neighborhood children. He and his four brothers and sisters were un-doubtedly poor; he had to drop out of school in the sixth grade to learn the craft of rug making to help support his family. He looked on in dis-gust at the other poor workers, who wore rags and worked for pennies. He vowed that when he was grown, his own family would never suffer such an indignity.

And thus arose a success story of sorts. It was true that Zahir's father did rise out of the slums of Marrakesh and establish his own rug trading company. It was true that his wife never worked and his only son Zahir never went without anything. It was also true that he owned a very fine house in a superior neighborhood and had gained a certain amount of status. But all of this came at a high cost. Zahir's father had long ago stopped talking to his siblings, who, in his high-minded opinion, he considered "a bunch of beggars and peasants." He had turned into an unscrupulous businessman, ruining two business partners and several competitors along his path to glory. If he saw a potential customer, he could not stoop low enough to gain their favor. Customers, in his mind, were greater than Allah himself. They afforded him his lifestyle and there was nothing he would not do to earn their business. His God was not Allah, as he proclaimed as a Muslim, but the almighty dirham—the Moroccan currency. He never let an opportunity pass by to demonstrate his wealth, always buying the flashiest clothes and the gaudiest jewelry. His right pinky even displayed a diamond-encrusted ring made with stones from the mines of Zimbabwe.

Because of all this, Zahir had never known poverty or had wanted for anything. His father and mother ensured that he had the best of everything and would never know the pangs of hunger. They had even decided to just have one child so they could afford him the best of all things.

Walking the streets, Zahir did not see the beauty of his city. He did not notice the jujube trees and the flocks of Spanish sparrows diving for bugs in the red sky. The beauty of the Moroccan architecture was lost on him. Money, and things that cost money, were all that mattered to him. They were the only things he noticed.

He walked along until he came to a small betting stand. At this stand, the bookmaker accepted bets on all sorts of things, but mostly futbol games and camel races. The stand was also a haven for card and backgammon games. Most days, dozens of men sat across from one other, playing and screaming and exchanging money. Zahir had always been intrigued by the betting stand and spent countless hours watching the men bang down backgammon chips. Mostly, he liked the shiny coins they flashed. Money was constantly changing hands at the betting parlor, and from a young age that held a particular fascination for Zahir.

Zahir walked in and went straight up to the owner of the betting parlor, a young man of twenty-two who was now running the parlor for his father.

"I want to play," Zahir said.

"This is no place for children, go home," the owner replied.

"I can play. I have money."

"This place is for men. I'm busy, now go," the man replied annoyingly.

"I have money, look!" Zahir said and flashed his gold coin.

The owner did a double take at the gold standard. It would take most men in the parlor a week to earn such a coin. Still, Zahir was a boy, and the owner wanted no business with a child.

"No, it is bad for me. I cannot take money from children. Allah would not be pleased. Now go, and take your money."

"But I want to!" Zahir yelled and stomped down his feet, causing a couple of backgammon players to look up from their boards.

"Go bet with someone else," the owner said, turning his back to Zahir and walking away.

Zahir's face turned red and his cheeks puffed out. He was accustomed to getting his way with most everything and could not fathom a simple betting parlor owner turning him down. He stared at the backgammon players with furrowed brows and steely eyes, but nobody paid him any notice.

Except one.

He was older, perhaps fifty, with a skinny face, gray whiskers, and yellow teeth. He wore a black turban on his head and smelled of cod.

"My boy, I see you like to bet. I will bet with you," the man said.

Zahir eyed the man suspiciously. He had never seen him before.

"What kind of game?" Zahir asked.

"A simple game—which you have an excellent chance of winning. I will place three cards face down. I will shuffle the cards, and you try and find the card with the diamond on it. Do you understand? Here, I'll give you one for free," the man said and shuffled the three cards easily.

Zahir watched the diamond card with the eye of a falcon. When the man stopped, he pointed to the middle card. The man flipped up the diamond card.

"Hey, you're too good. I can't play with you," the man said and began to walk away.

"But you promised!" Zahir whined.

"No, no. I will lose all my money and my family must eat."

"No, you said that would bet with me!" Zahir yelled and placed his gold coin on the table.

"You are right, little boy. I did promise, and a man must always keep his promises," the man agreed and sat back down across from Zahir.

Again, he shuffled the cards in the same easy manner. Zahir followed the diamond card all the way. Finally, the man stopped.

"It is the card on the right," Zahir yelled excitedly.

"Are you sure?" the man asked.

"Yes, yes, I'm sure," Zahir giggled.

The man shrugged, flipped up the card on the right and—it was not the diamond, but the donkey card.

"I am sorry, my friend. Maybe next time," the man said simply, pocketed the gold coin, and quickly exited.

Zahir sat stunned. His precious money was gone. Worse, a simple peasant man had beaten him. In his world, this was a travesty.

Zahir spied the owner in the back preparing some coffee.

"That man took my money," Zahir told him.

"What man?" the owner asked.

"I don't know. We played a card game. The first time I won easily, but the next time I couldn't pick the diamond card and I lost."

Zahir started to cry.

Usually with his parents, a few tears would reduce them to bidding any favor. But this man was not his parent. He cared not for Zahir's troubles and he certainly wouldn't reimburse such a handsome amount to a little boy.

"I told you not to gamble. It is your loss. Do not look at me, little boy. Now, go home. If I see you here again, I'll make trouble for you," the owner scolded.

Zahir cried harder and stomped his feet and his cheeks puffed out and turned red.

The men in the parlor looked at the boy throwing a tantrum and began to laugh. Even the shop owner could not contain himself and began to smirk at the petulant and spoiled Zahir.

"Go home now. I have work to do."

Zahir went up and started kicking and hitting him. At first, the man was merely annoyed but Zahir caught him a good one in the shin and the man winced in pain. He grabbed Zahir by the collar and tossed him out of the parlor. Zahir landed on his stomach on the ground outside.

Walking back to his coffee, the parlor owner shook his head, wondering how someone could raise such a spoiled young boy. His wife, a pretty girl pregnant with their first child, came and sat next to her husband at the table.

"Who was that boy?" she asked.

"I don't know. He lost his money to some swindler and now he's whining about it. I told him not to bet around here. Serves him right."

The girl looked at Zahir who returned her stare with a look of disdain.

As Zahir was dusting himself off, he continued to cry; only now his tears were tears of shame. He had never been treated in such a disrespectful manner. The servants and merchants around his house always treated him with a certain amount of pomp because of his father's standing.

That night Zahir could not stop thinking of the gambling shop owner and the patrons laughing at him. He would plan his revenge on the shop owner if it took ten years.

It wouldn't take ten years. It wouldn't even take ten days.

Two nights later, Zahir wandered around his house during one of his father's infamous parties. His father spared no expense for his parties, hiring the most expensive caterers and entertainers. Platefuls of delicacies and desserts lay stacked upon oversized tables. Zahir's mother took delight in pointing out the cost of everything, from the wine to the drapes.

Zahir found his father talking with the Chief of Police on the patio.

"Zahir, my son, please let me introduce you to Hazzam Kabil. He is a very important man here in our city. You see, he is the Chief of Police," Zahir's father said.

"Hello, Zahir, and how are you this night?" Hazzam Kabil asked.

"Fine, thank you. How are you?"

"I am having a very pleasant time. This is a splendid party."

"I know a secret," Zahir said.

Hazzam Kabil and Zahir's father looked at one another.

"What kind of secret, Zahir?" his father asked.

"Where the bad men are," Zahir replied.

"What bad men?"

"The resistance bad men."

Hazzam Kabil was about to take a drink of water when his arm stopped in midair.

"What did you say?" he asked.

"I know where the resistance men are hiding. They are bad men, right? Papa always said that resistance men were bad."

Zahir's father suddenly took notice of his only son. This was not a trifling matter. The resistance men were tribesmen dedicated to overthrowing the Moroccan government. For the most part, they were little more than a nuisance. But, lately they had gotten more organized and had gone about killing a few government officials.

"Where do you know of such men?" Hazzam Kabil asked.

"At the betting stand."

"What betting stand?"

"The betting stand by the mosque with the wooden fountain out front. I was playing the other day and I heard four men sitting at a table talking about killing someone in the government. A minister or something."

"This is no idle threat, young man. Are you sure?" Hazzam Kabil asked.

"Yes, I think the parlor owner was one of them. They kept talking because they thought I was just a stupid boy. They didn't realize that I'm smart and could hear them. "

"What did they say?"

"They were talking about the police—about a man they did not like—and they were making a plan to ambush and kill him this weekend. Also, they talked about the security around a court house."

"Could you point out the men?" the police chief asked Zahir.

"Of course," Zahir said proudly.

"I would like you and your son to join me first thing in the morning," said Hazzam Kabil to Zahir's father. "He will take me to this gambling parlor and point out the men."

"No problem at all. Zahir is a very smart and honest boy. If he said that the men were of the resistance, it is surely true."

"Okay. Zahir, thank you," Hazzam Kabil said before excusing himself. Zahir's father kneeled down to his son.

"Zahir, are you sure of what you say? This is a very serious matter," his father emphasized.

"Yes, Papa. I heard it correctly," Zahir replied in his most wholesome and honest voice.

"Well, you have been an excellent patriot to our country today. You will go far, my son," his father said proudly. Secretly, he understood that turning in resistance fighters would gain him many favors within the police and the government.

Zahir nodded, kissed his father on the cheek, and returned to the party. His plan was not an elaborate one. It was, truthfully, very elementary and his lies could have been discovered with some basic questioning. Unknown to Zahir, his lie's greatest strength was that it played upon a point of view held by both his father and the police chief; because of this, they assumed guilt rather than innocence without questioning Zahir further.

The next day Zahir, along with his father, a dozen policemen, and the Chief of Police, stood a block from the betting parlor.

"That is him. The one with the apron," Zahir said, pointing out the young owner.

"Okay, you two. Please keep out of sight. If you are seen with us, it could put your family in danger. Men, arrest the owner and everyone else at the parlor for questioning. Follow me!" the police chief barked.

Zahir and his father hid behind a pillar as the police chief and his men marched to the parlor. Zahir kneeled down low so he wouldn't be spotted by the owner.

The police chief was overzealous in his arrests. He threw the owner down by the throat and kicked him in the head. The policemen were equally as rough with the betting customers. One policeman broke a man's wrist with his billy club when the man tried to resist. The owner's wife came from behind and threw herself on her husband, proclaiming his innocence. The police chief just shoved her away.

After being rounded up, the betting customers and the shop owner had their hands tied behind their backs and were marched off. Hazzam Kabil and his men went about destroying the betting parlor, smashing chairs, overturning tables, and pocketing whatever money they found. The wife of the owner cried and screamed as she watched their livelihood being destroyed in front of her eyes. Zahir did not feel empathy for the owner and his wife. They were beneath him and yet had ridiculed him. He felt nothing but contempt.

A month later, Zahir asked his father about the betting parlor owner.

"Oh, he got what he deserved," his father mumbled, irritated that his son interrupted his reading of the newspaper.

"What does that mean?" Zahir asked.

"It means he will no longer be running any betting parlors—or anything else, for that matter."

Zahir understood immediately. Justice was swift and cruel in Morocco. The man had probably been tortured for days or even weeks. When he refused to provide information about the resistance, the police would have just killed him. It was interesting that the police chief never asked to see Zahir again. Not even for a moment. Perhaps the man had been a resistance fighter after all? Perhaps Zahir was a hero? This was how Zahir justified his crime in his head, as all criminals do.

Zahir couldn't have known it, but the man did not die. He lay rotting in a prison cell, forgotten. His wife moved back in with her parents a shamed woman—her husband was now branded a traitor to the state. No facts were ever presented against the man. It was assumed he was guilty.

Word of Zahir's action reached the highest levels of military and formed the beginnings of a relationship with the Sultan. That would be how Zahir would come into favor with Caid Ali Tamzali years later—by one little lie told by an angry child.

CHAPTER
— 10 —

THE DAY OF THE RACE

Tariq slept fitfully, awakening almost every hour. He was fully awake by five o'clock in the morning. He stared through the jail bars and could just barely make out the sun as it slid up in the sky. He felt the warmth on his face and closed his eyes. Would this be the last time he felt the sun? Would this be his last sunrise? He was placing his life, his fate, in the hands of total strangers. His plan had all seemed so impossible. How was it possible that Zahir did not suspect him? Any moment, he expected Zahir to bust through the dungeon door and drag him off to the gallows. But Zahir never showed his face. The rest of the prisoners slept peacefully.

Water dripped from the dungeon ceiling, smacking Tariq on the cheekbone. He did not move. The cool water felt good on his skin. He stuck out his tongue and felt the cool drips wet his mouth.

He stared out onto the sand and felt scared. Who was he? Just a simple orphan boy. He was worthless in the eyes of most. He was nothing. He had no real family. He had nobody that believed in him. Why was he even trying to escape? Maybe being a slave was the best thing for him, like Jawad. He looked at the sleeping boys. Maybe this was his place on the earth, maybe he was destined to be a poor and starving camel jockey and die an early death.

Sighing, he sat down and felt the weight of his troubles on his small shoulders. He did not understand his emotions. He should have been overjoyed with the thought of escaping this place. But what did he have to escape to? Where would he go? His future was entirely uncertain. Worse, he had dragged Fez and Aseem into this mess. What if he got them killed as well? He was no leader.

He thought about calling off the plan, but that was impossible. If he did not escape, Zahir would kill him for sure, once he figured out Tariq could not ride well. He had to go through with it. But maybe he didn't need to get his friends involved. Maybe they could go about with their lives and he could simply die in the desert?

He decided to leave his friends out of it. That was his plan. He would tell Aseem and Fez that things had changed and to ride hard as usual rather than stay back with him. He would face this danger alone. And suddenly, he felt alone. All the adrenaline of the past month had subsided and he now felt terribly alone in the world.

In the harem quarters, Margaret also lay awake. But her thoughts were not of self-doubt, they were of her family. She could not stop thinking of them. How she missed their smiling faces. She saw her father's face in her mind. His blond hair flowing in the sea breeze. The crow's feet around his blue eyes. How handsome he was. She suddenly realized how much her father meant to her. Even though he had been largely absent in her life, it was his voice she heard in times of fear and doubt, instructing her to be strong. She had always known the unconditional love of her family, and that gave her a real strength. Amazingly, she didn't find herself afraid. In fact, she was looking forward to the escape. She hated this place and found herself dreaming of home. She thought of breakfast at her family's home—fresh eggs, bacon, and biscuits with fresh butter and strawberry jam. Her mother's voice coming from the kitchen. She missed the simple things the most. This place, this harem, seemed like a bad dream to her, like a nightmare from which she would wake at any moment.

Margaret promised herself she would escape even if it meant killing someone. No matter the cost, she would see her home and her family again.

At seven o'clock in the morning, the monkey woke the sleeping boys. They quickly arose and waited to be marched to breakfast and a bath. It was race day! Although it was infinitely dangerous, it was also a detour from their meager day-to-day existence and a chance for a little glory.

Jawad walked up to Tariq.

"How are you feeling, Tariq?" he asked.

"Not bad, and you?"

"Just two more races and I have my freedom. I could not be happier," Jawad said.

"Jawad, I am truly happy for you, if that is what you want."

"Thanks, Tariq. Have a good race."

"You too."

Jawad walked away and Tariq was joined by Aseem and Fez.

"So what's the plan for today?" Fez whispered.

"Nothing. It was a mistake. Please, both of you ride as hard as you can. I will be fine," Tariq answered.

"Tariq, I've seen you ride. You will not be fine. We are your friends and we will help you," Aseem said.

"No, everything is fine. Please do not worry. Both of you race well," Tariq said.

Aseem looked at him and did not believe him. His head was down and he could not make eye contact. He did not understand Tariq's sudden change of thought and it troubled him. First, he was expecting them to finish behind with him and now he wanted them to race hard? It made no sense.

"Tariq, what has happened? You seem different. Please tell me."

"Aseem, it was just a dumb idea, that's all. You and Fez finish as fast as you can."

Aseem stopped and looked Tariq directly in the eye.

"Tariq, if you are planning to escape, then you must take Fez and me with you. We will not last long here, do you understand?" Aseem said.

"Maybe you would be better off here, Aseem. Did you ever think of that? Your own father sold you out. What do you have to go back to? You're probably better off being a camel jockey and living here. At least you have a place to sleep and food to eat!" Tariq yelled at him.

Aseem cocked his right hand and punched Tariq square in the lip, knocking him down. Tariq felt the blood ooze from his lip. Thankfully, the soft sand cushioned his fall.

"You are not my friend, Tariq," Aseem said and walked away.

Fez stood over Tariq and offered him his hand.

"We're all scared, Tariq. We're just kids. I don't know what's going on with you, but you're still my friend."

Tariq glanced at Fez, who looked so young and innocent. He was so small and had such a good heart. The sting of the cut had jolted Tariq back to reality.

"You're a good boy, Fez. You are my friend as well."

Fez walked off and Tariq felt lonelier than ever. Had he done the right thing? He had been sure of it this morning, but now he had his doubts. All this stress was taxing him and preventing him from thinking clearly. He didn't know what he would do next. He didn't know if he even wanted to escape anymore.

At the harem quarters, Margaret was fully dressed and waiting with the other girls.

"Has anyone seen Fatima?" someone asked.

Nobody in the harem said anything and just looked around at one another.

"She went to bed last night, but was not there when I woke up," one of them said.

"Perhaps she has special privileges and went ahead of us?" another surmised.

The mystery of Fatima soon faded to the background. She was not particularly well-liked within the group, so her disappearance was not seen as a tragedy.

Margaret spied Sanaa up in front, but neither of them made eye contact. Margaret simply kept her head down, her eyes focused on the ground.

Soon, the door opened and the harem women were shuffled out. The progression of the harem was quite a spectacle. A group of sentries surrounded them for security as they walked through the kasbah streets. Three younger girls walking in the front spread flower petals along the ground for the harem to step on. The oddest thing was that the entire crowd had to turn their backs to the harem as they marched past them. It was eerie—forty or fifty women dressed all in white passing through walls made by people's backs. Everyone yelled and cried and whooped and hollered as the harem walked by. They were not allowed to look at them as they passed, which only added to the mystery.

After a long walk through the streets, the harem was escorted to a large stage with dozens of rugs decorating the floor. Hundreds of kilim pillows lay around the stage for the harem to lie upon. A large white canopy protected them from the sun. Assistants used peacock feathers to fan the girls. In front of the stage sat the Caid's throne. This time, however, a smaller throne was placed alongside the Caid's—this was the throne of his son. Crowds had already gathered outside. Dozens of sheiks and warlords had arranged their own tents alongside Caid Ali Tamzali's.

Margaret lay down upon some pillows and watched as the sheiks set up their tents and officials prepared the race stage. Usually, the harem would wait for an hour or so before the entrance of Caid Ali Tamzali.

Sanaa came and lay next to Margaret.

"Just before the Caid arrives, we will excuse ourselves by saying we are going to the bathroom. We will be escorted by a guard. It is very important that you stick close to me," she whispered.

"What happens then?" Margaret asked.

"Do not worry about that. Just ensure that you accompany me to the restroom. We have a plan. I am going to go now. I don't want to look suspicious by talking with you."

Margaret lay there and felt her heart pounding. All she knew was that Sanaa had an escape plan and it would be very dangerous. As her heart beat fast in her chest, she heard her father's voice in her head.

Do not be afraid, Margaret. You are protected and I am looking out for you.

At once, Margaret felt a calm come over her. She pictured her father's face in her mind, and his confidence seemed to channel itself through her body. She was not afraid. She was exhilarated.

She was going to escape.

The boys saddled and prepared their camels. Tariq talked to no one—not Fez, not Aseem. He felt a huge weight on his body and his heart felt very,

very heavy. He couldn't have known it, but he was allowing a deep, insecure part of himself to control his actions—the scared, fearful part that is in almost everyone. Only instead of suppressing it, he was allowing it to rule him. His fears overcame his common sense. The weight of these fears caused him to have trouble breathing. He felt like he might cry.

"I am nothing, I am nothing," he repeated in his head. Negative thoughts overtook his thinking.

The camels marched in single file through the streets and took their place at the starting line. Moments later, trumpets sounded as the arrival and entrance of the Caid drew near. Tariq could barely look at his friends. He stared at the ground. In a few moments the race would begin.

"That is our cue," Sanaa whispered to Margaret after returning to her side. The trumpets meant the Caid was only moments away from arriving. They went to the head guard.

"My friend is having some girl problems. We must go to the restroom," Sanaa said.

"The Caid has not arrived. You must stay until he has arrived."

"If you don't want a mess on your hands, then you'd better let us go!" Sanaa asked sternly.

The guard understood immediately the problem at hand.

"Please escort these two to the ladies' room," he instructed a nearby assistant.

The guard assigned to accompany them was a young boy of about twenty. He stood in front of the girls and marched them through a side alleyway to a restroom reserved for members of the harem. It was intentionally secluded, away from the crowds to ensure the privacy of the harem. The guard stood outside as Sanaa and Margaret entered the restroom.

Once inside, Sanaa was quick to act.

"Here, put this on. You will look like any other Arab woman," she said, tossing Margaret some common clothes.

The two of them quickly undressed and changed into their new outfits. They would fit in perfectly with the crowd. The veils covered their faces so nobody would recognize them.

Sanaa produced a twelve-inch dagger from her waistline. She slowly made her way along the wall opposite the sentry. Quickly checking to be sure there were no witnesses, Sanaa stepped up, covered the man's mouth with her left hand, and slit his throat with the dagger. The man struggled and convulsed and tried to fight, but Sanaa's technique was perfect. Her wrists carefully twisted his neck so he couldn't use his torso to pull away. She stood close to his body to avoid being hit by flailing elbows and feet. In a matter of seconds, the man was dead.

"Help me drag him," Sanaa ordered.

Margaret assisted in dragging the corpse into a stall in the bathroom. Margaret stared at the man's lifeless eyes staring back at her. She had already steeled herself for anything that might happen and did not allow a dead body to rattle her, as it might have a week ago. Locking the bathroom door behind them, Sanaa performed a quick cleanup of some of the blood and covered the rest with sand.

"Let's go. Follow me!" Sanaa ordered.

The two women, now in disguise, quickly made their way out and hurried to a nearby building. The crowd and guards were thoroughly entertained by the entrance of the Caid and eagerly awaited the beginning of the race. Sanaa and Margaret easily crept by undiscovered until they found themselves at the stables.

"You said you could ride a horse, right? A camel is not much different. Just put your feet in the stirrups and hold on. Let your body ride with the animal. You will be fine," Sanaa instructed.

Sanaa went about saddling the camel with some help from Margaret. Within minutes, both camels were saddled. But before they could climb into the saddles, Margaret heard footsteps.

"Someone is coming. We must hide," Margaret whispered.

The two women took their saddled camels and hid behind two water barrels in the end corral. Within moments, a guard came waltzing into the stable. He wasn't particularly alert and seemed to be making his rounds.

Nonchalantly he walked down the length of the stable, gently tapping his hand with a hard wooden stick. He casually checked each stall until he spied the two saddled camels in the back. Alerted, his footsteps picked up and he made his way to the end stall. As he stood with his back turned to the water barrels he scratched his head, puzzled as to why two camels might be saddled.

Sanaa sprang into action, grabbed the man by the neck, and plunged her dagger across his throat. But the man was quick and managed to partially block the dagger with his hand. Blood spurted from his palm and he winced in pain. If his wits had been about him, he would have yelled and alerted some other guards. In such a surprise attack, he was merely trying to fight for his life.

Sanaa jumped on his back; he kneeled down and threw her to the ground. She landed hard, losing her grip on her dagger. Immediately he was on top of her. The two struggled until the man overpowered her, pinning both her arms to the ground. He reached for his own knife and slowly brought it down to her throat. Sanaa struggled to keep his weight off her, but he was too strong. Seeing the murder in his eyes and the contentment on his face, she realized she could not escape. She prepared herself for the moment when the blade would slice her exposed throat.

"Please...," she muttered, but the man did not care. He was going to kill this woman.

The Caid entered the grounds to his usual fanfare and pageantry. The crowd's attention was completely focused on him and his entourage. He was flanked by his son and also by Zahir, who acted as the Caid's personal security guard. Zahir looked stoically about the crowd, thoroughly pleased with his prominence. The Caid appeared tired and bags formed under his eyes. His son was quite a bit younger. He was tall and thin and walked with an air of arrogance, refusing to make eye contact with anyone in the crowd. The two sat in their respective thrones. The Caid gave a gentle nod to the headmaster to start the races. In an instant, buglers began playing and the racers escorted their camels to the starting line.

Tariq looked over at Aseem and Fez. Aseem refused to meet his eyes, while Fez gave him a small smile. Jawad seemed to be thoroughly enjoying the affair and smiled at the crowd.

The headmaster fired his rifle in the air and then shots from a hundred rifles from the tents of the sheiks rang out. The camels dashed off in an instant, and the race was on.

For the first mile, the group rode in a pack as everyone settled in. They rounded a sand dune and were soon out of view of the kasbah. On the ridge of the dune, security sentries could be seen on their own camels with glints of their rifles reflecting in the sun.

Tariq, holding his own amongst the pack, suddenly felt the pain return in his wrists and thighs. With each passing minute, it became more grueling to hold on, and he had to slow down his camel. The other riders surged past him, including Fez and Aseem. The pack sped ahead. Soon, Tariq was left alone—twenty, fifty, a hundred, and then two hundred feet from the last rider. He rode as hard as he could, but the pain was excruciating. After two miles, he saw no sign or hope of a rescue, just choking dust from the other riders and sentries on either side of him.

He was trapped, with no way to escape.

Zahir wandered among the tents saying his "hellos" and paying special attention to the more important sheiks. Finally, he made it to the tent of Hari Kazim. The sheik was hosting a small party, and several other prominent sheiks were in attendance.

"Zahir, my dear friend, come join us for some pomegranate juice and delicious lamb," Hari Kazim said, welcoming Zahir.

"Don't mind if I do. Your lamb is some of the best," Zahir said warmly. He was feeling extra confident.

"Everyone, Zahir and I have a small wager on today's race. No doubt he is coming to pay me my winnings in advance, considering his rider," Hari Kazim said to laughs from the crowd.

Zahir, always hating to be embarrassed, smiled and announced boldly.

"Actually, I was coming to see if you wanted to double the wager."

There were small gasps from the crowd and a bit of grumbling. This was just the sort of drama that people loved to see at the races.

"Do you have that kind of money, Zahir?" Hari Kazim asked.

"It is a pittance to me," Zahir said casually, more than a little upset by the rudeness of the inquisition.

"Then consider it done. My dear Zahir, you are as bold as you are courageous. I like a man of daring. Let us toast to our wager and laugh at our winnings or losses," Hari Kazim raised his glass with Zahir and the rest of the crowd.

Hari Kazim knew that Zahir would lose, and he had to be delicate in his proceedings. Once he won the bet, he would have to collect from Zahir, which would take a good amount of finesse. His toast was a gentle offer to Zahir's good graces. He didn't want to publicly embarrass him too much. News of his losses would spread, and that would be embarrassment enough.

"Yes, and you are a man of courage as well, Hari Kazim. Let us toast our good fortune as allies."

Like most gambling addicts, he was addicted to the adrenaline of the wager. In his vivid imagination, he had scammed Hari Kazim and his winning outcome was assured. The thought of losing never really entered his mind— he was blinded by the delusion of winning and the feeling of power.

Zahir wanted to be in this tent when his rider came across the winner. He wanted to see the look on Hari Kazim's face and the admiration on the faces of the crowd.

Raising his glass and feeling the sweetness of the wine trickle down his throat, he secretly laughed at the idiot Hari Kazim.

The dagger was only inches from Sanaa's throat. She felt the warmth of the man's breath on her face, and felt his heavy weight beginning to crush her. She had only seconds left, and she began to panic. She was sure this would be her death. Her breathing accelerated and she began to hyperventilate. Tears streamed from her cheeks.

The dagger edged closer when...

The man collapsed on her—he let out a coughing spasm and took his last breath—dead. All his weight was on Sanaa as his dagger fell harmlessly to the floor. She rolled the man off of her and saw Margaret standing above them, holding Sanaa's bloody dagger. The girl looked as if she had gone into shock. Her face was white, her eyes wide with excitement.

Quickly, Sanaa composed herself and stood up. Taking the dagger from Margaret's hand, she wiped off the blood and returned it to its hiding place within her robe.

"Thank you, Margaret. You saved my life," Sanaa said, eternal gratitude in her voice.

Margaret swallowed hard, nodded her head, and began breathing normally. She *had* saved Sanaa's life, and somehow that made complete sense. The man would have killed Sanaa for sure, and then probably killed Margaret as well. If she hadn't acted, Margaret never would have seen her father again. Never would have tasted her mother's homemade biscuits or slept in her own bed in the English countryside.

She did what she had to do in the moment. Actually, a bit of pride came over her as they mounted their camels.

"Put your veil on and follow me. No matter what, do not stop. Do you understand?" Sanaa instructed.

"Yes."

In an instant, the camels were out of the stable and riding through the streets. Sanaa had a route pre-planned—to circle to the back of the kasbah where there were no crowds and few guards. They wouldn't really gain attention, and most guards would simply think they were a couple of women out riding for an errand.

But after they made it through the streets, the plan became dangerous.

Their route took them directly past the Caid's tent and followed the racers into the desert. Hopefully, the chaos would be enough of a distraction that the two women would pass unnoticed.

They gathered momentum and soon the camels were almost sprinting. Margaret proved to be a very capable rider and easily moved with the rhythm of the camel. Eight years of horse riding back in England had served her well.

Sanaa saw the crowds of people in the distance and followed their planned route. Two small fences about twenty feet apart marked where the racers had entered and made for a perfect segue into the desert.

There was only one problem. A small piece of wood had been placed between the fences as a barrier. Sanaa had not counted on this.

"Can you jump?" She yelled at Margaret.

"On a horse I can!" Margaret replied.

She saw the barrier and immediately understood the issue. Giving a small nod to Sanaa, Margaret loosened the reins and urged the camel to go on faster. As an equestrian rider she had jumped her horse hundreds of times. But a camel?

Sanaa was the first to jump and easily cleared the barrier. She looked back at Margaret, who took the jump in perfect stride. The landing went well, but her right foot came loose from the stirrup. Her entire body shifted to the right and she was suddenly halfway off the camel. The camel, feeling less weight, decided to go into a full gallop and sped by Sanaa and her ride. Margaret was holding on by just a strap. She had to summon the strength to pull her entire body up with just her left hand. As she began to panic, she again heard her father's voice in her head and saw her mother's smile in her mind's eye. In an instance, Margaret calmed herself, focused on the strap, and pulled with every bit of strength she could summon. Slowly she edged up the saddle, finally pulling herself all the way up. She was now square in the saddle. She placed both feet in the stirrups and kept riding as if nothing had happened.

The Caid and his son looked at one another. Zahir had returned and was standing directly behind the Caid.

"What was all that about?" the Caid asked.

"I'm not sure, my master," Zahir replied.

"Send some soldiers after those two. I don't think they were part of the race. They were dressed like women."

A murmur came through the crowd, who watched the two riders jump the barrier and race across the sands. Zahir made his way down to a cavalry sergeant, ordered him to take ten riders and follow the escaped camels. Unfortunately, the sergeant and his men had been busy watching the races and were unprepared to mount their camels. Zahir barked and threatened each of them as they fitted their mounts with bridles and prepared to ride. After three or four minutes, the Sergeant had his unit together and they rode off after the escaped riders.

Watching the cavalry ride in pursuit only added to the crowd's excitement, and soon the murmur had escalated to complete exhilaration. The crowd was wild with gossip, and rumors flew, speculating about who the mystery riders were and why the cavalry was following them.

Tariq lagged behind even further, but valiantly tried to ride his mount as fast as possible. The dust made his eyes itch, but he was unable to wipe them because his hands were tied. He finally came into a rhythm and actually managed to ride well for a while; unfortunately, he had lost much too much time to catch the others. He continued to ride until he saw something in the distance.

It was a camel.

No, it was two camels. One of the riders was on the sand. The other rider leaned over him.

Someone had fallen.

As he rode closer, Tariq saw that the fallen rider was Jawad. His crimson colors were easily identifiable. The rider bent over him was Fez. Tariq stopped his camel; unfortunately, he could not dismount because his hands were tied.

"Is he okay?" Tariq asked.

"No, he is barely conscious," Fez answered.

"How did it happen?"

"I don't know. I was in the back of the pack. I came around the bend and saw his camel was stopped and he was over on one side—unconscious and bleeding. He's been hit on the head very hard. It's amazing he's not dead."

"How did you get your hands free?"

"I have small hands, and they were sweaty."

Tariq looked around. They were in a valley and the sentries were nowhere to be found.

"Where is the security?" Tariq asked.

Fez looked up. He hadn't thought of that. Surveying the area, he also saw no security.

"I didn't notice."

"Fez, help me get my hands free."

Fez found a sharp rock and began cutting at the rope like a scissor. After a few moments, the rope came untangled and Tariq was able to free his hands. They were raw and bloody. He then took the rock from Fez and cut his ankles free, dismounted, and walked over to the fallen Jawad.

Jawad's body lay in the sand, bloodied and lifeless. Tariq put his head to Jawad's chest. He was breathing slowly.

"I'll take him," Tariq said quietly.

The two boys took Jawad's body and slid it on the front side of the camel's hump, leaving just enough room for a rider to mount. Tariq then tied Jawad's ankles and wrists together under the camel's belly so he wouldn't fall off. Satisfied the limp body was secured, Tariq mounted his camel.

"Fez, stay with me," he ordered.

"Why?"

"Because there *is* an escape plan. I just don't know if it will work."

"What's the plan?"

"I'm not sure exactly. Only that we were to ride in the back of the pack and, at some point, we would be rescued."

"Why didn't you tell Aseem and me earlier?"

"I wanted to, but I was instructed to share the plan with no one. Then, I just got scared. I worried—what if it didn't work? What if I ended up killing both of you? I just lost faith."

Fez nodded.

"I know how it is to lose faith, Tariq. But what are we going to do about Aseem? He will be all alone if we escape."

"If we escape, I promise, I'll come back for Aseem."

Again, Fez nodded. If Fez possessed one quality it most certainly was empathy. Being small and picked on growing up gave him the ability to feel for others. He understood that Tariq felt awful about his decision. He was, after all, just a boy and suddenly found himself responsible for two other lives. His heart may have even been in the right place. It was not an easy decision.

"Let's just ride and see about this rescue."

The two boys galloped away on their camels, far behind the rest of the pack. Jawad lay unconscious on the front of Tariq's ride. They rode silently, but Tariq was glad to have a companion. His heart lightened a little. He realized he was not alone after all.

Sanaa and Margaret sprinted through the desert with perhaps a four-minute head start on the pursuing cavalry. They both tossed off their veils, allowing their long hair to fly in the breeze behind them. Margaret felt free. She felt alive. Riding a camel wasn't that much different from riding a horse, and she took to it naturally. Sanaa looked on in amazement—Margaret was actually a faster rider than she was—and Sanaa had been riding camels her entire life!

Looking back, Sanaa saw the approaching cavalry behind them.

"We've got visitors!" she yelled.

Margaret looked back, also saw the oncoming cavalry, and urged her camel even faster. In the distance, about three miles away, was a mountain range. If they could make it to the mountain range their chances of survival would dramatically increase. They could ride up ridges, crisscross canyons, and use the mountain countryside to confuse their pursuers.

The two women rode faster as they edged closer to the canyon. Their pursuers were gaining ground on them quickly, as the largest and fastest camels were reserved for the cavalry. In a matter of minutes, they would catch the women with orders to kill.

After ten minutes, the women could see that the cavalry was only a hundred yards behind them. Margaret heard their shrill shrieks and tried to ride faster, but her camel was already in an all-out sprint. For the first time since they had escaped, she felt afraid.

The cavalry riders closed in on the two just as they entered the canyon. Only twenty yards behind now, Sanaa could hear the hoofbeats of the camels gaining on them.

Up ahead she saw two riders. Could it be Tariq? None of the other racers could be this slow.

"Tariq—Go!" she yelled.

One rider up ahead turned around, and then the second, and Sanaa saw both of them trying to urge their camels to gallop faster. However, one rider seemed to have something tied to the camel's back, slowing it down and preventing an all-out sprint. Within moments, Margaret and Sanaa had caught up to the two boys.

"Ride, Tariq! Ride!" Sanaa yelled as she pulled even with him.

Fez looked white with fear as he glanced at Sanaa. Soon, she saw the problem. Another boy was tied to the front of Tariq's camel. Not only was the weight slowing them down, but a sprint might cause the boy to become untied and plummet to his death.

The cavalry was only ten yards behind them now. The leader drew his sword and raised it. He swiped at Margaret's back and the blade fell only six inches short. Margaret, sensing the danger, leaned forward and urged her camel on. The lead rider stood tall in his stirrups, gained ground on Margaret, raised his sword again, and was about to slice her neck. The sword came around and…an arrow, seemingly from nowhere, struck the man square in the forehead. He fell from his camel—dead before he hit the sand.

A volley of arrows followed, piercing the remaining cavalry riders. Most pulled up and stopped, some fell from their rides, tumbling and crunching in the sand. A group of masked riders emerged, as if by magic, from behind a canyon wall—a sneak attack! The fugitives rode straight through them, and the cavalry riders stopped in their tracks, completely caught by surprise.

The masked riders converged on the remaining cavalry riders, cutting them down, ensuring they could not report back to the Caid.

Sanaa, Tariq, Fez, and Margaret stopped their camels ahead on the trail. They watched as the rebels cut down the cavalry quickly and efficiently. These rebels could fight, and they could ride. They were not a disorganized group of bandits. These people were organized and efficient. This was a planned attack, executed ruthlessly and precisely.

After surveying the carnage, the rebel group rode up to meet them. The lead rebel yelled at Sanaa.

"Are you okay?" he asked, his face covered by a brown scarf.

"Yes, we're all fine."

The man nodded his head and soon the entire group was on the run. The Caid's army would no doubt send reinforcements quickly that would greatly outnumber the small group of rebels. They would need to make their way in the mountains and hide their tracks by nightfall.

CHAPTER

— II —

THE STORY OF ZIJUAN

The old master, Zhao Ning Qiang, sipped his hot green tea, observing the sunrise and the morning dew that dripped from the palm leaves. He sat on a porch made of bamboo—a porch he had built himself more than thirty years prior, just as he had built his house, dug his well, and farmed ten acres of rice. He had, in fact, not one possession that either he or his wife had not crafted themselves. The clay mug warming his hands, the tan robe on his body, even his sandals made of cowhide. Purchasing something was, to him, a ridiculous notion. What could he ever need that he himself could not build or make? And, if there was such a thing, he couldn't see a use for it.

He stared at the view of the valley where he was born. It was the valley of his parents and their parents and so on, reaching as far back in his lineage as anyone could remember. This was the only land he had ever known, and this never bothered him. He never felt the need to travel or to explore new countries. He had so much still to learn about his own land. So much still surprised him. Just yesterday he discovered an anthill filled with tens of thousands of red ants. He sat in wonderment watching the ants work and organize, scavenging the droppings of the nearby jungle for food. He was constantly in awe of the world around him.

The tea was a bit hot this morning and he allowed it to cool.

At first, he felt a quiet disturbance. Something in his body ached. Something was not right. He was in tune with the rhythms of the land. When something was foreign, or different, or just not right, he felt it. An instinct, developed over years of inhabiting a land so completely that it was as much a part of him as his arm or leg.

He listened, and after five minutes, he heard it.

Horses. Riders. Maybe three or four.

They were coming over the ridge and would be on him in minutes.

Ning didn't run. He didn't really even move. His body just shifted as a snake might prepare to strike. His shoulders hunched down a bit. His eyes lowered into slits. He watched the horizon carefully.

And he sipped his tea.

A tiny smile formed on his face.

Finally, the riders—four of them—appeared, about one hundred yards from his house. They were not dressed in the style of this region or any region close to him. Slowing to a trot, they rode to the porch and began circling him. All of them were armed with long swords, sheathed at their sides of their mounts.

Dirt kicked up from the horses' hooves as the riders made a spectacle of their entrance, purposely throwing their horses around like a heavy-weight fighter warming up in the corner. The horses' heads nodded and snorted, their long necks sweating in the heat. Their legs kicked high, their tails swiftly moving back and forth.

The riders eyed the man and expected him to jump up or run or say something. He said nothing. He simply sat drinking his tea.

Finally the leader, tired of this game, dismounted, grabbed his scabbard, and walked up to the porch. Stopping four feet in front of Ning, his posture was aggressive, like a predator—legs spread wider than shoulder length, chest out, arms down and exposed.

Ning appeared defenseless. In his arrogance, the bandit thought the old man to be a victim. The hunted.

That was the bandit's first mistake.

Before even uttering a word, Ning had produced a dagger from beneath his robe, risen to his feet, and slashed the throat of the bandit leader.

Blood spurted from the man's throat. He fell to his knees, grabbing his throat, blood gushing through his fingers. The wound had been perfectly executed—six inches wide, just under the larynx, cleanly puncturing the artery.

Slowly, the bandit rose to his feet in a stupor, stumbling in the dirt. In desperation, he tried to get away, walking just fifteen feet before dropping to his belly—dead.

The other bandits watched in amazement at the quick death of their leader.

That was their mistake.

Ning drew the dagger behind his back, aimed, and with perfect accuracy threw the dagger into the throat of a bandit directly to his left. The man pulled up on the reins of his horse, causing the animal to rear on its hind legs, and the bandit fell, dead before he hit the ground.

Quickly, Ning picked up a nearby bamboo stick almost seven feet in length. It was not there by accident. He took three steps and jabbed the hard staff into the eye socket of a bandit on his right. The man fell to the ground and, in a split second, Ning brought the staff down, crushing the bandit's skull.

The last bandit remaining, disorganized and completely taken by surprise, attempted an attack. He kicked his horse in the ribs, sprinted forward, unsheathed his sword from its scabbard, brought it over his head, charging the old man at full speed.

Easily taking two steps to his right, Ning lowered his bamboo staff and caught the man square in the jaw, breaking it. He took a step back, whirled the staff around, and brought it down full force on the back of the man's skull, breaking his neck.

Ning finally stopped. The horses, sensing his calm, slowed their pace. Steam rose from their breath. It had taken Ning less than a minute to take apart their masters. The horses looked to the old man with a kind of awe. The men had not been kind to these horses. They had beaten and whipped them unmercifully. Ning, however, gathered their reins and spoke to them softly. They sensed his kindness as he led them to his small stable in the back.

That's when he heard it—the unmistakable sound of a crying baby.

It was coming from the gray mare.

The old man cautiously went to the horse. On its saddle was a large hump covered with a blanket. Lifting the blanket, the old man saw a small baby gazing up him with large brown eyes. The baby had been a bit suffocated by the blanket and, once uncovered, immediately stopped crying.

Astonished, the old man untied the baby cradle and took the baby in his hands. He and his wife had never borne children, in spite of their efforts. His wife, away visiting her relatives across the valley, would no doubt be overjoyed when she returned. She had always wanted children and now an orphan had dropped into their laps.

Cradling the baby and rocking it back and forth, he could see it was a small girl.

"I will call you Zijuan after my mother," he whispered to her, smiling.

The years passed and the old man and woman raised Zijuan as they would their own. They loved her, but could never force themselves to tell her the truth—that she could be the baby of a bandit killed by her adoptive father. They simply loved her and treated her as their own daughter. Her mother taught her to read and write and gave her an education. Her father taught her to fish, to farm rice, and, above all, to fight. By age ten, she could handle a staff better than most grown men. By fifteen, she was equally as deadly with her hands and her feet. At twenty, she could defeat ten men in a fair fight.

Zijuan was, however, a wild child. She frequently wandered outside the safety of their valley and would sometimes be gone for as long as a week at a time. By the age of eighteen, she enjoyed exploring the coastline and camping in the wilderness. She even ventured to some cities and enjoyed sights and sounds far different from the slow pace of their valley. She could always handle herself and, on more than one occasion, had broken the bones of some poor fool who thought her a harmless girl.

She found herself in the city of Jiangsu one Sunday morning. She had just left a spice market and now sat by herself at a café eating quail eggs and roast duck. It was, for the most part, an ordinary Sunday, with the hustle and bustle of people doing their weekend shopping. She smiled while watching a family of four haggle with a fisherman over the price of a brook trout.

Out of the corner of her eye she noticed something not right. Something out of the ordinary.

In the back alley of an apartment building, two men shuffled a child through a door. It happened quickly—maybe half a second—but Zijuan could see there was something undeniably criminal about the scene. The men didn't appear to be the sort to have children. They were hard and dressed in shabby clothes.

After paying for her meal, Zijuan slowly walked to the door of the apartment building. Opening it, she peeked inside. A large hallway, barely lit with candles, extended for about fifty feet. A dank smell of mold filled the hallway. It felt cold—not just the temperature, but the entire feeling of the place. It emanated evil. Zijuan felt this strongly, but decided to enter anyway. She produced a small dagger from her waist belt and held it in her right hand.

The corridor was long and, oddly, there were no windows or doors on either side. Shadows danced from the torch flames that produced a little light. Otherwise, the corridor was dark and still.

Slowly she walked until she saw another door and the very end of the hallway. As she stepped closer, she heard muffled voices from behind the door. At first, they were barely murmurs but grew louder as she approached the closed door. Putting her ear to the door, she could distinctly hear a man's voice. He was counting or something, but the sound was muffled for her to be certain. She listened for a few minutes, and the man kept counting. Once in a while she heard other shouting.

Then, she heard it. The inexplicable sound of a child's scream.

She had two choices. She could leave and live the rest of her life knowing she could have helped an innocent child. Or, she could open that door and deal with whatever lay behind it.

Concealed in the small of her back was an eighteen-inch staff made of petrified bamboo. She placed the staff in her right hand, held the dagger in her left, took a deep breath, and opened the door.

Directly in front of her was a guard with his back turned to her. Behind the guard were dozens of seated men in a large, dank room. In the center were a blindfolded girl about ten years old and an auctioneer. The girl's hands looked to be tied behind her back.

Quickly Zijuan whirled her staff in a three-sixty and hit the guard squarely in the back of the head. He fell, face first on the floor with a thud. The room grew quiet. All eyes stared at her as she slowly took three steps inside. Her eyes shifted from right to left, scanning the room. Another guard, this one bigger, charged at her from the far-right corner of the room.

Waiting, she watched the movements of the running guard and instantly calculated the length of his steps and the speed of his run.

The guard kept running until he was only a few feet from Zijuan. He lunged at her, no doubt thinking his overpowering strength would easily subdue a slight woman.

In the time it takes a hummingbird to flutter its wings, Zijuan brought the staff straight up, where it met the man's forehead right between the eyes. He stumbled, momentarily stunned, and she drew the staff twelve inches back, bent her back leg, and flung the staff around like a baton, smashing it down on his skull.

Blood dripped from his forehead as he dropped to his knees. His eyes swelled with tears. Before he had a moment to act, Zijuan jabbed the staff solidly into the man's ear, breaking his eardrum and knocking him unconscious.

She gingerly stepped over his body and approached the auctioneer.

Everyone in the room stared at her.

"You all have ten seconds to clear out. Then, I will begin taking each and every one of you apart," she sneered.

Nobody moved. There were maybe twenty men in the room and she intimidated every last one of them.

"One," she began.

"Two.

"Three."

"What about our purchases? We paid good money for these slaves," a fat man yelled out, his fist in the air and his long, full moustache cascading down each side of his lips.

She smiled at the suggestion and, before even finishing her thought, had broken the auctioneer's neck with a blow from her staff. He crumpled to the floor—dead.

"Whatever bargain you had with this man died with this man.

"Four," she continued.

The men began to scramble for the door, some jumping over the others.

"Five."

More scrambling and clawing ensued, until someone finally opened the door and they began spilling out into the hallway.

"Six.

"Seven.

"Eight."

By the time she'd gotten to eight, the room had emptied.

The little girl stood still. She'd stopped crying. Zijuan quickly untied the girl's blindfold and cut the rope that bound her wrists. She could see the rope had dug into the child's skin, scraping and tearing it until a bloody red band was left where the rope had been tied.

The girl was not Asian. She had brown skin and though her face was dirty, her big hazel eyes gazed up at Zijuan. She wore rags as garments.

"Hello," Zijuan said.

The girl just looked at her. It was obvious she didn't understand a word of what Zijuan was saying.

"My name is Zijuan. Zijuan," she repeated.

"Ziwah," the little girl whispered.

Zijuan began to wipe the girl's cheeks with the fluff of her shirt; multiple layers of dirt came off. This was the dirtiest child Zijuan had ever seen.

The little girl was obviously in shock. She stared at Zijuan and then slowly pointed.

"What? What is it?" Zijuan asked.

The girl continued to point to the far corner of the room, which was mostly concealed by shadows. The little girl took Zijuan's hand and led her to the corner.

An outline of a door presented itself.

Zijuan slowly unlocked the hinge, opened the door, and saw thirty pairs of tiny eyes staring up at her.

None of the children was older than twelve.

The children quietly stared at her. Their features resembled those of the girl she had rescued—none of them looked to be Chinese.

"Come, come," she motioned to them.

Taking the girl by the hand, she continued to motion for them to follow her.

"Come, come."

Cautiously, the children stood and followed. A couple of them had their hands tied—these were the ones who had already been sold. Zijuan quickly untied them and motioned for the entire group to follow her.

Once out of the building, the group of them ran across the waterfront, to the wonderment of onlookers. Shoppers stopped and pointed and merchants talked amongst themselves.

Zijuan knew she must get the children out of town and into safety. No doubt some of the buyers had police connections and would soon be looking for her and the children. Hurriedly, she shuffled them down a path that led out of the city. The group walked in single file for an hour. The children said nothing, dutifully following their newfound liberator.

The children were lost and hungry, yet grateful to be free. Each of them looked at Zijuan with a look of admiration and deference, as a Catholic schoolgirl might look upon a saint.

Zijuan was unaccustomed to this sort of attention, but she couldn't help but be humbled and warmed by the innocence of these desperate children. A tiny girl took her hand and looked at Zijuan as a baby kitten gazes at her mother.

"Z-I-J-U-A-N," she said phonetically, saying her name slowly so the little girl would understand.

"S-A-N-A-A," the little girl whispered and Zijuan smiled.

The group walked in single file without saying a word. No doubt they were starving, but had apparently learned to ignore their hunger. Zijuan enjoyed the warmth and tenderness of little Sanaa's hand. She couldn't have been older than six years old. Her long, dirty brown hair dangled over her eyes like a lazy curtain hangs down from a windowsill. Her dress was barely a rag, covered with soot and grease. In spite of her filthy exterior, she remained a sparkling and curious little girl.

Zijuan marched the orphan train for another three hours, until she began to see fatigue in some of their faces. Noticing the sun would be down in another hour, she decided to stop for the night in a clearing by a stream. Working diligently, she showed the children how to make their own beds out of nearby palm leaves. She deliberately established their camp under a stand of hackberry trees in case the heavens opened up and drenched the group with rain.

Next, she separated the children by gender—boys in one area and girls in another—and had them take swims and wash themselves. Her Chinese upbringing demanded proper hygiene.

While the group bathed in the stream, she prepared a large fire from a bundle of firewood, hoping to keep them warm throughout the night. Taking care to pick only dry wood, she enlisted the help of the children until the stack of wood stood three feet high.

Finally, she noticed some wild kiwi trees and goji berries. She pointed to the fruit and berries, motioning with her fingers and mouth that these were edible. The children then went about in search of food, bringing their finds back to the fire area.

By dusk, Zijuan had managed to build a raging fire and portioned out fruit and berries for each child. They ate in silence, happy to receive some kind of nutrition in their starving bellies.

In the glow of the fire, Zijuan looked into their eyes and, for the first time in her life, felt a genuine sense of purpose. Up to this point, she had always been searching. Now, she had found something she truly believed in. The Creator had placed a bushel of homeless children in her care and she would not let them be thrown to the wolves of the world.

After dinner, before each child slowly fell asleep, Zijuan went to each of them, placed a giant palm leaf over their tiny bodies, kissed them goodnight, and told them a Chinese prayer. This was the first time many of them had ever felt the safety of an adult who genuinely cared for them. Although it was a little cold and they were outside, every child fell into a deep, restful sleep.

Zijuan, however, could not sleep. She did not know what to do. Could she raise a group of foreign children in her village? The local villagers would not take kindly to such an intrusion. She didn't know anything about them. Not their country, or their names, or even what language they spoke. How could she return them home?

She gazed up at the sky full of stars and suddenly felt at peace. She did not have the answers yet, but that was not important right now. She knew she would eventually find an answer in all this.

The following morning she awoke early to pick some berries. She even managed to trap a hare, build a fire, and provide a couple of mouthfuls of protein to the children, who were most appreciative.

And then they started the long journey to her village.

It was a two-day walk. Zijuan kept the group off the main roads to avoid drawing attention. They camped and built fires and foraged for food along the way. Zijuan was able to catch some wild trout for a feast on the second night.

On the third day, the caravan arrived at Zijuan's parents' home, dragging their tired bodies, relieved to be stopping at last. Her father was tending to a crop of rice when the group appeared over the hillside. At first, he saw the head of his daughter and then, slowly, the little bodies of dozens of children. He dropped his rake, called to his wife, and they both greeted the group.

"What is this? Who are these children?" her mother asked.

"I'm too tired to explain. We need to eat and sleep and then I'll tell you everything," an exhausted Zijuan said.

Her parents fed the children a hearty meal of stew and rice. Each child ate at least three courses and then fell into a deep slumber, the group bundled together around a fire in the living room.

Ning was a naturally patient man. His years gave him a certain amount of wisdom in worldly matters. He knew there was a story behind the children; he simply waited for his daughter to explain, which she did, after a nice meal and a nap.

"What are you going to do?" he finally asked.

"I do not know. The children cannot stay here. It would create too much of a distraction," she said.

Her father nodded his head in agreement. Although he was considered a leader of his village, he also understood the insular nature of his people. They did not appreciate outsiders. They were simple and, in many ways, very ignorant and racist. There was harmony, but it was delicate.

"I think, perhaps, you should consider returning them to their homeland," he finally said.

This was quite unexpected. Most fathers, with all their good intentions, attempted to suffocate and protect their daughters.

"You have always been wild, Zijuan. Since you were a very young girl, I've known this village is too small for your wandering heart. I think, perhaps, your destiny lies outside our valley. I think these children were placed in your care for a reason."

Zijuan listened to her father. It was true, she had always sought adventure. It was something deeper. She had always longed for a meaning to her life that her parents couldn't provide—a purpose higher than herself.

"How would I do that?"

"Find out where the children came from and then go to Shanghai and find a ship."

"None of the children speak our language. I have no idea where they live. And what ship would be willing to take a group this large?"

"Zijuan, your greatest trait is your resourcefulness. Surely you will find a way."

That night Zijuan slept outside, alone with her thoughts. All she had ever known, except for her little adventures, was this valley. It represented safety and familiarity. But she knew her father was right. She could never be satisfied in such a place. She found no contentment in gardening or fishing or tending to rice paddies. Her heart yearned for the unknown.

She decided to leave for Shanghai in three days. Provisions would have to be made. She would require a wagon with an ox for the journey and enough food to feed the children for a week. This would require money she didn't have.

Zijuan slept little that night. In the morning she told her father and mother her plans. Both nodded solemnly in agreement. Her mother had been against the plan from the beginning. Such a young girl out in the world! As a mother, she was naturally protective, but understood the wisdom of the plan. Zijuan had always been uncontrollable, even since she was a small girl. It is a kind of crime to hold a person against their true nature, and she wanted nothing more than for her daughter to follow her soul and heart.

"I have some money for you, Zijuan. I don't know if it will be enough to get you a ship, but hopefully it will," Ning told her.

Zijuan was both eternally grateful and tremendously sad. She loved her parents more than anything or anyone. To leave them would break her heart.

The next three days went by quickly. The children took to learning some basic words and phrases. Zijuan learned their names and bits of phrases in their language as well. She made a point to have class for two hours each day, as they would need to continue to learn to communicate with one another. Her father helped supply the wagon and food with some extra clothes for the children.

Finally, she was ready to say goodbye. The children were crammed everywhere—inside the wagon, some on top, some in the front with her, and still others walked alongside.

The journey was slow and arduous. Zijuan took care to avoid busy cities, sticking to country roads and small towns. The children never complained. Every two hours, they would stop for a light stretch and a bathroom break. Three times a day, they would stop for food breaks, which mostly consisted of rice and some cabbage or leeks. Other than that, they never stopped moving.

On the morning of the fourth day, Zijuan stood atop a mountain overlooking the sprawling city of Shanghai. Wooden buildings crammed together like worms in a can. Freighters and trawlers endlessly entered and exited the Shanghai harbor. The busy city streets were infested with peasants, wagons, and every type of merchant.

She instructed the children to stay in the camp until she returned, which would probably not be until the next day. The city was still three miles away, so she left the camp at a quick pace. She would need as much time as possible to search out a ship and a trustworthy captain.

Within two hours, she had made it to the city borders. Although she had ventured to some cities, nothing compared to the sights and sounds of Shanghai. Every manner of beast, fish, and plant was openly sold in the many outdoor markets. A six-foot shark was being auctioned off at the fish market. A live cobra was having its blood extracted. Chirping monkeys swung from cages. The stench of human waste almost caused her to gag several times—Shanghai was in dire need of a sewer system.

After getting lost and finding her bearings several times, she finally arrived at the marina, staring at miles of docked ships. Workers hauled bags of spices from the West Indies, barrels of molasses from Jamaica, bales of cotton from India, and many hauls of different fish. The marina was a bustling mess of workers carrying hundred-pound bags on their backs while bosses yelled and even whipped them. Vessel owners inspected their cargo and conferred with captains. Merchants eagerly purchased from the ship's containers and their own workers carted the wares to their stores or factories.

Zijuan wandered for hours among the ships, trying to find the right one. She had learned the children had come from a land called Morocco and was listening for a dialect similar to the one spoken by the children.

But no opportunities presented themselves. Most of the ships' captains were white and spoke very odd languages.

Frustrated and hungry, she spotted a seaside bar and made her way inside.

The bar was named "The Grey Gull," noted by a small wooden sign hung just over its rotting red door. There was one tiny window of green stained glass in the center of the wall.

The inside was dark and lit by candlelight. The floorboards, wooden and wet, harbored the dank smell of rum, beer, tobacco spit, and salt.

Everyone inside appeared to be sailors, either in good spirits if they'd just returned from sea, or in a sour state if they were about to embark. A group of Dutch sailors stood in the far corner, six deep, hugging one another and singing a Dutch sailing song. An English sailor snored in his cup of soup, dead drunk. Other nationalities drank and talked in the many corners of the Gull.

Zijuan made her way to the bar counter and asked for a green tea and a bowl of noodles. Finding a seat, she smelled the warm broth and it brought a smile to her face. The fish oil, lemongrass, coriander, chili peppers, honey, and soy mixed together to form a delightful aroma. She slowly sipped the broth and allowed the warmth to settle in her stomach.

"Not bad soup, eh?" a voice behind her said.

"Not bad," she agreed.

"Haven't seen you in these parts before. What ship did you come in on?" the voice asked.

"I didn't come in on a ship," she slowly answered, suspicious of the sudden attention.

"Hmmm, what are you doing here, then?"

"Eating."

"Now listen here, missy…," the voice answered angrily, grabbing her by her arm.

Before the voice could make another movement, Zijuan had produced a dagger from beneath her coat and held it to the man's neck. She looked into his black eyes, felt his saggy skin on her blade, and smelled the considerable amount of rum on his breath.

"Old man, you had best behave yourself or I'll slit your throat like a beached trout," she whispered in his ear.

The man, obviously drunk, suddenly sobered and let out a slight whimper. Zijuan let her blade up from his throat and the man slinked away as she casually returned to her soup.

She finished the meal without further incident, paid her bill, and was making her way to the door when she heard it—a dialect like the children's. It was coming from the corner. She stepped up and saw the owner of the voice—a tall man wearing a towel around his head, a gold earring in one ear, and a pitch-black goatee on his chin. She ventured up to his table.

"Do you have a ship?" she asked.

The man, sitting with a group of men, looked startled to see her.

"Do you have a ship?" she asked again.

"Yes, I have a ship. Why do you want to know?" he replied in perfect Chinese.

"Where are you from?" Zijuan asked.

"Excuse me?"

"What country?"

"I am from Algeria. Have you heard of it?"

"No."

"So, why do you need a ship?"

She studied him. He had green eyes, with light wrinkles of crow's feet—probably from being in the salt and sun. His face was tanned and dark and his teeth white. He looked like a sea captain.

"I have some cargo that needs transporting," she replied.

"To where?"

"I don't exactly know."

"What is the cargo?"

"I can't tell you that."

"Well, it will be difficult to give you a price if I don't know the cargo or where it's going."

"I need a miracle, it as simple as that. Are you a good man?" she asked.

He studied her for a moment. He wasn't accustomed to such boldness from a woman. He had observed with admiration how she handled herself with the drunk. He immediately liked her.

"That depends upon who you ask if I'm a good man."

"Can you spare a few hours?"

"For what?"

"I need to show you something, but only you."

He paused suspiciously.

"There are Shanghai artists in these parts. You're not going to drag me to an alley and knock me out are you?"

"No, nothing like that. But I need to show you to explain."

Zijuan needed to introduce this captain to the children. If he spoke their dialect then he could help her find out where they lived. More importantly, she needed time to judge his character and to decide if she could trust him.

"When?"

"Now!"

"I've just sat down after a month at sea. Can't I have a beer or two? Why don't you join us?"

"I don't have time for that. I need to show you this, and then you can drink all you want."

The captain let out a heavy sigh, nodded, grabbed his coat, and bid adieu to his comrades.

"This better be good," he said.

"Don't worry about that."

"Where are we going?'

"About three miles out of town."

"And you plan to walk?"

"Of course."

"Oh no, we're taking a rickshaw."

"I don't have any money," she replied but without shame. She didn't have time for pleasantries.

"It will be my pleasure."

"Okay, then."

They flagged a horse-drawn rickshaw and began the trek out of the city.

"What is your name?"

"I am Zijuan. What is yours?"

"I am Captain Basil."

"Where did you learn Chinese?"

"My parents lived in China when I was a boy. My father was a captain, as well as his father and his father before that. You see, the sea is in my blood."

"And what is it you transport?"

"Anything that brings a price. From the Chinese, we purchase tea and spices and ship them to the English. From India, we purchase salt and cotton, which we sell to the Spanish."

"Do you have a family?"

"Yes, a beautiful wife and two lovely sons."

"How often do you see them?"

"When I am in port, perhaps every two or three months. Not as often as I like."

"So why don't you quit to be closer to home?"

"As I said, the sea is in my blood. If I am not sailing, I'm afraid I'll wither away and die."

Zijuan liked the fact the captain was married and had children. That was the mark of a stable man. She also liked the fact that he was in the same craft as his father and grandfather. That meant he'd probably been instructed well. His manner was calm and confident, and she held a good feeling about him.

"So now are you going to tell me about this cargo?"

"A week ago, I rescued about thirty children from a slave trader. They speak the same dialect as you. I need to return them to their home."

The man's face expressed complete shock.

"That wasn't the answer you were expecting?"

"Honestly, no. I thought perhaps you wanted to ship opium."

"And would you have agreed?"

"No. If I am boarded by authorities, I could lose my ship. And, I don't approve of drugs."

They sat in silence awhile. Finally, Captain Basil spoke.

"These children, they may not have homes or families. Have you thought about raising them here?"

"They belong with their families or, at a minimum, with their people. Besides, what if they *do* have families? If your children were kidnapped, would you not want to see them returned to you unharmed?"

"I see your point."

The rickshaw wound around a bend and the horse struggled a bit with the incline.

"There. It is just over that hill to the right," Zijuan instructed the driver.

The rickshaw made its way up the hill and turned right into a grassy field. About a hundred yards down, there was a grouping of trees with a small creek. As they edged toward the trees, Zijuan and Captain Basil could see the outlines of small children running for cover.

Finally, they reached the trees. Several children came running when they saw it was Zijuan. Soon, all the children had surrounded the rickshaw. Captain Basil looked in amazement at the innocent eyes staring up at him.

"There are so many," he stammered.

"I know."

Captain Basil stepped off the rickshaw and studied the children's faces. They were undoubtedly Arab but he couldn't tell exactly which country. Seeing the eldest one, he began an inquisition.

"Where are you from?" he asked her gently, in Arabic.

"Morocco."

"How did you come to be in this country?"

"We were kidnapped and sold."

"Are you orphans?"

"A few are but many of us have families."

"How long have you been gone?"

"I do not know. Perhaps a month, perhaps more."

The girl was tall and lanky, and her accent revealed she came from an upper-class upbringing. It held a touch of nobility.

"What does your father do?" Captain Basil asked.

"He is a merchant."

"And where did you go to school?"

"The Misri School."

"It was a private school?"

"Yes."

"And you probably speak English."

"Yes."

This girl was definitely from an upper-class family and no orphan. Captain Basil went to Zijuan.

"They are from Morocco. A few are orphans but most have families. This one here is from a well-to-do family. I can tell by her accent and education. Just as you suspected, they were captured and sold as slaves."

"So will you help me?" Zijuan asked.

Captain Basil assessed the situation.

"How much money do you have?"

"About a thousand yen."

"Not nearly enough. We are sailing for Algeria, but it would be another two weeks, round trip, to drop them off in Morocco. I have the cost of my crew, food…"

"What if their families would help?" Zijuan asked.

"I was thinking the same thing. It's a risk on my part."

"I'll say it again. What if these were your children?"

He eyed her—the guilt of a woman! He took a few breaths but already knew his answer.

"You will need to watch them. I can put them in a hold. It will be cramped. I don't want them disturbing the crew."

"You won't even know they are on the ship."

"I highly doubt that. Be at the docks in two days at daybreak. The name of my ship is *The Constantine Ghost*. It is at Dock 21."

"Please. I need to trust you. If you say you will be there, you must be there. All these children and their families are counting on you."

"Madame, I am a man of faith. I believe that you and these children were delivered to me by Allah, and it is my sworn duty to see them delivered safely to their families. We will worry about the money at another time."

"Thank you," Zijuan said and, in spite of her nature, bowed deeply in respect.

Captain Basil returned the bow.

"I only have a day in port to celebrate. I will see you in two days."

Captain Basil loaded himself back onto the rickshaw and disappeared over the hill. Zijuan was sad to see him depart. It felt safe to have someone, anyone, to talk with and share just a bit of her burden.

Two days later, in the early morning darkness, Zijuan and the children made their way through town. She retraced her steps to the marina and headed straight to Dock 21. Sure enough, *The Constantine Ghost* sat at the dock like a dog awaiting its master. It was a handsome boat, with golden mahogany for paint and a wooden gull at the front of the bow.

An hour later, Captain Basil emerged from his quarters with sleep in his eyes, stretching as the sun beckoned over the horizon. He looked up, yawned, turned and immediately found thirty sets of eyes on him. He was so startled he started laughing.

"Good morning," he said.

"Good morning to you," Zijuan replied.

"Well, no dawdling; let me set you a ladder and welcome you aboard."

Captain Basil placed a wooden ladder between the ship and the dock. Slowly, each child made their way onboard, followed at last by Zijuan.

"Come, your quarters are waiting. Have the children eaten?"

"Not much, just some cold rice and seaweed."

"Well, we'll get them fed. I have purveyed separate quarters for you. The children will be allowed on deck from the hours of seven to nine in the morning, two to three in the afternoon, and seven to nine at night. These orders are to be followed. They will be allotted two meals a day. It's not much but it's all I can spare."

"You are very generous. What about chores?" Zijuan continued.

"What about them?"

"Please. Put the older ones and myself to work. We can cook, clean, launder, anything to make the voyage more pleasant."

Captain Basil hadn't considered this.

"I'll talk with my first mate. Perhaps we can have a work detail. That is a very generous offer."

"It is you who is making the generous offer," Zijuan corrected him.

Soon the children had eaten a breakfast of eggs, rice, and biscuits. Captain Basil had never seen little mouths move so fast. The cook, an old salt named Rigby Jones, came out to greet his new customers, and even he was touched by their appetite.

The rest of the crew wasn't yet onboard. Captain Basil showed the children to their quarters in the stern, the rear of the boat normally used for prisoners of war captured at sea. Pillows and rugs had been carefully laid and Captain Basil had even purchased some toys and trinkets to entertain the children. The quarters were tight, but soon the children were fast asleep, practically on top of one another.

Zijuan was shown to her quarters. It was a small room with a bed, a bowl for washing, and a small desk. A small porthole allowed the sunlight to creep in and could be opened to view the ocean, splashing ten feet below.

"You are too kind," said Zijuan, sincerely grateful.

"It is nothing. A woman should have her privacy. Now, if you will excuse me, I have a ship to prepare for sail."

"Thank you, Captain," Zijuan said as he walked away.

She lay down on her bed, and a tremendous sense of relief came over her. For the first time in days, she allowed herself to relax and drift into a deep sleep as *The Constantine Ghost* set sail and headed for open water.

CHAPTER
— *12* —

FROM CITY RAT TO
RESISTANCE FIGHTER

Through the day they rode without stopping. Zigging and zagging through mountain paths surrounded by cedar, juniper, and Moroccan fir trees. The mountainside was especially steep, but there were so many valleys and gullies it was difficult to keep any sort of direction. The group followed a small creek for a while and then cut over and up a steep embankment. Snow was still on the ground in most places.

Tariq rode slowly and everyone was constantly forced to wait for him. Fortunately, these rebels knew the mountains better than their own homes, and they left a trail that was impossible to follow except by the most expert of trackers.

At nightfall, the group sought refuge and a needed rest. They strategically chose a location on high ground that would allow them to defend their position against a much larger force. The camp was camouflaged by the overhanging trees and bushes. Two sentries, expert archers both, stood watch on either side of the trail below. The rest of the group quickly set up camp, which consisted mostly of laying down some rugs on the hard ground, pitching tents, and tying up and feeding the camels and horses.

Tariq, Margaret, and Fez all watched this activity from a distance. Someone from the rebel group offered them a snack of cold pigeon and dried apricots, which they gratefully accepted.

As the rush of adrenaline from the day's events began to ebb, Margaret found herself starting to cry. They had escaped! Her dream had come true. She was no longer a slave in a harem. Against all odds they had made it out alive. She hugged Fez and Tariq and both of them cried as well.

"Where is Aseem?" she asked.

"He didn't make it," Tariq said slowly.

"Is he okay?"

"Yes. I'd rather not talk about it right now."

Margaret saw the shame in his face and decided not to broach the subject. Obviously something had happened between the two of them.

Sanaa approached the group with one of the rebels. He was young, maybe thirty, and handsome. A three-day black beard grazed his face. His skin was bronze and his eyes dark. He possessed the stature of a nobleman.

"Everyone, this is Malik. Like all of us, he is a sworn enemy of the Caid," Sanaa announced.

Malik stepped forward, looked all the children in the eyes, and smiled broadly.

He spoke in a soft voice.

"My friends, I cannot express to you how astounded I am of your bravery. For children, you showed the heart of lions. What you did was courageous, and I am proud to be in your company."

Malik went to each of them, hugged them, and kissed them on both cheeks. His embrace was warm and genuine.

"Come and rest your tired bodies. Tomorrow we will make our village, where you will all be accepted as one of our own."

That night, Tariq lay on the ground by himself, away from the others. He gazed at the sky full of stars and planets. He tried to keep count of the falling stars and meteors but his mind drifted and his thoughts kept returning to Aseem.

"Something on your mind?" Malik asked, and lay next to him.

"Have you ever done something you regret so much but can't take back?"

"Yes."

"What?"

"When the Caid was gaining power, my father wanted me to join the resistance and fight him, as he and my brother did. I refused. They were killed by the Caid, who then pillaged my town."

"How do you live with it?" Tariq asked.

"By learning from my mistake and making a difference each day. There is not a day that has passed that I do not think of my father and brother. The good, however, is that it lit a fire in me to fight the Caid—each and every day until he is defeated."

Tariq thought about this for a moment.

"I want to see the Caid defeated as well."

Malik didn't say anything for a few moments. There was something he needed to discuss with Tariq but he didn't know the best way to bring it up in conversation.

"Tariq, your friend Zijuan asked me to rescue you," Malik finally admitted.

Tariq had known this, because Sanaa had told him when he was a prisoner.

"How do you know Zijuan?"

"Oh, Zijuan has been fighting with us for as long as I can remember. She is like a mother to Sanaa. She is as good a friend to me as I could ever imagine."

"She is like a mother to me as well."

"She specifically asked that I look out for you. But she asked me something else as well."

"What was that?"

"That if we rescued you, I would take you as my apprentice and teach you to fight with us."

"Why would she ask that?"

"Because, Zijuan wants something better for you than being in an orphanage."

Malik allowed Tariq to think about this for a moment before continuing.

"The choice is yours, of course, Tariq. You can return to the orphanage in Tangier or stay here with us and begin your training. But, life might be very dangerous for you in Tangier. You are a wanted man now, and the Caid's spies will be searching for you."

Tariq thought about this for a moment. He looked at the encampment. He was a city rat and had never even been outside of Tangier.

"What would I need to do?" Tariq asked.

"Well, first you must learn to live as our people live—how to live off the land, how to hunt and how to live in the desert and mountains. Then, you must learn to fight. Not just with your hands, but with your head."

"And you would teach me?"

"Yes."

"Could my friends stay with us, if they want?" Tariq asked.

"Of course."

This all made Tariq very happy. He didn't need to give it much thought, as his mind was already made up. In fact, he had already planned to approach Malik to ask about staying with his group.

"I will join you, Malik. I am proud you have chosen me as an apprentice."

"Tariq, I must warn you. The training is not easy and it's not supposed to be. Our goal will be to prepare you for the hardships of battle and the difficult life of a resistance fighter. You may want to quit, but I will never let you. In fact, the more you want to quit, the harder I will make you train."

"I will not quit, Malik. I will be your best student ever!"

The two shook hands and hugged. Tariq, for the first time in a long time, smiled very broadly. He felt much better after the conversation. He decided he would dedicate the rest of his life to freeing Aseem and to fighting the Caid. He could not wait to begin training—even though he had no idea what that training entailed.

Tariq got up to go tell his friends leaving Malik by himself.

What Malik held back was what Zijuan had told him—that Tariq was a natural leader, as athletic and courageous a boy as she had ever seen. Malik didn't tell this to Tariq, of course, because he didn't want to swell the boy's head. Too often, gifted boys and girls will take the attitude that their gifts are enough, without being challenged to develop them.

Malik wanted to see for himself what the boy was made of.

The next day, the group arose before the sun showed itself over the mountains. It was completely dark and bitter cold. Everyone wrapped themselves in blankets and broke camp. They didn't bother to build a fire.

176

It would have slowed them down, and, if the Caid's soldiers were nearby, they did not want the smoke from the fire to reveal their location.

The group headed silently back up the trail. There wasn't the rush from the previous day, so they took their time. Many parts of the trail were too steep to ride, so they walked single file, cutting through narrow valleys and up steep embankments.

By nightfall, they had made it to the village.

It wasn't so much a village as dozens of tents pitched in a circle. There were perhaps one hundred and fifty inhabitants, including many women and children. These were Berbers; mountain tribes of Morocco who had been roaming these mountains for thousands of years. There was fierceness, but also generosity, in their eyes. Their skin was brown and tough, but somehow there was elegance to each one of them, as if a light shined from within.

Tariq, Fez, and Margaret were soon surrounded by all manner of men, women, and children who shouted, sang, and shook their hands. They were greeted as conquering heroes. After five minutes, the three friends were shown to their tents; Fez and Tariq would share one, while Margaret would have her own. Jawad was still very injured and placed in a medical tent where the local doctor could tend to his wounds. The tents were small but cozy, with a number of rugs and furs to keep them warm in the cold mountain nights. That night, there was much dancing and a feast to welcome their new inhabitants.

The following morning, just as the sun was hovering over the horizon, Malik woke Tariq. Without hesitation, Tariq threw on his shirt and was immediately at Malik's side. He watched his breath in the cold morning air. He liked waking up in the cold; it somehow made him feel more alive.

The first thing Tariq noticed was a falcon on Malik's shoulder. A small hood covered its head and eyes.

"What are you doing with that bird?" Tariq asked.

"This, my friend, is your first lesson. Meet my trusted friend Babr Al Jaraz. He is a very noble and very proud Peregrine Falcon."

"Hi, Babr Al Jaraz."

"Come, we have a bit of walking to do."

The two walked for about a mile, up to a high ridge. From that vantage point, they could see the entire valley and the adjacent mountainsides covered with trees and snow. It was beautiful and enormous. Malik slowly took the hood off Babr Al Jaraz. The falcon cooed with satisfaction. Malik slowly untwisted the leather strap attached to the bird's talon. Babr Al Jaraz chirped with gratification, playfully nipped at Malik's ear, and took a few steps to ensure he was free.

Malik then gave a series of hand signals to the bird. Babr Al Jaraz nodded once in understanding and then took off in flight.

"I gave him instructions to make one pass around the camp and then hunt for food."

"What do you mean one pass?" Tariq asked.

"Falcons are our scouts. It takes years to train them, but once trained, they are invaluable. They can see a mouse flying half a mile over the desert and swoop down to grab it silently. We train them to alert us to enemy movement. Many times we will have them fly over the Caid's camp as a spy. They fly so high that the Caid's rifles cannot hit them. Our falcons are a primary reason the Caid's men can never find us. We are alerted to their locations far before they are able to find ours."

"Doesn't the Caid have falcons as well?"

"Ah, but he has nobody to train them. Falcons can easily be trained to simply hunt and return to the same spot. But training them to act as scouts and spies takes an artist's touch and a priest's patience. It is an art that has been passed down for hundreds of years among our people."

"May I train a falcon?" Tariq asked.

"That is an honor you must earn, my friend."

"How do I earn it?"

"By first proving you can work hard without question. That, you must learn with hard work and sacrifice."

Tariq nodded in appreciation.

"Being an apprentice means performing all the menial chores for me. This includes sharpening my sword, making new arrows, cleaning my clothes, minding my horse, and even cooking my food. This is meant to teach you what it is like to perform manual labor so you may appreciate those who do this sort of work for a living. You must never look down on such people, for they make our lives easier."

"Okay."

"Being an apprentice is also meant to teach you how to take care of yourself."

"Okay."

"When you have proven you can do this work with a positive attitude and without prodding, I will begin teaching you the way of the warrior and the way of battle. I will teach you how to lead and how to scout. How to fight the Caid. How to hunt and fish. How to live in the desert."

"Okay."

"Now, considering this will require very long hours and demand your constant attention—do you accept these terms?"

"I do."

"Have you thought about it?"

"Yes."

"Why do you accept these terms?" Malik asked him.

"It is like a baby bird in a nest. The fledgling must first learn to fly and may fall from the nest. To fly takes much struggle and much learning. But once the bird learns to fly, it can soar in the heavens."

Malik smiled; he liked this answer very much.

"That is very good, Tariq. Today, please rest and play. Tomorrow we will start your true training."

"Malik, there is one thing I must discuss with you."

"What is it?"

"That boy Jawad, he did not want to join us."

"What do you mean?"

"He wanted to stay with the Caid. He was about to join the Caid's cavalry. He is only with us because he fell off his camel during the race and I did not want to leave him."

"Hmmmm. I will need to consider this."

"There is one other thing."

"What is it?"

"My friend Aseem is still with the Caid. He was left behind. I must rescue him."

"I cannot allow that, Tariq. The Caid will be extremely angry with us. Any day now, I expect him to begin patrols to scour these mountains looking for us. He will increase his security details. It will be very dangerous in the coming months."

"Okay," Tariq answered and held his head low.

"I will figure out how to deal with Jawad. In the meantime, hold your head high. You are no longer a slave. You are a free man."

Tariq smiled. They stood on the ridge for another hour talking and watching as Babr Al Jaraz hunted—he finally scooped up a small squirrel and hungrily devoured it on a nearby ledge. Afterwards, he dutifully flew to Malik's shoulder and rested—content and full from the morning's hunt.

"So, what did you and Malik have to talk about?" Margaret asked Tariq.

"He has taken me as an apprentice," Tariq answered proudly.

"That is wonderful—congratulations!" Margaret said and hugged him. Tariq turned red with embarrassment at this display of affection.

"So when do you begin?"

"Tomorrow."

"Well, that gives us today. They are planning a feast and party for us again tonight. I can't wait. I could use a nice bath and some good food. It's not right for a proper English girl to get so dirty like this."

"You look fine Margaret."

"Tariq, there's something we need to discuss."

"Yes."

"What are you going to do about Jawad?"

"I don't know."

"Perhaps you could talk with him?"

"He's still pretty bad. I will wait until he's healthy."

"And Aseem?"

Tariq thought about this for a minute.

"I must go back for him. It is my fault he's not with us."

"How will you do that?"

"I don't know, but I must save him."

Margaret did not push the subject. She could see Tariq was in considerable pain. To push the subject further would only add to his sorrow. She figured he needed a pat on the back more than a kick in the behind.

"What are you going to do, Margaret?"

"I need to return to my parents—to England."

"How will you do that?"

"I'm not sure yet."

"I will help you."

Margaret smiled at that thought.

"Tariq, you're just a child."

"None of us is a child any longer. I will help you return to your family. I promise."

"Thank you, Tariq."

Fez joined them, waking up from a nap.

"Fez, are these the mountains of your tribe?" Tariq asked.

"Yes, but my tribe lived much further north. I do not know this area."

"It's beautiful country," Margaret said.

"Do you know that there are apes in these mountains?" Fez asked.

"Apes?" both Tariq and Margaret said at once.

"Yes, Barbary apes, but they are just a nuisance."

"Anything else?" Margaret asked.

"Oh yes. Wild boar, mountain sheep, goats, gazelles, and more birds than one can imagine," Fez said excitedly.

Margaret looked at the trees spread around them.

"Fez, what kinds of trees are these?" Margaret asked.

"The tall bushy ones are called fir trees. The longer, skinnier ones are called cedars."

"Any snakes?" Margaret asked.

"Oh yes! The cobra, viper, and puff adder are some of the most dangerous," Fez answered, even more excited.

Margaret looked at Tariq and gulped. They didn't have snakes in England. Although she had lived in Egypt, where snakes were plentiful, her life had been in Cairo, in the safety of the city. As a child in Cairo, she had witnessed a snake charmer, and she remembered the white markings on the back of a cobra's hood.

"Anything else?" Margaret asked slowly.

"Just watch for the scorpions. They're small buggers and can crawl into your blanket at night for the warmth."

With that, Margaret went almost completely white.

"Do not worry, Margaret, snakes and animals are more afraid of you than you are of them. It is very rare to die from a snake bite. Just don't provoke them and you should be fine. If you are bitten, cut a little incision around the wound and suck out the poison," Fez explained.

"Well, I don't want to run into any of them. I don't like snakes or scorpions."

"Oh, I like snakes; in fact, I was going to learn to charm snakes. Not like in the cities, where they use defanged cobras and vipers, but a real snake charmer."

"Fez, you're kind of weird," Tariq said.

All three of them laughed, and Fez continued to tell them stories of the countryside. He was a little encyclopedia, and went on at length about star constellations, bird species, different kinds of plants and flora, and even gave them a long lecture on the benefits of limestone.

After fifteen minutes, Tariq and Margaret both had a headache from all the information they had just absorbed.

"I feel like I'm back at school," Margaret finally said.

"Fez, you could be a professor at a university," Tariq remarked.

"That would be a dream for me," Fez answered.

"Well, I'm going to take a bath and relax. Thank you for all the information, Fez," Margaret said and retired to her tent.

That night they feasted on roasted goat, prickly pear, and a fig dessert. They danced and played drums along with the entire clan. Finally, everyone collapsed from exhaustion under the stars. The three friends felt like part of a family. The Berbers, always known for hospitality, were nothing but smiles and affectionate greetings to their new companions. Margaret had never experienced anything like this. Even Tariq, who was from

Tangier, was warmed by the generosity of their spirit. They all seemed to have smiles on their faces, and their hearts seemed so true. The women were beautiful, even after living in the mountains, with bronzed skin and inquisitive chestnut eyes. Everyone wore colorful garments and head-dresses. The men, who were constantly under the stress of war, possessed a whimsy and honesty in spite of their hardships and oppression.

"The training begins."

Tariq, before the sentence had ended, was up from his bed, putting on his shirt. In another instant, he was out of his tent, standing face to face with Malik. It was so early the sun had not yet risen.

"So, you're a willing apprentice," Malik smiled when he said it.

"Yes, sir."

"Let's have a walk."

"Okay," Tariq said and dutifully followed him.

"Tariq, why did you leave your friend Aseem behind?"

"Well..."

"Think before you answer."

Tariq already knew the answer but was ashamed to admit it.

"I was afraid, sir. Afraid I wouldn't succeed. Afraid I might fail."

"Exactly. Fear is in all men."

"Even you?"

"Especially me. It's what you do with that fear that determines if you are a leader or follower, a brave warrior or a coward. Fear is like fire. Control it, and it can cook your food and keep you warm at night. Let it rage out of control, and it can burn down your entire village."

"How do I control my fear?"

"Tariq, why do you think you were afraid?"

"I felt weak."

"Weak?"

"These feelings deep inside of my stomach kept coming up to me. They forced me to lose my breath, to tremble."

"What feelings? Describe them."

"I am an orphan. What good am I? I am poor—even my own parents did not want me. I was an accident. What good could I ever do?"

Malik listened to Tariq, and he felt for the boy. It was a heavy burden for such a young one to bear.

"Tariq, you have shown the heart of a lion, and you are a good person. However, you have something to prove. You have a hunger inside of you. Never, ever let that hunger be extinguished. It is your edge over all others."

"I don't understand."

"A boy who has parents and a comfortable life has no reason to reach beyond his boundaries. He can be perfectly content with his life and never strive or risk for anything greater. A boy who comes from nothing, and has nothing to lose, has something to prove to himself and the world. This is a boy who can do great things."

Tariq listened intently; it was the first time a man had ever had anything good to say to him.

"However, you must learn to conquer your fear. In the face of great danger, allow fear to be your friend and let it fuel you."

"How?"

"First, by repeating it to yourself. Now, repeat after me, like this—I will never show fear."

"I will never show fear."

"If I am facing the biggest warrior with the largest sword and I only have my bare hands, I will never show fear."

"If I am facing the biggest warrior with the largest sword and I only have my bare hands, I will never show fear."

"I am not afraid of pain. I am not afraid of getting hit."

"I am not afraid of pain. I am not afraid of getting hit."

"I will give to my enemy twice as hard as he gives to me."

"I will give to my enemy twice as hard as he gives to me."

"Now, are you ready?" Malik asked.

"Yes," Tariq answered, but before he could say more Malik had swiftly kicked his ankles out from under him. Tariq hit the sand hard on his side.

"Now, get up and try to hit me."

Tariq rose and lunged wildly at Malik, missing him completely. With his palm open, Malik swung his right hand and slapped Tariq upside the head, sending him tumbling.

Tariq was thrown face first onto the sand. He shook his head and got back up slowly.

"Come on, you aren't hurt. You're much tougher than this," Malik urged him.

Tariq gathered himself, lunging to tackle head first into Malik, who simply moved to one side and shifted his weight so that Tariq went flying into the sand.

This continued for five minutes until Tariq was bloodied and tired. His shirt was ripped and sand stuck to the open wounds on his elbows and chin. He breathed heavily and fell to his knees. He spit a combination of saliva and blood.

Malik went to him, extended his hand, and lifted him to his feet.

"That was very good, Tariq. You were with a stronger and more experienced opponent, yet you never quit. You were sloppy, but you never quit. That is the most important lesson of all—never quit."

Tariq nodded, bloodied but happy.

"The first thing you must learn is balance. If you are unbalanced, you will be easily beaten. Stand with your feet about shoulder-width apart and bend your knees a little. Good; now, bring your arms up and keep your elbows at your ribs. Yes; this position protects your body from attack. When you attack, don't lunge so much; bend your knees and twist at the waist for power. Never, ever lose balance."

Tariq did as he was told, and the two of them practiced sparring for over an hour. Malik taught him balance and knocked him to his butt when he was off-balance. Tariq learned quickly to keep his weight centered and his arms close in to protect his ribs. He improved greatly in just a short amount of time.

"Now, I would like for you to prepare my horse by putting on his saddle. Also, feed him and bring him water. After that, go to my tent, collect my dirty clothes, wash them, and have them folded in my tent by sundown. When you are done with that, I will show you how to make an arrow. I will need one hundred arrows made by the end of the week."

"Yes, sir."

"When you are working, think only of the job at hand. Think of nothing else. Do not think of other things you would like to be doing. Do not think about how hard your task is. Just focus on the job at hand and nothing else."

"Yes, sir."

"Then, let's get started."

CHAPTER
— *13* —

TO BE A FRIEND

Aseem was held upright with his wrists and ankles bound like a crucifixion. The rope dug into his wrists and blood slowly dripped down his arms. He was barely conscious.

"You have been sentenced to die," the guard told him.

Aseem said nothing. He had no more tears to cry.

"Since you know nothing of the rebel filth and their plans or where-abouts, you will die for our entertainment."

Aseem said nothing. He was alone. He had been abandoned by his friends and had nothing left to give or to live for.

"When?" he asked.

"Seven days," the guard replied with a sneer. "You will be an example at the next race for any other riders who have ideas of betrayal."

Again, Aseem said nothing. He looked ahead with a distant, blank stare. He knew he was going to die. He thought of everything in life he wished he had done. Wished he had experienced.

His life had been so short.

Fat Zahir stumbled through the desert. The blistering sun beat down on his brown face. He sweated profusely through his robe. On his back was three days' worth of water that would quickly be reduced to two days. Zahir had never rationed before and his thirst knew few boundaries. He carelessly drank and gulped water every half an hour, even spilling some of it in the red desert sand.

After the camel race, and his loss to Hari Kazim, Zahir had bundled up as much food and water as possible and escaped in the night. The Caid blamed him for the camel race escape and, generally, people not liked by the Caid rarely lived long. His debt, compounded by the loss to Hari Kazim, totaled more than he would earn in a year.

In a fit of desperation, he had slinked out of the camp at nightfall with no plan and nowhere to go.

He stood in the heat, then fell to his knees and started to cry. He wished he could be home with his mother and father, with none of these worries. He missed his mother's dove casserole and cashew nut pie. He missed his father. He was not ready for responsibility. He was a grown man, yet such a child.

Like most bullies, once the façade of his toughness was broken, his true colors showed—a spoiled little boy who would run home to his parents at the first glimpse of trouble.

He was weak, and he knew it.

Continuing to stumble along, Zahir blubbered like a toddler. Looking down at the sand and feeling sorry for himself, he walked aimlessly ahead until he felt something sharp in his chest.

Looking up, he saw a rider dressed completely in beige as camouflage in the desert. The rider's face was covered with a cloth to protect his eyes from the sand. He held a rifle with a long bayonet at the end.

"Look what came crawling in the sand," the rider laughed.

Zahir, terrified, starting crying and blubbering even louder.

"Oh my goodness, stop your stammering," the rider scolded Zahir, annoyed.

"Please don't hurt me."

"And why not? Obviously you come from the Caid's kasbah. You're wearing his colors."

"I can help you," Zahir answered.

"How?"

"I know everything about the Caid's kasbah. I can provide you with detailed plans of every nook and corner in the kasbah. I can tell you everything you need to know about his army."

The rider, considering this piece of information, decided to do the most logical thing. He descended from his horse, took the butt of his rifle, and hit Zahir squarely in the head, knocking him unconscious.

Next, he hog-tied Zahir's wrists and ankles, blindfolded him, shoved the fat man up onto his horse, and started for the resistance camp.

"Do you know who this is?" Malik asked.

"He is the man who tortured us," Tariq answered.

Zahir kneeled on the ground, a rag covered his mouth to prevent him from speaking; he was blindfolded, and his ankles and wrists were bound with a leather rope.

"Mmmmm," he mumbled.

Malik took the rag from his mouth.

"What is it? You have thirty seconds before we end your pitiful life."

"I was the head guard at the kasbah. I can help you."

"How can you help us?" Malik asked.

"I know secret passages. Ways to get in and out of the kasbah completely undetected."

"This sounds like a trap," Malik heard someone say.

Malik thought about this for a moment. He motioned to the scout who found Zahir.

"Are you absolutely sure you were not followed?" he asked.

"Yes, Malik. I made sure I was alone."

"If it's a trap, then it's a very bad one. We have the fat one here as a captive."

Malik rubbed his chin and stared at Zahir. He studied him for three long minutes.

"Okay, fat one, provide us with a detailed diagram of the kasbah. Give us every bit of information, including secret passageways, exit points, ammunition depots, guard details, and anything else we ask for. If you provide us with this information, and it turns out to be valuable, your life will be spared."

"What will happen to me then?" Zahir asked.

"We will drop you at a port city far away from here. That is the deal. Agree to it, or we slit your throat right now."

Zahir breathed in and nodded his head.

"I agree."

The next eight hours was spent interrogating Zahir and obtaining more valuable information than Malik ever thought possible. Zahir explained underground tunnel systems for entering the kasbah completely undetected. He provided details on guard posts and the timing of guard changes. He explained how to enter the weapons and provisions storage areas. He told them that food arrives once every month and described the exact route of the caravan. He even provided the keys to crack the Caid's codes.

Malik exited the tent where Zahir was held captive and spoke with Sanaa.

"Do you realize the value of the information he is providing us? We have every bit of intelligence to defeat the Caid."

"I guess the fat man really wanted to live," Sanaa laughed.

"Yes, he doesn't sound like much of a soldier. I'm amazed the Caid would entrust his security to such a buffoon," Malik said.

"But, he does have one quality. He knows how to appeal to the Caid's ego," Sanaa surmised.

"I've found that most powerful people are the most insecure with themselves. This might be the weakness we've been looking for in defeating the Caid."

Sanaa smiled at this. There was a reason Malik was their leader. He was wise beyond his years.

Malik called the entire resistance force together around a campfire. He was sure to keep out of earshot from Zahir, who was sleeping off a large meal and coconut whiskey as reward for his confession.

"We have been provided with extremely valuable intelligence from the fat man. We have detailed plans for exactly how to enter and exit the kasbah undetected. With this information, we can plan an attack that will cripple the Caid's forces. I will convene with our leaders on the exact details. We will plan on executing the attack in three days' time. Prepare yourselves!" Malik ordered.

There was a considerable amount of excitement amongst the resistance fighters. For years they had eked out a meager existence fighting the Caid. Their victories were measured in tiny increments—small food raids and perhaps the killing of a foot soldier or two. This attack was an opportunity to inflict serious damage on the Caid.

Immediately, the camp was buzzing, as fighters sharpened their swords and prepared their horses. Men, women, and children all had a role to play in preparing for this attack. Nobody was spared from a detail. Everyone worked.

Tariq diligently worked at Malik's side to help sharpen his daggers, wash his clothes, and prepare his meals for the desert ride.

"Will I be going?" Tariq asked.

"No, you've had enough excitement for now. You'll be staying behind," Malik answered.

Tariq hung his head in shame. He felt he'd proved himself as a warrior and should be included. Malik saw the change in his attitude.

"Tariq, you're a very brave boy. What you did to escape was truly courageous. But, you're not ready to be a soldier. You have so much training to complete. Please be patient and listen to what I say."

"I will."

"Good, now go see your friends and get a good night's sleep."

Tariq went and joined Margaret, Fez, and Jawad.

"How are you, Jawad?" Tariq asked.

Jawad had been steadily improving for days. He could eat now and could sit up. However, he still had bouts of dizziness and fatigue from the blow to his head.

Jawad just stared at Tariq.

"Jawad, please do not be upset with me. You had fallen from your ride. The Caid's men may have killed you if they thought you were part of the escape plan."

"I was going to be a cavalry soldier in the Caid's army. Now what am I? A rat with a bunch of villagers," Jawad answered.

"Jawad, you should be thankful that we saved you," Margaret said. "I doubt the Caid would have taken such good care of you. These are very good people who just want their freedom."

Jawad said nothing, folded his arms, and stared straight ahead.

"Suit yourself," Margaret said and looked at Tariq and Fez.

"Quite a bit of excitement in the camp, huh?" Fez remarked.

"Yes, fat Zahir really did in the Caid this time. Too bad we can't go," Tariq answered, still pouting a bit from his dismissal.

"Yes, it is too bad. But, there are other ways we can provide value," Fez answered.

"What do you mean?" Margaret asked.

"I've been thinking about the code that Zahir provided to us. If we can intercept the messages without the Caid's knowledge, we can change the orders."

"I don't get it," Margaret said.

"Well, let's say a message comes from a scout that he's found our secret camp. We could change the message to an entirely new location and ambush the Caid's men."

"That would be fabulous!" Margaret exclaimed.

"Yes, it would disrupt all the operations of the Caid. We could spread out his troops as we wanted, interrupt food caravans, and even give him misinformation about our size and our numbers."

"You should discuss this with Malik."

"I plan to in the morning."

Throughout this banter and conversation, Tariq barely said a word.

"Tariq, what are you thinking about?" Margaret asked.

"Oh, nothing…just daydreaming."

In fact, Tariq *was* thinking of something. He was thinking of Aseem being stuck in a cell. He was thinking of how he had failed his friend and of the shame it brought upon him.

But he was also thinking that he had a plan.

The next morning the camp awakened early. Fires were built and breakfast was made. Malik immediately went about diagramming a map and developing a strategy for the coming raid on the Caid's kasbah. There was an underground tunnel that emerged just in front of the weapons storage. He could have a small band of soldiers arrive there under the cover of darkness, steal a great many weapons, and burn the remainder.

He could have another band of soldiers set fire to the food warehouse to severely cripple the Caid's rations and supplies.

He continued to think strategy and tactics when he noticed that Tariq was not at his side. This was unlike Tariq, as he had proved to be a willing and accountable apprentice.

Nor had he prepared breakfast or provided laundry.

Malik, upset at this tardiness, went about searching for Tariq. Instead, he happened upon Margaret.

"Margaret, have you seen Tariq this morning?"

"No, he was not in his bed when I woke up. I thought he was with you."

"No, I have not seen him all morning. I don't know where he could be."

Malik and Margaret began scouring the camp, asking everyone if they had seen Tariq.

Nobody had.

After fifteen minutes, they stood in confusion, wondering where he could have gone.

"I found Tariq," Fez came up to them.

"Where?"

"Here," he said, and handed Malik a note. It read:

> Dearest Malik,
>
> You have been an inspiration to me. I cannot express my thanks enough for taking me on as an apprentice. But I have something that I must do. I left a friend in prison at the Caid's kasbah. I must rescue him. It is my fault he is imprisoned and mine alone. Do not worry, as I will not spoil your plans.
>
> Your humble servant,
>
> Tariq

Malik took a moment to take in this news. As with all things, he didn't rush to judgment or act in haste. He considered all consequences before deciding upon a course of action.

"If he took a horse, which I'm sure he did, there will be no catching him. He has at least a five hour head start on us," Malik thought out loud.

Margaret and Fez watched him. They could feel his anger and said nothing.

"Your friend is very brave. But, if he is caught we cannot rescue him. Most likely, he will be tortured and forced to reveal our plans and whereabouts. We must move the camp immediately."

"What about the raid?' Fez asked.

"I do not know," Malik said and walked away.

Malik walked to a mountaintop overlooking the valley. The sun was just coming up and it was growing hot. He thought of Tariq and couldn't help but feel a tinge of pride. It was a courageous and, yes, stupid act. But he admired that the boy was willing to risk his own life out of loyalty to his friend.

Still, if he were caught, he would ruin their entire plan for a raid. It was a once-in-a-lifetime opportunity, and it rested on the shoulders of a young boy.

Tariq had taken a horse and made his way down and out of the mountain camp just before midnight, after everyone had fallen asleep. He had ridden hard to ensure he was not followed. He rode for several hours until the Caid's kasbah appeared in the distance. Tying his horse to a prickly pear behind a string of rocks, Tariq was sure to provide plenty of water and shade for the animal. If all went well, he wouldn't have to endure the heat of the desert sun.

Tariq had only a fifty-yard run to reach an underground entrance just outside the southern wall of the kasbah. He knew exactly where the guards were posted, thanks to Zahir. Under the cover of darkness, he was completely invisible.

Walking in the sand, he circled for twenty minutes, trying to find something that signaled an entrance to the tunnel. A door? A rope? He grew more and more frustrated. His plan depended upon finding this tunnel and moving in and out of the kasbah completely unnoticed.

As he grew more frustrated, a nagging thought entered his head.

What if this was all a trap? What if listening to Zahir lead him right into the hands of the Caid?

He would be caught, tortured, and then sentenced to die.

The escape would have been for nothing.

As these negative thoughts entered his head, his hands found something as they scurried through the sand.

An iron handle.

This was it! This was the entrance!

Tariq's pulse quickened and he could feel himself beginning to sweat.

His fears, the same fears that prevented him from saving Aseem, now devoured his thoughts once again.

What if he was caught?

What if he couldn't do it?

He was just a stupid orphan, never destined for anything.

Shaking his head, he pulled with all his strength, opening a wooden hatch below the sand. He saw torch with a cinder at his left. Lighting the torch, he descended down some steps to a rather large dirt tunnel. The ground was wet and muddy, and shadows danced around corners from the light of the torch. The ceiling was at least two feet above his head. There was plenty of room on the sides. It was a tunnel made for a group of people rather than an individual.

Slowly, Tariq made his way through the tunnel. He heard nothing except the splash of his own footsteps in the muddy water. He felt so alone at that moment. He missed the camp and his friends and the instruction of Malik. He missed Zijuan.

He kept moving forward.

In the shadows, he heard nothing but his own breathing and the steps below his feet. At any moment, he kept expecting a guard to capture him. The tunnel was mostly a straight line, but the torch only illuminated a few feet in front of him, so it was like walking into darkness every couple of seconds.

After ten minutes, the tunnel ended and a wooden ladder leaned straight up against a wall. Tariq extinguished the torch and tied it to the ladder.

Slowly, ever so slowly, he climbed up the ladder.

At the top, another latch was attached to a wooden hatch-type door. He used his shoulder and the weight from his legs to push up on the latch. It opened gently. One centimeter at a time, he eased it up until it was open just a tiny amount. He climbed out on his belly and closed the hatch behind him.

Just as Zahir had said, the ladder led to a storage area. All around him were crates of fabric, chairs, curtains, and anything else the Caid might need.

Tariq took out a map he had made from Zahir's explanation of the kasbah.

There was a window to his east, and the prisoner's quarters were only two buildings away.

It would be daylight in another hour. It didn't give Tariq much time.

Tariq opened the window enough to slide his body out. It was a three-foot drop to the other side. He let his body scrape the side of the building until his feet hit solid ground.

Closing the window behind him, Tariq made his way along the building's side, among the shadows. Immediately, he recognized the prisoner's building where he had been held captive.

Looking in all directions, he didn't see any security patrols, so he quickly ran across a pathway into the shadows of an adjacent building.

Moving along the side of the building, he was directly across the path from the prisoner's building. There were no guards outside, but that wasn't extraordinary. Generally, there was only one guard on the inside watching the locked prisoners—and that monkey.

Quickly, he ran across the pathway and began scaling along the wall of the prisoner's building. He made his way to the east entrance where he knew there was a window; more importantly, he knew the window was completely open, without so much as bars or even glass to get in his way.

The window just fit his slender body. He squeezed his way through it, dropped down to a corridor, and from that point could see the entire jail.

To his right, the monkey slept on its perch. Just below the monkey, the guard slept on his chair.

Tariq stood up and scanned the jail. There were about thirty prisoners, mostly children. Tariq recognized most of them, but he could not make out Aseem. He remembered there was an isolation cell just outside the front door. It was possible Aseem would be kept there.

Placing his hand in his pocket, he took out a tiny parcel of desert herbs. One of the mothers in the tribe told him she used the herbs in her tent when her children could not sleep. It was very soothing and, when lit like incense, immediately placed them in a deep slumber.

Tariq only hoped it would also work on monkeys.

He lit the herbs with a pocket flint, waited until a small amount of smoke began wafting up to the ceiling, and then slowly slid the lit herbs under the perch of the monkey. While waiting for a few moments, he himself began to feel drowsy; quickly he shook it off. Tariq took out a scarf and wrapped it around his face to conceal his identity and prevent the sleeping herbs from entering his nostrils.

He would have to take his chances, as he was running out of time.

Descending on his belly, Tariq saw exactly what he was looking for.

The cell keys were on a hook just to his right.

Slowly, ever so slowly, he crouched on his knees, ready to pounce and grab the keys. He wasn't worried about the guard so much as the monkey waking up. He decided to count to three before he would grab the keys.

One.

Two.

Three.

He quickly moved up the wall with his left hand, grabbed the keys so they wouldn't clang against one another, and just as quickly moved back to his hiding spot.

The guard and monkey didn't make a sound.

Tariq felt his pulse throbbing in his throat. He closed his eyes and forced his breathing to slow down. He was going to hyperventilate if he didn't relax.

He had a decision to make.

He wasn't sure if Aseem was being held with the other prisoners. If he was not, the entire plan was for nothing.

He had a feeling.

He had a feeling that Aseem wasn't in with the other prisoners. If the Caid discovered he had been friends with the escapees, Tariq and Fez, he may have deduced that Aseem was a co-conspirator.

The Caid would have had Aseem tortured.

Or worse. He might have executed Aseem on the spot.

Tariq didn't even know if his friend was alive.

He decided to take one last chance.

He kneeled down and then placed his belly on the floor of the cell. It was cold and hard, but he slithered past the guard and monkey, past the prisoners, and down the hallway to the solitary cell. As he stood up, his eyes took some time to adjust as it was darker here than it had been in the jail.

That's when he saw Aseem dangling by his wrists—asleep, or unconscious.

Tariq could scarcely believe his luck—he had found him.

Gently, he opened the door and quickly made his way to his friend.

"Aseem!" Tariq whispered.

No movement.

"Aseem!" he whispered even louder.

Still no movement.

Tariq unlocked his wrists and Aseem fell to the ground in a lump.

"Ugghhhh," he mumbled.

"Shssshhh," Tariq whispered.

"Ugghhhh," he mumbled louder.

"Aseem, it's Tariq, I've come to rescue you, but you must be quiet."

Aseem slowly opened his eyes, his left eye so swollen it would barely open.

"God, do not wake me if I am dreaming," Aseem muttered.

"This is no dream, but I need for you to walk. You're too heavy to carry."

Aseem, in a haze, made his way to his feet, putting all his weight on Tariq's shoulders. Slowly, the two exited the cell, made their way up the main stairs, unlocked the gate, and emerged outside.

It was still dark outside, but they would only have about thirty to forty more minutes of darkness in which to pass undetected. Tariq led Aseem to the west wall of the prison building, where there was another window to the main cell that held the prisoners. This one, however, was covered in bars.

Tariq put Aseem down and quickly went to the window. Looking down, he saw a boy sleeping directly beneath the window.

He took the cell keys in his hand and dropped them directly on the boy's head.

The boy awoke from his deep sleep, took a moment to see what had woken him, rubbed his head where it was sore, and finally found the keys.

In his sleep-deprived state, he couldn't make out the meaning of two keys in his hands.

Then he heard the voice from above. It was a boy's voice, and just a whisper.

"Those are the keys to the cell door. Free yourself and the others. You must move quickly. You only have about thirty minutes before it is light out. Head directly west to the stables. The gate next to the tower is unguarded right now. You all know how to ride. Make sure you bring water for yourselves."

Then the voice was gone.

The boy rubbed his head, looked at the keys, and took a moment to realize what had just transpired.

This was a chance to escape!

He silently went to his friends, woke them, whispered in their ears, and had them follow him. After five minutes, all the boys were awake and crowded around the cell door.

The boy with the keys gently opened the cell door from the inside, and the rest of the boys tiptoed out the cell, up the stairs, and outside. There, they crept in single file and as instructed, ran to the stables to the west. Silently, they went to their camels, filled a canteen with water, and rode single file to the west tower. As Tariq had explained, there were no guards.

The lead boy quickly got off his camel, unhinged the bolt closing the gate, opened the gate, and quickly got back on his ride. The boys walked their camels silently through the gate. Once outside, they immediately brought them up to a full gallop to make as much space between themselves and the kasbah.

Tariq and Aseem, however, headed east, back to the tunnel.

Aseem, barely conscious, hardly knew what was happening. His feet moved more out of determination than anything else. Tariq guided them through the shadows, checking for sentries, until they were back to the building with the entrance to the tunnel.

Urging Aseem on, Tariq lifted him on top of his shoulders and then dropped him through the window onto the floor on the other side. Hoisting himself up, he also made his way through the window and then locked it from within. Winded, he managed to get Aseem to his feet once again and they made their way to the tunnel entrance. He didn't know how Aseem could possibly make it down the steps. He was in and out of consciousness. Tariq decided to tie a rope around both his and Aseem's waists. Tariq could just barely support his friend's weight as they gently made it, step by step, to the tunnel floor.

Closing the hatch behind him, Tariq lit the torch and began leading Aseem down the muddy tunnel floor. Almost immediately, a sense of relief and exultation came over Tariq. He had made it this far! A plan with so much risk had come off beautifully.

Now, he just had to make it back to the camp without being followed or captured.

The prison guard barely opened his eyes after a long and deep sleep. Smacking his lips, his vision slowly came into focus.

Immediately, he stood up, gasping for breaths.

All the prisoners were gone.

All of them.

The door was open and not a trace was to be seen.

Scrambling for his emergency whistle, he began blowing and blowing and ran out of the jail. Ocho the monkey screamed in disbelief as well.

Running through the kasbah, the prison guard blew his whistle over and over until finally a captain in the Caid's army by the name of Hassan came out of his tent, sleep still in his eyes.

"What is it? What is it?" he asked.

"The prisoners. They are all gone. Every one of them," the guard managed to stammer out.

"What?"

"They escaped last night. I don't know how. I woke up and they were gone."

"Where are your keys?" Captain Hassan asked.

The guard fumbled around his person, his hands finding nothing.

"I don't have them."

"Bloody fool, they've stolen your keys. I'll put up a search party and begin scouring the area!"

Captain Hassan threw on some clothes, went to the barracks, and arranged a posse of forty soldiers. They were preparing their rides when another guard approached him.

"Sir, the slaves took their camels and headed west. We managed to track them out the gate."

"Damn, they may have hours of a head start on us."

Looking at his troops, he controlled his horse and brought his whip out.

"They are probably headed for the coast. We will ride at a full gallop. Hopefully, we can catch them by mid-day."

The group of soldiers galloped through the kasbah streets, out the west gate, and began following the tracks of the escaped prisoners. It was quite easy to find the camels' hoof prints. In the sand, there was almost no way for the prisoners to hide their tracks. It was all rolling sand dunes for a hundred miles. After that, however, the prisoners would run into some hills, then mountains, and eventually the ocean. If they rode hard, they could make it to the coast by midnight. The advantage of the cavalry was they were on horses and could ride faster than riders on camels. If the prisoners only had a one- or two-hour head start, by noon they should be in the hands of the Caid's troops.

Tariq and Aseem made it to the end of the tunnel. Aseem, still groggy, kept mumbling incoherently. Tariq ignored him and focused only on the escape. They weren't in the clear yet, not by any means. The kasbah would be abuzz with excitement once they learned of the prisoners' escape. The Caid might send out a search party in all directions just as a precaution.

Climbing up the steps, Tariq opened the hatch to the outside, half expecting to find the Caid's soldiers surrounding the two of them. Instead, he felt a cool breeze on his cheeks and heard the distant chirping of a cricket.

The horse was well hidden, standing in the shade. Tariq closed the hatch behind him and dragged Aseem to the horse. He untied the rope from his waist and managed to hoist him belly first up and over the haunch, then tied his wrists and feet to the saddle. It was a sloppy job, but Tariq hoped it would keep Aseem from falling during the ride ahead.

Finally, he carefully covered their footprints by taking a rag and wiping the sand. After three minutes, any trace of them had been erased. Tariq untied the horse, and, in a second was at a gallop, heading back to the resistance camp.

The Caid was not accustomed to being awakened at such an early hour. Generally, he liked to sleep in until noon, have his lunch and tea, and then conduct business.

It was not even seven o'clock in the morning.

"What is it?" the Caid asked.

"There has been an escape, Sire," the Caid's aide stammered out.

"What?"

"The prisoners have all escaped. Apparently they stole the guard's key and escaped by camel. Captain Hassan has led a party of forty cavalry soldiers to find them. He left five minutes ago."

The Caid sat up and rubbed the sleep from his eyes. He was accustomed to emergencies and making quick decisions.

"Bring me the head of the prison guard responsible for this."

"Should we increase our security around the kasbah?" the aide asked.

"What for? They've already escaped! Besides, we are now short forty cavalry soldiers. Once the prisoners are found, we will make an example of them."

"Yes, Sire!"

The Caid fell fast asleep. He was unconcerned with the escape of some petty criminals and child slaves. He had much bigger concerns.

Captain Hassan led the forty cavalry soldiers in pursuit of the escaped prisoners. The tracks were easy enough to follow; thirty or so camels in the desert left quite a trail.

They were flying along at a full gallop when he noticed it off to his right.

Clouds forming. In the desert, that could only mean one thing—a sandstorm.

His group wasn't prepared to withstand a major storm. They didn't have water provisions or tents, or anything to assist in withstanding the onslaught from that amount of sand. They would just have to ride faster in hopes of outrunning the storm.

Digging his heels in, Captain Hassan urged his horse to run even faster over the rolling dunes.

An hour ahead of the captain and his posse, the prisoners themselves rode hard. They were scared and tired and had absolutely no idea where they were going—only that it should most certainly be better than where they had been.

"How much farther do we ride?" one asked.

"Until nightfall. The Caid's troops will be after us on horses. We must make as much time as possible."

With that, nobody said anything else. They focused on staying on their camels and tried not to think about the fear paralyzing their little bodies. If they were caught, surely the Caid would kill, or at the very least, torture them.

Tariq rode hard for three hours. Having Aseem on the back made the ride considerably slower, and he continually checked in the rear to ensure he wasn't being followed. He had been navigating through a series of small hills and sand dunes. Now he was at the foot of the mountain. His horse began climbing, almost from memory. The trail was extremely difficult and there were no tracks to follow. In fact, Tariq had to double back many times because he forgot his way. After climbing for half an hour, he stopped briefly to rest. After drinking some water, he put some on Aseem's lips as well, which seemed to rouse him a bit.

"Where are we?" Aseem mumbled.

"We have escaped!" Tariq replied.

"You can let me down now."

"No, you're too injured."

"I'm feeling much better. Besides, the rope is cutting into my wrists."

Tariq dismounted, took out a dagger, and cut the rope holding Aseem onto the horse. Gently, Tariq helped Aseem slide off so he could stand on his own two feet.

"How do you feel?" Tariq asked.

"Groggy and tired, but much better. I cannot believe you came back for me," Aseem said and hugged Tariq tightly.

"It was my fault you were in prison. I couldn't allow you to die."

"Where are we?"

"Heading to a resistance camp—the people who rescued us the first time."

They were on an edge that overlooked the entire desert. In the faint distance, perhaps twenty miles away, the outskirts of the Caid's kasbah could barely be seen. Aseem and Tariq stared at it.

"I hate that place," Aseem whispered.

"I do as well."

"I want to destroy the Caid," Aseem said, looking wistfully at the desert. Still not quite believing he escaped the clutches of certain death.

"We will my friend, we will."

It was late, and getting hotter. They both took another gulp of water. Tariq looked into the sky to see the position of the sun. That's when he saw the falcon. They were being tracked, most certainly by Malik and the resistance.

That was good. They were expected.

Captain Hassan and his group felt the heavy winds first. Each rider pulled a scarf over his face to shield his eyes from the sand being blown about. The wind, unfortunately, was coming straight into them, causing the horses to slow down. The group formed a tighter circle so the inside riders would be sheltered by the outside riders. Each rider took turns on the outside to absorb the punishment.

At once, Captain Hassan saw the prisoners. They were far off, very far off. Perhaps two or three miles, it was difficult to calculate the distance through the dunes. But it was certainly the escaped prisoners, a small group of riders like specks in the distance.

The captain's group huddled tighter and braced themselves against the wind. The storm would be on them in ten or fifteen minutes. If only they could ride faster, they could outrun it and be on the prisoners in no time at all.

The boys were panicked. They had seen Captain Hassan and his group following their exact trail. Some were shrieking at their camels to go faster. Others simply wore shock and panic on their little faces. It seemed certain they would be captured. The older boys attempted to placate and calm the younger ones. Some of the boys were beginning to cry. They were confused and worried and absolutely scared. They didn't want to be slaves any longer. Most of them had escaped only because they had just followed along. No one had a plan, or anything or anyone to escape to.

In their panicked state, none of them noticed the impending sandstorm.

The scout had been tracking Tariq and Aseem for over an hour since they'd reached the desert, and had watched their movements even as they left the kasbah. Malik had given orders to simply observe and not engage. He had followed them up the mountain trail, watching safely from a distance. The scout's most important task was to ensure that the boys were not followed by the Caid's men, in which case he was to intercept the two boys and lead them away from the camp. However, nobody from the Caid's army followed the pair. In fact, the scout had observed the prison break and thereafter, watched the posse following the large group of slaves in the exact opposite direction from the mountains. But, nobody followed Tariq and Aseem.

Tariq was lost. He had taken a series of turns through a cavern and was completely turned around. Now he was in a tight valley with walls of red clay, thirty feet high on both sides, with no way to scale them. They needed to keep moving forward, but Tariq knew this wasn't right. These mountains were huge and disorienting. He was worried they wouldn't find the camp and would need to stay the night outside.

"You're going the wrong way," the voice said behind them, echoing in the cavern.

Tariq and Aseem froze in their tracks. Behind them, the scout stood in his desert camouflage. His face was covered by rags and his desert attire stood out against the red clay.

"Follow me, I'll lead you to the camp," he said.

"Who are you?" Tariq asked.

"My name is Ragga. Malik asked me to watch and wait for you. I was expecting only one. It looks like your rescue attempt was a successful one."

Tariq smiled a bit at this.

"Don't be happy with yourself. Malik is extremely upset with you right now. You have jeopardized the entire camp," Ragga said sternly before turning around.

"You didn't tell them you were going to rescue me?" Aseem asked.

"They never would have gone for it."

The two followed Ragga, and Aseem was even more impressed with his friend than he had been before. He was banged up, injured, and his head felt like it was swimming in cobwebs. But the adrenaline of being rescued kept him awake. The realization that he wasn't going to die motivated him and woke his senses.

The storm was upon Captain Hassan and his riders. They kept riding, trudging through the circling sands. However, visibility was extremely poor—they were only able to see about four or five feet in front of them. If they could just push through! If they could make it to the edge of the storm, they would be safe. Captain Hassan knew they were near the edge. He could see it as the storm bore down on them. Only a couple of hundred yards and they would be through. He urged his horse and his riders to push through. They could make it. He knew they could make it.

The group of boys looked back at the storm. It was only five hundred yards behind them. A giant wall of sand covered the desert. But it hadn't reached them. They were outside the storm's edge.

None of them fully understood what was happening. They had seen Captain Hassan and his men closing in on them, and they had given in to being captured. Now? The men were gone. Blocked from view by sand.

None of them stopped. At any moment, they expected to see Captain Hassan and his men ride out of the storm to capture them. But they saw nothing and kept riding.

Ragga led Tariq and Aseem through a series of turns and dips and valleys. Tariq, if left on his own, would never have found the camp. Getting out had been easy; just head down the mountain and eventually hit sand. As much as he'd tried to memorize the way, it was impossible to find his way back.

Finally, they made it back and Ragga led the two boys into the encampment. People stood up from their fires and came out of their tents. They didn't know what seeing the two boys and the scout meant. Had they been followed? Who was this new boy? What had happened?

Ragga led the two boys directly to Malik's tent, where all three dismounted.

Tariq hung his head and his eyes stared at the ground. He didn't want to confront Malik. He knew what he had done was reckless and could have endangered the entire camp.

Malik came from within the camp and stared at the two boys.

"What happened?" he asked.

"They were riding fast from the Caid's kasbah about seven hours ago. I followed them until they were lost at Lost Dog Ridge. I led them here."

"Were they followed?"

"No."

Malik heaved a huge sigh of relief. He could see the worry on Tariq's face. He should scold him and tell him how reckless and stupid he had been. He could see Tariq already realized that he had put the camp in a predicament.

"So, you must be Aseem?" Malik asked.

"Yes, sir," Aseem quietly replied.

"You don't look too good. We'll get some food into you and get you bandaged up."

"Thank you, sir."

"Tariq, what you did was foolish and stupid. You jeopardized the safety of the entire camp."

"I know. I'm sorry. I didn't think about that. I just wanted to save my friend."

Malik thought about that answer before replying.

"What you did was also extremely brave and courageous. I could use more friends like you in my life. Now, the two of you go get washed up and find something to eat. Your friends were worried to death about you."

Tariq and Aseem scampered off in search of Margaret and Fez, a little skip to their step. Tariq had expected a much harsher punishment from Malik. He suddenly felt completely exhausted, and the adrenaline from his body had now materialized into a deep numbness. He wanted nothing more than to lie down and sleep for an entire day.

Ragga went to Malik after the two boys had gone.

"There's something else."

"What?"

"A group of prisoners escaped to the west, followed by a posse of the Caid's men. Apparently, the boy covered his tracks by having the army follow the escaped prisoners. I watched the Caid's men ride west just after daybreak."

Malik considered this for a moment. That was extremely smart of Tariq. Extremely smart!

"Another thing. The posse was riding right into a sandstorm. I could see it forming on the horizon."

Malik stepped away and thought about this news for a second.

"How many riders followed the prisoners?"

"Difficult to tell, thirty or forty perhaps."

"The Caid will be short of troops. He has already dispatched a division to the south."

"Yes," Ragga replied, as if reading Malik's mind.

"But we can't be sure if the Caid knew how the boys entered and exited the compound undetected, or if he knew about the tunnel," Malik said.

"I wouldn't think so. I watched the tunnel entrance after the boys escaped. Nobody emerged."

"With the Caid short-handed and the sandstorm approaching, this would be a perfect time for a raid," Malik thought aloud.

"It would appear so."

"Tell everyone to prepare themselves. I want to see what happens with this storm. If it engulfs the kasbah by nightfall, we may perform the raid tonight, sooner than planned."

The scout nodded, and went off to begin talking to the camp inhabitants. Their movements quickened, and soon, the entire camp was bustling with preparations for the raid. There was a palpable excitement in the air.

Captain Hassan and his men were completely engulfed by the sandstorm. They had been forced to stop riding and lay huddled in a circle. At first, the sand was merely an annoyance, as despite their efforts, it managed to get into their eyes and mouths. The riders coughed and spat out sand, and it took every effort to keep the horses down on the ground.

Then, gradually the ground began to rise—at first just to their elbows, and then to the tops of their bodies. The riders stood on their knees, even allowing their horses to stand. The horses, panicked, began running and bucking in the storm to no avail. Chaos ensued and the riders lost all sense of direction and discipline in the presence of so much sand. Men scratched their eyeballs until they bled. Scarves blew everywhere. The sand reached their knees and then their waists.

The men, in spite of every effort, couldn't move. The fast-moving sand engulfed their bodies until it covered their armpits.

Then it covered their shoulders. The men screamed and held their hands over their heads. Their screams were drowned out by the swirling sands and wind. Finally, mercifully, the sand inched up and buried their faces and heads, muffling their screams.

A few minutes later, the screaming stopped altogether.

The prisoners kept riding. They continually looked back at the storm and realized it wasn't gaining on them. In fact, they kept distancing themselves from it until it was farther and farther in the distance. They never saw Captain Hassan and his men emerge from the storm.

Relief came over the boys.

"God is looking out for us," one of them said.

The others agreed.

The group continued to ride, trying to put as much distance as possible between themselves and the kasbah. The boys were relieved to be freed from slavery, but being lost in the desert with no home and no family didn't feel like much of a relief. Their state of mind was more of shock than anything else. Still, not having the Caid's troops on their backs was reason enough for a brief celebration.

"Aseem, it's so good to see you!" Margaret said and hugged her friend.

"I can't believe you're here! There's so much to tell you," Fez said.

Aseem sat on a pillow and took a big gulp of water.

"It was because of Tariq—what he did was very brave."

"How did you do it Tariq? The entire camp will be talking about your bravery!" Margaret gushed.

Tariq, not wanting any attention, shrugged his shoulders. He wasn't expecting this sort of reception. For weeks he had felt nothing but shame, now he was just glad to have his friend back with him. In fact, he was embarrassed by the adulation.

"Yes, you're a hero, Tariq!" Fez exclaimed.

"No, Aseem is the hero. He was tortured and scheduled to die. Please, I don't deserve any of this praise. I'm just glad that Aseem is back with us."

Aseem smiled at that and soon fell asleep. The buzz and rush of the escape was finally subsiding, and his body desperately needed rest. Margaret covered him with a blanket and began washing the wounds on his wrists with soap and water, then covered them with bandages.

"There's talk we will launch an attack tonight," Fez told Tariq.

"Really?"

"Malik feels now is the best time. There's a sandstorm approaching the kasbah. The Caid would be caught by surprise."

Tariq thought about this for a moment.

"It's a good plan. The Caid wouldn't be expecting an attack so soon. He might be disorganized."

"How did you get into the kasbah?" Margaret asked.

"I watched and listened as fat Zahir provided detailed plans, and I made a map of the kasbah tunnels on my palm. The hard part was getting in and out of the prison without being detected."

"That must have been scary."

"It was. I still can't believe we escaped. I was more worried about that stupid monkey than anything else. I think…I think that I had help."

"What do you mean?" Margaret asked.

"I don't know. A guardian angel or something, guiding me and looking out for me."

"You believe in guardian angels?" Margaret asked.

"I don't know. I just felt an incredible sense of calm, almost like someone's voice was guiding me."

"I believe in guardian angels," Fez answered.

"You do?" Margaret asked.

"I believe my father is watching out for me. Sometimes, I can feel him with me. Like a calmness in me when I should be scared. I think that's him standing with me."

"I don't know if my father is alive or dead," said Margaret.

"I'm sure he is alive and is looking for you. Don't lose faith, Margaret. If our adventures have taught us anything, it's that the impossible isn't nearly as impossible as we thought."

"I hope so. I dearly miss him and the rest of my family."

"You will be with them soon," Fez answered, and Margaret managed a small smile in return.

Just then, the group heard a clapping sound, which was used to bring everybody around the main fire pit. Every inhabitant of the camp was soon huddled around the fire, perhaps one hundred and fifty people strong.

Malik stood in the middle, waiting for everyone to gather. After a few moments, he began to speak.

"The time has come for us to launch an attack on the Caid. We have detailed plans of the kasbah, including secret passages to get in and out without being detected. A group of fifty of us will lead a raid at dusk. We think the Caid will be caught unaware. This is an opportunity to strike a blow against our hated enemy!"

The group was completely immersed in the speech, watching Malik's every move. Every man, woman, and child had been waiting for this opportunity.

"I want to also thank our Tariq for his incredible bravery in rescuing his friend. It was foolhardy, but showed great courage and resourcefulness. He and his friends are a welcome addition to our people."

Tariq blushed a deep red. He had never, ever been singled out for any kind of accolade. Most adults in his life had ridiculed him or put him down. He was accustomed to being thought a kind of sneak. Now he was being hailed as a hero.

Fighters, many of them hard men with eyes of steel, smiled and congratulated Tariq. The women blessed him.

He blushed even more.

"I have already spoken with the warriors that will accompany me on the raid. The rest of you, simply prepare the camp for evacuation. We will be changing locations and meeting at a new rendezvous. If any of us is captured, it will be too dangerous to stay in our current encampment."

The group began to disburse and Tariq went to Malik.

"Malik, am I going on the raid?" Tariq asked.

"I'm sorry, Tariq. Although what you did was extremely brave, it was also extremely lucky. You need much, much more training and to grow a bit older. Do not worry; you have an important role in assisting with moving the camp."

"But..." Tariq started. He felt he had earned the right to participate in the raid.

"Tariq. You were lucky once. If you were to be killed or captured in this attack, I couldn't live with myself. You have proved your valor and your bravery. Be patient—there will be many, many more chances to defeat the Caid. If we are successful in today's raid, it will be like stepping on the toe of a lion. It will hurt the lion, and he will squeal in pain, but it will not kill him."

Tariq shrugged his shoulders. He knew Malik was right. He had been lucky, and it would not be smart to push his luck any further.

"Okay. I will do my best to move the camp."

"Thank you, Tariq."

Tariq then lurched forward and hugged him, tears coming from his eyes. Malik, caught by surprise, hugged him back.

"Be careful, Malik," Tariq said.

Tariq, who had been holding in his emotions for such a long time, suddenly felt a deep closeness to Malik—the closeness he wished he had felt with his own father. He had been searching for a father his entire life, and he now felt as if he had finally found one. The last thing he wanted was to lose him.

Malik realized Tariq was still just a boy.

"I will be very careful, Tariq. Do not worry. I will see you in a day's time."

Tariq released the embrace, looking at Malik with a dirty face streaked with tears.

"Now, go wash yourself and get something to eat."

"Okay."

Tariq went off in search of his friends and to prepare for evacuation.

It was going to be another eventful twenty-four hours.

CHAPTER
— *14* —

THE SAGA OF CHARLES OWEN

The *Dove* was outmanned and outgunned. Charles Owen had done his best to escape the clutches of the crew on the *Angelina Rouge*. His plan had worked; his family had escaped and was now swimming to safety.

A shot from the *Rouge* went across the bow of *The Dove*. This was standard pirate practice. One warning shot, and then they blow you to pieces.

Charles heaved-to directly into the wind and let down his mainsail. His boat was now bobbing in the ocean.

The *Rouge* sailed up beside her and stopped about fifty feet upwind. Fifteen or twenty crewmembers pointed their rifles at Charles. He simply held his hands above his head and avoided eye contact.

A small rowboat with five passengers left the *Rouge*, made its way across the bumpy waves, and finally made it to the port side of *The Dove*. A line was attached to the forward and aft cleats, and soon the entire boarding party was staring Charles Owen in the face.

A man in perhaps his mid or late forties looked back at Charles. The man was tall, about six foot two. His face was thin, his hair dark and his skin even darker. A black goatee, peppered with gray, made him look Spanish. His clothes were not of the finest tailors, but not peasant garb, either. His white cotton shirt was unbuttoned, and a silver cross hung from a leather strap around his neck. The man's face was weathered and tan, but in a good way. Crow's feet flanked the most inquisitive, excited green eyes Charles had ever seen.

"Where is your family?" the man asked.

"They escaped," Charles replied.

"You're sure they're not hiding?"

"Search if you like."

"You think we would have done something with the women? Sold them, perhaps?"

"Yes."

"Hmmm," the man snorted.

He began walking around the ship, interested in the details, taking note of the lines.

"She's a fast one. Took us a while to catch you. You're a good sailor, my friend. You know your way around the sea."

To this, Charles said nothing. The man had a perfect English accent, which Charles found surprising. The dialect was difficult to identify. Perhaps it was Moroccan? But, it held a distinct French flavor as well.

"It's true, we are, as you say 'pirates,' and yes, we will take your ship and sell her for a nice profit. But, we are not slave traders. We are not rapists or murderers."

"That's not what I hear," Charles answered to that.

"What do you hear?"

"You must be Captain Basil, yes?" Charles asked.

"That is correct."

"I hear you're a pillager of villages, rapist of innocent women, trader of civilians, and brutal murderer."

Captain Basil smiled at this.

"You sound like a very smart man. You sound like a man that attended fine schools and universities growing up. I suppose you come from a rich family?" asked Captain Basil.

"My education was adequate. My family was far from rich."

"Compared to the Queen of England? Perhaps. Compared to a peasant in Morocco, you're a king!"

Charles said nothing to this.

"As far as my being a slave trader, a rapist, a pillager? All lies, spread by your government. I will admit to taking ships and goods that do not belong to me and selling them. However, the money from those proceeds goes directly to helping our people."

"The British government does not lie," Charles said, slightly angered that a peasant would lecture him about his own country, which in his mind was the greatest country on earth.

"The British government does not lie? For an educated and experienced man, you have the innocence of a child."

"What are you going to do with me?"

"First, unfortunately for you, we are going to take your ship. Second, I am going to show you a different side to your British government. Then, we will see."

The crew ordered Charles into the rowboat, and finally onto the deck of the *Rouge*. Three crewmembers stayed back and commandeered *The Dove* as it followed the *Rouge*.

Charles was taken below deck and locked in a room. It was actually quite comfortable, with a good-sized bed and cotton sheets. After an hour or so, he was brought a dinner of rice and fried mullet fish with a little rum to wash it down. Soon after, with nothing else to do, he fell into a deep sleep.

"We're home, wake up!" a voice yelled at Charles.

He awoke with a start. He had no idea how long he had been asleep, but if felt like a long time. With hands tied, he was led to the top deck and outside. The ship was now docked, and the crew had begun unloading boxes and trunks of captured booty. Charles stood on deck and looked at the scene in front of him.

They were in a protected cove. From the open ocean, the ship was hidden by a stretch of hillside. On the beach in front of him was a sizable village. Wooden huts lay on top of one another, just off the sand and into the jungle. At the beginning of the dock, a long line of villagers stood waiting patiently.

"These are my people. Everything we steal goes to them. Some of it they keep for themselves, and the rest they sell at markets or to traveling caravans. This is their primary source of income. We used to be a thriving fishing village until your government imposed fishing restrictions on us. We can't even fish our own waters now! Apparently, we were too good at it and your British ships weren't catching enough fish, so the government sought to even the score."

"Where are we?" Charles asked.

"Do not worry about that. Come, I will show you what your government has done to our people," Captain Basil said with disdain.

With that, Captain Basil untied Charles's hands, led Charles off the boat, down the dock, and through the long line of villagers patiently waiting for their share of stolen goods. They went past some huts, then paused and went into one.

The hut stank of rotten flesh and filth. Charles almost threw up from the stench. On tables were men with an assortment of injuries. Some were missing hands. Others had severe saber wounds down their chests. Still others were missing ears and eyes. Some were just shy of death.

"What is this?" Charles asked.

"This, my friend, is the work of your British government. These are all fisherman who defied your country's law against fishing in our waters. Some were beaten to an inch of their life. Others had their hands chopped off."

Charles walked up to one of the men. An old man in his sixties was missing his right hand.

"Do you speak English?" he asked.

"Yes, a little," the man replied. He had a kind face and high cheekbones. His head was practically bald, with the exception of some gray hair just above both ears.

"What happened to you?" Charles asked. He wanted to hear an account firsthand, from someone other than Captain Basil.

"My sons and I were fishing off the coast. That is where the schools of marlin can be caught. That is how we make our living. The English captured us and killed my sons and left me for dead."

"How did you make it back here?"

"Captain Basil found me floating on a piece of driftwood. Another five minutes and the sharks would have had me."

Charles felt sorry for the old man. He liked him. He had gentleness about him, the simple nature of a man who has lived his entire life from one day to the next. Charles appreciated that.

"I am sorry for the loss of your sons and your hand. I don't know who did this to you, but I intend to find out," Charles said, shook the man's good hand, and walked out of the hut with Captain Basil.

"Is that why you untied my hands?" Charles asked.

"You might escape, but where would you go?" Captain Basil asked.

"I can't believe the British government is responsible for this."

"It gets much worse. If I were responsible for one-tenth the amount of piracy I was accused of, I would have more wealth than the King of England."

"What are you saying?"

"That British ships are acting as pirates and blaming it on me. That they are responsible for more looting and pillaging and raping than anyone else."

"I can't believe that."

"Whether you believe or not, it is the truth."

Charles looked at line of villagers in front of him. Poor people waited in turn for something they could sell to feed their family. The image of the "hospital" remained etched in his thoughts. The poor old man missing a wrist—simply for trying to fish.

Charles had always been a patriot. He loved his country and his government. In his mind, Britain was a light in a room of darkness. Yes, they were conquerors. But they also improved any conquered people. They introduced a court system, an educational system, a transportation network, and even a mercantile system of trade to any area they occupied. That was the British way. Yes, the government could be brutal, but only in the interest of progress.

What he saw sickened him. What he saw was senseless brutality and a sick abuse of power.

"I am sorry about your family," Captain Basil said.

"What?" Charles answered, startled from his deep frame of thought.

"If you and I could have had this conversation, we could have taken you and your family to a safe port. I hope they are alive and well."

"I hope so as well."

"We will take you to a port where you can make it to Tangier. Of course, you won't be allowed to see our location for our safety. But, I wanted you to see firsthand the actions of your government."

"What about my boat?" Charles asked.

"Consider it a contribution to the poor and unfortunate. There are other boats, my friend."

Charles didn't like that response one bit, but he had no choice in the matter. He had cared for *The Dove* for almost ten years. Sanded and varnished and painted its hull and decks. Personally rigged every single line. Even sewn the mainsail. His family had spent many vacations laughing on her deck and playing in the hold. She would be sorely missed.

Just then, with the sudden impact of a lightning bolt, a shed to their right was annihilated in a loud explosion and cloud of dirt. The ground shook, and Charles was thrown to the ground by the force of the impact. Four more explosions happened around them.

Captain Basil grabbed Charles by the right arm and began dragging him to his feet.

"We are being attacked!" Captain Basil screamed.

"By whom?" Charles screamed back.

"The British Navy!"

Charles looked out and saw two British steamships just inside the harbor. They had managed to sneak up the coastline and into the cove without being detected. For once, Charles wished that Britain didn't have the best navy in the world, or the most experienced naval captains.

Flashes from deck cannons dotted the ocean horizon. All around, chaos ensued. Explosions rocked the beach, creating a mist of sand and smoke. Villagers ran in all directions, panicked and scared. Just in front of Charles, a woman died as a cannon shell blew a hole through her.

Many more villagers died as the bombardment became more intense. Dead bodies littered the beach. Blood drenched the incoming tide. The smell of sulfur filled the ocean air.

Charles and Captain Basil began urging villagers to retreat to the jungle behind them, out of range from the ship's cannons. It was a natural instinct for Charles to protect innocents. These villagers were not soldiers, rather people simply wanting food and shelter. He grabbed a woman and her daughter and ran them further up the beach, pushing them towards the safety of the jungle. People continued to run all around them.

Charles looked out and saw four large dinghies full of British soldiers. The bombardment stopped as the boats reached the shore. The soldiers dispatched, charging the beach and shooting or bayoneting anyone in their path.

Captain Basil and his men fired at the soldiers from behind some of the huts. A couple of soldiers were cut down and the rest continued to storm the beach. One ran right at Charles, screaming his lungs out with murder in his eyes, his bayonet blade charging toward Charles's stomach.

Acting on instinct, Charles shifted his body and as the blade just missed his mid-section, he grabbed the rifle around the barrel and brought his leg out to trip the onrushing soldier. The soldier flipped over Charles's leg, landed on this back on the sand, and let out a loud "uummpphh." Twisting the rifle out of the soldier's hands, Charles brought the butt of the rifle down on the soldier's temple, knocking him unconscious.

A group of soldiers, seeing their comrade down, began firing at Charles from about forty feet away. Bullets whizzed by his head. Ducking for cover, he couldn't bring himself to fire back at his countrymen; instead, he crouched down and ran toward the shacks. Bullets nipped at his ankles, his running slowed by the slick sand. It seemed like forever before he reached the shacks, briefly safe from the oncoming soldiers. Five of them had followed him up the beach and were now running in his footsteps in the sand.

Hiding behind the back of a hut, Charles quickly considered his options. He could run to the jungle and hope he wasn't followed, or he could begin firing on the troops. He didn't like the second option, as they were his countrymen and he was outnumbered.

He had only seconds to decide.

He decided on one last option. He would surrender.

"I'm with you. I'm a British citizen. Don't fire," he yelled.

The soldiers, thankfully, were running slowly in the sand and in a position to make a sound judgment. They heard Charles's voice and saw him emerge from the back of the hut with his hands over his head in a position of surrender. Charles walked towards them slowly and kept shouting, "Don't shoot, I'm a British citizen!"

Soon, they were on him and had him surrounded. The soldiers, all boys younger than twenty years of age, were caught a bit off-guard.

The youngest one, a boy named Will Smythe, only seventeen years of age, was full of testosterone and rage. Without thinking, he brought the butt of his rifle directly into the back of Charles's skull, knocking him to the ground unconscious. He was about to beat Charles to death, but was stopped by his comrades.

Charles lay on the sand, bleeding profusely from the back of his head...

An hour later, Charles woke up. He was seated at a wooden table with his hands tied in front of him. On the other side of the table, a man came into focus. He appeared to be an officer, a well-dressed British officer, a Lieutenant, and he was smoking a cigarette. He had a very skinny face, slits for eyes, and a little black moustache covering his lips. The officer was looking out a window when he heard Charles moan.

"You're awake," he said, casually.

"Who are you?" Charles asked.

"Lieutenant Dreyfuss."

Charles looked around; he was in a hut, most likely on the beach.

"Are you in command of this expedition?" Charles asked.

"Yes," Dreyfuss said, extinguishing his cigarette, and for the first time, placing his full attention on Charles.

"Do you mind explaining to me why the British navy is attacking a village of innocents?"

"I'd hardly call them innocents. This is a pirate's den. Just like clearing a wasp's nest, we wiped them out," the response was cool and breezy, as if Dreyfuss was explaining how he had cleaned his chimney.

"Wiped them out?"

"Well, we can't have them returning to their pillaging and looting ways, now can we?"

"And the women and children?"

Dreyfuss didn't like this line of questioning. He was unaccustomed to having questions directed at him. He was much more comfortable being the one doing the asking.

"Who are you?" Dreyfuss asked.

"Colonel Charles Owen. I'm a British officer," Charles replied wearily.

"I doubt that," Dreyfuss replied.

"Why do you doubt that?"

"You don't have any military clothing or identification. Why would a British colonel be in the middle of Morocco with a group of pirates?"

"I was on a pleasure cruise with my family. My family escaped, while I tried to outrun the pirates. Eventually, they caught me."

"Where is your family now?"

"I don't know."

"Where is your boat?"

"I don't know that, either."

"How convenient."

"It's the truth." Charles looked Dreyfuss directly in the eye. He outranked Dreyfuss and was completely unimpressed by these interrogation tactics.

"So, you have no proof and nobody to verify your identity?" Dreyfuss asked.

"I was—am—with Cornwall's light infantry. I was stationed in Ceylon and then Cape Colony after that..."

"Who is your commander?" Dreyfuss interrupted.

"Lieutenant General Stapleton."

"I've never heard of him," Dreyfuss responded.

"You're the only one who hasn't, it seems. The man is practically a legend."

"I'm still not convinced," Dreyfuss added, thoroughly enjoying his position of power.

"Yes, you are," Charles answered back.

Dreyfuss took out another cigarette and took his time lighting it. For the first time, he felt intimidated by Charles. It was true. He did believe that Charles was a colonel in the British military. He had that air of superiority that only the British possess, especially British officers.

"Perhaps I am," Dreyfuss admitted.

"Then why don't you untie me?" Charles asked.

"Because."

"You're afraid I might report what I've seen."

"Partially, and, you might just interfere."

"Interfere with what?"

"I'm here on orders. My orders are to protect the interests of British merchants. I highly doubt the British press and public would respond favorably to our tactics."

"You mean terrorizing and murdering innocent civilians in a country we're not even at war with?"

"Very perceptive."

"All so British nobles can line their pockets. With what? Profits from fish?"

Dreyfuss continued to puff on his cigarette.

"Not exactly."

"Then what?" Charles asked.

"My dear friend, as much as I hate to see one of my countrymen cut down, I'm afraid you're going to have to be a casualty of our little battle."

"You mean massacre," Charles corrected him.

Charles had experienced war. He had seen, firsthand, the brutality of combat. But his soldiers, British soldiers, were always disciplined. They didn't loot. They didn't pillage and murder. They followed an honor code that he based his entire life upon. The military had been his life since he was thirteen and a cadet at a military boarding school.

Charles watched as all his beliefs were torn down right in front of him.

Dreyfuss avoided eye contact with him, showing a sign of weakness. He extinguished a second cigarette before speaking.

"I'm sorry, but your time has come," Dreyfuss said before standing up. He went outside to fetch a guard. No doubt, he didn't want to do the dirty work himself.

A young sentry followed Lieutenant Dreyfuss inside. A boy, only eighteen, named Steven Terry.

"Young Seaman Terry. The man in front of you is a pirate. He is a conspirator. He is responsible for the deaths of countless innocent civilians. He has been tried, judged, and sentenced to death."

"Yes, sir!" Seaman Terry answered.

"Seaman Terry, it is your sworn responsibility to carry out his sentence," Lieutenant Dreyfuss barked.

"Sir?"

"You are to execute this man and then burn this hut."

"Sir...I...?" Cadet Terry stammered out.

Charles could sense the boy's confusion at receiving such an order. He looked the boy in the eyes. He wasn't a cold-blooded murderer like Dreyfuss, just a young soldier trying to do his best. Dreyfuss was obviously covering his tracks. If this young man pulled the trigger, it would be his word against that of Dreyfuss if it ever got out that they had killed one of their own. Dreyfuss would have his hands clean.

"Son, I'm a colonel in His Majesty's Service. This man wants you to commit murder."

"Kill him, Seaman Terry!" Lieutenant Dreyfuss interrupted.

"You don't have to do this, son. You're not a murderer!" Charles yelled at the young man.

The young seaman, confused and scared, raised his rifle and pointed it at Charles, while continuing to look at Lieutenant Dreyfuss. He had been drilled to always, always follow orders. Not obeying orders for even the most trivial things, like shining his shoes a shiny black, could result in harsh discipline. The British military thrived on discipline, and that meant always following orders. His own conscience balked at such an order, but as a soldier he had been is brainwashed to bury his conscience somewhere deep within himself.

Don't Think!

Follow Orders!

Always!

"You don't have to do this, son. This isn't part of a being a soldier. This man can't order you to commit murder!" Charles screamed, tears welling up in his eyes.

"Do it now, Seaman Terry, or I'll have you whipped and court-martialed!" Lieutenant Dreyfuss barked right back at him.

Charles could see he was going to lose this battle. Seaman Terry was firmly in the grasp of Lieutenant Dreyfuss. He had one chance, and one chance only.

Terry looked to Lieutenant Dreyfuss for approval one last time. That provided Charles an opportunity to lunge forward, take both his shackled hands, and hit Terry square in the jaw. The boy fell backwards onto his rear end. Charles turned right and dove through the open window. Distantly, he heard a gunshot. He felt a sharp pain in his right shoulder when his body hit the sand—probably landed on it wrong.

Springing up, he began sprinting for the jungle. He didn't look back. He didn't know if Terry was chasing him, and he didn't care. All he cared about was surviving and making it to the jungle edge, where he might find some needed cover.

Sprinting through the sand and running between huts, he felt bullets whiz near him and heard shouting in the distance. No doubt more troops had been gathered to chase after him.

Thankfully, it wasn't a long distance to the jungle. He didn't look for a trail or opening or even a path, but just lunged through a thicket, almost losing his footing. He continued to sprint through the trees away from his pursuers. The ground below him now was dirt and mud. It was much darker now, with shade provided by the wall of trees overhead. It felt different. It *felt* darker.

Charles continued to sprint, hearing soldiers coming from behind him, perhaps only twenty feet away. He began to zigzag through the trees in an effort to slow them down. He was making good time, but he had no idea how many troops were following him.

For another minute it continued like this, with Charles running frantically, zigzagging, brush hitting him in the face, falling to his knees, getting up and continuing. He was beginning to get tired.

Then—disaster!

In his haste, and because the jungle overgrowth literally blocked his view in every direction, he had gotten lost. He realized had no idea where he was heading, except he was sure he wasn't headed back to the beach. He ended up at the foot of a large embankment. Not a huge mountain, only thirty feet high or so, but he would have to scale it in order to get away. With soldiers just seconds behind him, he would be an easy target.

Turning around, with his back to the hill and his chest to the jungle, he awaited the soldiers. He didn't have a plan. Surrender? Fight?

Three soldiers emerged from the jungle, running at a full sprint about fifteen feet in front of him. They crouched low, bayonets fixed in front of them, murder in their eyes.

There would be no surrender. These men were ordered to kill on sight.

Charles braced for the worst.

He heard gunfire. Had he been shot?

He watched as bullets ripped through the shirts of all three men, thrusting them backwards on their backs—dead!

But he was alive.

Looking around, he heard only the whistling of the wind through the jungle trees. After a few seconds, several men appeared from the jungle.

Charles immediately recognized Captain Basil.

"Do you believe me now about your British navy?" he asked.

"Of course I do. I had no idea of the level of corruption."

"We don't have much time. I'll tell you everything after we have our ship back."

"How are you going to do that? She's surrounded and outnumbered. You've got a sailboat, for the love of Pete. How do you possibly expect to outrun steamer ships?"

"The same way I have for three years. By using my head instead of relying upon technology," Captain Basil replied, smiling.

"Oh," Charles replied sarcastically.

Captain Basil had all of nine men with him—with Charles it made ten. The small group made their way single file through the jungle towards the ocean. It was getting darker and would be completely dark in about forty-five minutes.

After half an hour, the group had made a large arc and now sat safely camouflaged at the sand's edge. They nestled on a hill, overlooking both the village and the ocean. This perch provided a panoramic view of the British troops as well as the British ships.

"Okay, Aquina, you're up!" Captain Basil whispered.

Aquina, the first mate, had a leather backpack. He squirreled his way past the group, down to some rocks, and was soon at the water's edge. Captain Basil threw him the end of a tiny hose with a nozzle at the end. Aquina took the hose, placed it in his mouth, and was quickly submerged under water. The hose was hidden by the rocks and fed by another member of the crew.

"What the devil is going on?" Charles asked.

"An old pirate's trick. Aquina has a rope; he is going to tie the anchors of the two ships together."

"Are you kidding me?" Charles asked.

"No. The hose we have is crude, but effective—it acts as a snorkel, allowing him to breathe underwater. Unfortunately, it only works about half the time. Fortunately, even without the hose, Aquina can hold his breath for over three minutes. The ships are anchored adjacent one another, rafted up bow to bow, so luckily the anchors should be very close together," Captain Basil explained.

Charles watched the scene unfold in front of his eyes. He was unaccustomed to such clandestine missions. Most of his fights happened right in front of the enemy. He liked this. He liked outsmarting an opponent—even if that opponent was his own government.

Twelve minutes later, Aquina emerged from the ocean, exactly where he had entered. Soon, he was back with the group, dripping wet with saltwater.

"It was no problem. The water is shallow there, perhaps only fifteen feet."

Captain Basil smiled at this news. "Good. We wait until it's dark and then we move. Everyone knows their job, correct?" he asked.

The crew and Charles nodded in agreement.

"Even if their anchors are tied together, it might only give us a fifteen or twenty minute head start. Surely not enough time against those ships," Charles said.

"A storm is coming," Captain Basil replied.

Charles looked at the sky. He saw nothing but clear skies and the emergence of just a few specks of stars.

"I don't see anything."

"Just wait."

The group did wait, for another hour and a half. Lying completely motionless, they were still excited with anticipation. The plan was a simple one. Swim to the *Rouge* and board her under the cover of darkness. There was a southerly breeze that would allow them to hoist the sails and, hopefully, sail away without awakening the troops. If that didn't work, they hoped they could at least get far enough to be out of range of the ships' cannons.

Lying on his belly, Charles felt the chill in the air. He also felt the wind. Looking up, what had been a clear sky thirty minutes earlier was now covered in gray clouds.

"You were right about the storm," Charles whispered.

"It's going to be a gale," Captain Basil replied.

They waited another twenty minutes until the wind kicked up into a screamer and whitecaps formed on the ocean's surface. It was completely dark now, the clouds covering the light of the moon and stars.

"We go!" Captain Basil ordered.

One by one, the pirates and Charles entered the water, swimming about two feet from one another. They swam dog-paddle style so their arm movements wouldn't create a silhouette against the ocean waves.

The water was difficult to swim. The current was stronger than Charles had anticipated. He felt his body lift up and down with each new wave. A couple of times, a whitecap hit him hard in the face, forcing saltwater up his nose. A few times, he even lost sight of the man directly in front of him. The fact that everyone had on a full set of clothes along with weapons didn't help matters.

After perhaps ten minutes, the group rendezvoused at the starboard side of the *Rouge*. One after another, they climbed on deck, quickly ducked out of sight, and crawled along the floorboards to reach their positions. Every man knew his exact task. One man would unhitch the mainsail, and another would prepare to hoist it. Another man would un-hitch the jib, and another would hoist it. Charles's job, along with a man named Dwalu, would be to pull up the anchor. Captain Basil, of course, would man the wheel.

All the men watched Captain Basil intently; he would give them a hand sign and then it was a "go."

Captain Basil watched both British ships. One was to port and the other starboard. Both had soldiers on watch who walked along the deck of the ship. He was going to try to time his maneuver perfectly, when both men's backs were facing him. He spun the wheel around and al-lowed the *Rouge* to turn slowly, to about a forty-five degree angle into the wind with her bow pointed out to sea. In this way, all they had to do was hoist the sails and go without tacking.

The boat took about ten minutes to make the slow turn. Luckily, nei-ther watchman was observant enough to notice a boat turning complete-ly by itself.

Captain Basil kept an eye on the two watchmen, their figures bare-ly outlined against the dark night. He was timing their marches. One reached the bow as the other reached the stern, and both made their turns with their backs to the *Rouge* at the same time.

He brought his arm down three times. The crew immediately went into action.

Charles and Dwalu pulled the anchor up quickly, but quietly. The minute the anchor was raised from the ground, the *Rouge* began to drift ever so slightly. At that moment, the mainsail was hoisted, but only halfway. To pull it up completely would have made much too much noise. Besides, in this wind halfway provided plenty of power.

After a minute, the anchor was out of the water and on the deck of the ship. The *Rouge* sailed out to sea, protected under the dark sky and the noise of the wind.

Within thirty seconds, she had sailed past both boats.

A young sentry named Millwall was on watch that night. He was a young lad, only nineteen, and he loved being on watch. It meant he could be by himself for a few hours—a rarity on a boat—and be out with the sea and elements. Life at sea could be so dreary and monotonous. He loved to take his time, light a cigarette, pull up his collar, and squint into the wind.

Millwall walked slowly along the deck, smoking his cigarette, shielding his face from the wind. A couple of times he looked up, but mostly he was in his own head. He thought of his friends at home and how he missed his dog. He also thought of his return, when he would stroll into the local pub, order a round of drinks, and detail his many adventures at sea. That's why he'd joined the Royal Navy, to find adventure. It was the same reason most of the lads had joined.

He continued his walk, but something just didn't feel right. He looked up at the town. No, that wasn't it. He scanned the deck; everything seemed in place. He looked across at the other British ship.

Wait a minute.

Something wasn't right.

A ship was missing.

The pirate ship!

"Oh my God!" he sputtered.

Going to the side of the deck, he looked at the open sea. He could just barely make out the sails of the *Rouge*, perhaps two hundred and fifty feet away. She was on a full beam reach and moving fast.

Immediately, he went to the alarm and started ringing it. The alarm was a bell with a chain that, when rung, made an insane amount of noise. Within a moment, a petty officer by the name of Briggs emerged, putting his spectacles on.

"What is it, Millwall?" he asked, annoyed.

"The pirate ship. It's gone!"

"What?"

"It's gone!"

Briggs looked at where the *Rouge* was supposed to be.

It was gone.

He looked back at Millwall in disbelief. Millwall said nothing, but pointed vigorously to the outline of the mainsail of the *Rouge*.

A few other hands came on deck, rubbing sleep from their eyes and wondering what the fuss was about.

"Pull the anchor! Start the engines. The pirates have taken back their ship!"

Immediately, the deck of the ship looked like ants scrambling on a dirt hill. Sailors ran to and fro, each with assigned tasks of hoisting anchors, starting engines, and preparing cannons.

"What is going on?" Dreyfuss emerged from below.

"They've taken the pirate ship, headed out to sea at twelve o'clock!" Briggs answered.

Dreyfuss looked at where the *Rouge* should have been and had exactly the same reaction as Millwall and Briggs.

He couldn't believe his eyes.

Dreyfuss ran to the bridge and immediately took the helm. Pushing in the throttle, the engines whined in appreciation. He would be damned if that ship escaped. They had already allowed a certain English officer to escape to the jungle and had lost three good soldiers. He wouldn't watch their prize sail into the ocean night.

The ship turned and began to chug. The steam engines took a while to warm up.

Then suddenly, his ship lurched forward and stopped. Dreyfuss increased throttle to no avail. He put the ship in reverse, gunned the throttle again, and the ship lurched forward even more violently.

Briggs noticed the crew on the other ship waving their arms and yelling. He also noticed their boat was being pulled into the waves.

"I think our anchor is stuck!" he yelled.

He went down to two crewmen who were feverishly trying to pull up the anchor.

"She's stuck, sir!" one of them yelled.

Briggs took over, pulling on the anchor winch, but it didn't move an inch. She just wouldn't budge.

"What is happening here?" Dreyfuss had left the bridge and was standing in front of Briggs.

"The anchor's stuck, sir."

"Damn it, man—could anything else go wrong?"

"It looks like the other ship's anchor is stuck as well," one of the crewmen yelled.

Dreyfuss looked at the other ship. It wasn't moving either, and a group of sailors had converged over the anchor winch, just as their crew had been moments before.

It was obvious that sabotage was at hand.

"Cut the anchor!" Dreyfuss ordered.

"Yes, sir!"

The only problem with cutting the anchor was that it was held to the ship by a thick iron chain. Cutting it loose meant the difficult task of sawing right through the chain with a hacksaw. A sailor produced a hacksaw from a nearby storage container and immediately began sawing.

On the deck of the *Rouge*, the sails were in full flight. Charles glanced back at the harbor as the two British ships in the distance grew smaller and smaller, and were soon completely invisible through the rain and darkness.

"How soon before we jibe?" Charles asked.

"Another five minutes," Captain Basil replied.

Charles couldn't believe the escape had gone as planned. It also wasn't lost on him that the British navy now considered him a pirate and an escaped fugitive. Most men might dwell in melancholy; Charles, however, was a bit ashamed to admit he was having the time of his life. He had been an excellent military man for his entire career, and had enjoyed the many adventures and battles the military provided. But, the military life was an exercise in restraint. So many times he had questioned the methods and strategy of superior officers, only to hold his tongue and follow orders. The life itself was quite often tedious and routine. This was freedom.

"Get ready to jibe!" Captain Basil yelled.

The crew readied themselves and listened for orders. No one resented Captain Basil. The entire crew understood he was not only a capable and courageous leader, but also the best sailor, by a wide margin, of any of them. They trusted him with their lives. Charles could see his leadership qualities and his expert seamanship from the beginning. He would have made one hell of an admiral for the British navy.

"Now!" Captain Basil yelled.

The main and jib swung in as Captain Basil turned the wheel to port. The boat was turning against the wind and would now be running with the wind. They picked up additional speed, as they were now going with the current rather than fighting it.

Within moments the *Rouge* was sailing along at twelve knots.

"Now, it's time to pray," Captain Basil said to Charles.

It would be a matter of time before they knew if the ships had followed them. They were hoping to escape before the sun came up, so that it would take a wild guess for either British ship to turn exactly where the *Rouge* had turned.

The *Rouge* was a xebec, a three-masted ship designed by the Barbary corsairs for use in Mediterranean waters to outrun navies in the eighteenth century. The xebec's design was based upon speed and maneuverability. It wasn't the best boat for rough water, but in lighter winds it went unsurpassed. While this gale was certainly a good burst of wind, it was by no means a catastrophic hurricane or as rough as the seas in the northern Atlantic. In these winds, the *Rouge* was in her element. Basil had long ago mothballed all but two of the cannons for one sole purpose—to increase her speed. Without the added weight of cannons, artillery, and a full crew, the *Rouge* was as fast and agile as was possible for a ship of her design.

Unfortunately, she was trying to outrun a certain British ship named *The Walcott* piloted by Lieutenant Dreyfuss. *The Walcott* was actually a converted trawler of the larger Mersey design. Without a load, she weighed 438 tons and was specially outfitted with two Vickers machine guns mounted at the bow and stern. The Vickers gun was generally used by the British army on land, but its water-cooled design was perfect for use on the open sea. More importantly, it was the perfect gun for taking apart wooden ships at short or medium range. *The Walcott* carried a crew of thirty sailors, and although she wasn't a large boat by any means, she could outrun, and outgun, any fishing or merchant ship in the Mediterranean waters. She could easily overwhelm the *Rouge* in both speed and firepower.

Finally, after ten minutes, anchor chain was sawed in two on *The Walcott*. The sailor, flush with sweat and out of breath, gave a crewman the order to relay this information to Dreyfuss. In a moment, the ship began to chug along, slowly making her way out to sea.

The other ship was still trying to untangle her anchor and didn't have the judgment to simply cut it off, as Dreyfuss had. As a result, they only had one ship in pursuit, but that was more than enough to overpower a sailboat with a skeleton crew.

The boat picked up steam and was soon plowing through whitecaps. It was extremely dark and the wind was picking up. The waves steadily grew in size, bursting over the bow and soaking the crew. Dreyfuss had positioned four crewmembers at the bow, each with a set of binoculars. Their job was simple—scan every inch of the ocean in search of the *Angelina Rouge*.

On the bridge, Dreyfuss punched the throttle all the way forward. The boat chugged along, brazenly chopping through the open seas, frantically searching for her prey. Dreyfuss was, by nature, a highly vindictive man. He was also keenly aware of status. Twice in one day he had allowed the enemy to escape. A sense that he was somehow going to be embarrassed drove him to find the *Angelina Rouge*. He hated that he had been outsmarted; the fact that a glorified peasant had escaped his grip was unbearable to him.

Steadying the wheel was difficult in this rough water. Dreyfuss was breathing hard as his black eyes scanned the surface of the ocean. The boat fell and rose in the crests of the waves. Rain splattered down; softly at first, but then quickly changed into a violent, torrential downpour. Visibility became nonexistent.

Dreyfuss realized he would have to concede defeat. Finding a ship in these conditions was impossible unless they happened to run into it by chance.

"I'm turning her around and returning to port. I want the man responsible for the watch, and I want him now!" Dreyfuss screamed. Although he wouldn't find the *Angelina Rouge* that night, he would take his anger and frustration out on crewman Millwall by issuing ten lashes and confining him to kitchen duty below deck for a month or more.

After an hour, there was a feeling of relief on the deck of the *Angelina Rouge*. The storm had kicked up, and the rains descended on the men like a baptism. They knew it would be almost impossible for Dreyfuss to find them in this mess! The crew worked diligently and silently. Every few moments, each of them looked to the stern, half expecting to see the bow of the British warship steaming straight at them.

It never happened. They had escaped.

CHAPTER
— 15 —

RAIDERS IN THE NIGHT

The war room of Caid Ali Tamzali was magnificent. High, rounded ceilings topped the room, with stained glass windows depicting battle scenes on all sides. The walls were painted a dark orange, as the Caid wanted to provide the room with a forbidding feeling. A gigantic round wooden table, intricately inlaid with black marble, sat in the middle with perhaps twenty chairs around it. The chairs were wide and long in the back, made of varnished oak and fashioned with goose down pillows covered in burgundy silk. The room was inspired by King Arthur's court and the Knights of the Round Table. The Caid was always impressed with Western Civilization and the British in particular. He liked nothing more than to emulate his heroes. On most days, he loved to sit around the table and talk strategy with his generals.

However, on this day, the Caid was not happy. In fact, the Caid was furious.

The Caid paced back and forth in the war room. His generals and colonels sat nervously around the table.

He was missing an entire search party and one of his best captains. The prisoners had escaped, making him look the fool. To top it off, a sandstorm had descended upon the kasbah. Sending another search party was now impossible.

The Caid was a large and imposing man. His belly protruded before him. His bald head dripped with sweat under his turban. His black robe extended out over his arms and two gold necklaces draped from his neck into a bushel of black chest hair. His eyes, however, were his most memorable features. They were dark and devoid of emotion. To look into the Caid's eyes was to look into an abyss—an empty well missing any sort of feeling or humanity.

"So, they just up and walked out of our jail?" he asked again.

"It would seem so, Sire," a general replied.

"And then they stole camels, rode off into the desert, and escaped in a freak sandstorm?" the Caid asked yet again.

"Yes, Sire."

"And, this is the second escape we've had in a month?" the Caid asked.

"Yes, Sire."

The Caid paced some more, his hands behind his back, thinking.

"It's quite obvious our security forces are not only incompetent, but completely useless as well."

"If I may add something," a general asked.

The Caid said nothing; he simply glared at the general.

"Zahir was in charge of security. As you know, he has fled like a fugitive dog. With a new Security Supervisor, I expect that things will improve."

The Caid continued to glare at the general. He was not in the mood for excuses or explanations. In fact, the general had just made himself a target.

"We look like incompetent fools to our people and our enemies. Children escaping from our jails? Our security officer running off like a dog in the night? I think perhaps the problem is that I've become entirely too soft."

Nobody said anything to this. Nobody, anywhere, would ever have described the Caid as soft. In fact, he relished his reputation as a marauder and tyrant. He believed in instilling fear in his people. Without fear, there was no respect. Without respect, there was no power.

"I want these prisoners, all of them, captured and returned to the kasbah—dead or alive!" the Caid ordered.

"Yes, Sire!" the entire audience responded.

"I want a price of one hundred gold pieces on each prisoner's head. I want a price of one thousand gold pieces on that fat Zahir. Two thousand if he is brought back alive."

"Yes, Sire!"

"I want the guard details doubled."

"Yes, Sire!"

"I want a search detail scouring the mountains, destroying anything and everything in its path!" he screamed.

"Yes, Sire!"

The energy in the room was felt by each officer. Each of them felt the Caid's anger. Each of them fully understood the reach of his power and his capacity for destruction. If the Caid felt any one of his officers was weak or worse, a threat, he would order their execution without a second thought.

The winds howled outside the room, beating against the walls and ceiling, the sound of which provided a brief reprieve from the blasting of the Caid.

Outside, faint voices could be heard, barely audible through the doors and winds. Just then, a guard came rushing into the room.

"We are under attack!" he yelled.

"What?" the Caid asked.

"They are everywhere. The attackers have lit fire to two tents and have killed dozens of our soldiers!" the guard explained, exasperated.

The Caid looked at his officers. They looked at one another in disbelief. Each one thought exactly the same thing—*they were being attacked?*

The officers quickly stood up and went outside the war building, along with the Caid. The wind immediately kicked up sand into their eyes. Each man quickly covered his eyes and face with a scarf and braced against the swirling winds.

A man outfitted entirely in sand-colored camouflage stuck his sword into the chest of an infantryman. Another threw a torch onto a tent, and still another was trying to gather horses.

Each general, officer, and even the Caid drew swords and lunged into battle. Although most of these men were in their forties, fifties, and sixties, they could all handle a sword. One cut down a rebel as he was about to burn another tent. Six officers formed a circle around the Caid in the event of an attack.

The scene was confusing and chaotic, as soldiers scattered looking for rebels. There had been no time for order or organization. Soon, fires raged across several tents; with the help of the strong wind, the tents were quickly engulfed in flames. Rifle shots rang out in several areas at once.

"To the barracks!" the Caid yelled.

The group quickly ran to the military barracks. Soldiers were everywhere. One of the generals ran about, rounding up as many soldiers as he could find, and organizing a small army of forty soldiers into formation. They gathered ten cavalry soldiers, although the barn storing the horses now stood empty, burning to the ground.

Another general organized a smaller group of twelve soldiers and had them act as fire marshals, going from fire to fire and extinguishing each one.

The squadron of soldiers quickly marched throughout the kasbah grounds, looking for any rebels and attempting to restore order.

Malik held his blood-covered sword in his hand. The raid had taken place just after dawn. They had waited until there was civilian movement in the kasbah to further confuse the military. Sneaking in through one of the tunnels, a small group of rebels had first attacked the armory, stolen a cache of rifles, killed several guards, and then set fire to the remaining ammunition and weapons. Another group of rebel soldiers set fire to the food storage area, depleting the Caid's supplies, while another scattered the horses and set fire to the stable.

To the Caid's troops, it looked to be an unorganized and messy attack. But in fact, it was a well-conceived and perfectly-timed raid. Each rebel party understood its target and task. Everyone was on a time clock. Malik calculated it might take ten minutes for the Caid's military to organize a counterattack. Each unit was instructed to escape at the ten-minute mark. To further confuse the Caid's forces, each unit had a separate escape route. Some would leave through hidden tunnels and others via gates. Outside the kasbah, even more rebels were stationed to attack any troops that might try to follow.

It was as strategic as it was effective.

Malik blew a conch, a loud horn signaling for the rebels to withdraw. He and his team quickly met at the base of a hidden tunnel. Ensuring that nobody was following them, they each descended down the hole and began running through the tunnel. Reaching the end, they climbed back up the ladder, opened the trap door, and gathered their waiting horses. A small group of archers covered their flanks in the event they were followed.

They were not.

In a moment's time, the entire group rode off. They galloped at full stride, heading for the mountains. They expected to see a group of the Caid's riders following closely behind. Fortunately, none presented themselves. The raid had been a remarkable success. The Caid and his troops were so disorganized and preoccupied with putting out fires, they couldn't even mount a search party.

The rebels rode up through the mountain passes. The camp had been moved to a new location, and several traps had been set along the escape route. Not even an army of a thousand could catch or defeat them in these canyons and valleys.

Each separate group of warriors met at the rendezvous point. No one had been followed. They dismounted their horses, looked at their wounds, and dusted themselves off. Everyone was surging with adrenaline.

Malik made a pot of tea over an open fire; other warriors dressed their wounds and washed the blood from their clothes. They waited for over an hour, until at last, all the warriors were gathered.

Malik stood in the middle of a circle, surrounded by the beaming faces of his soldiers. They were tired, and some nursed serious injuries, but the look of pride in their eyes was immeasurable.

"They say a man is measured not by where he starts, but by how far he goes in life. They say not to measure a man by his lineage, or his nobility, but by his actions. I just witnessed a group of farmers and poor nomads perform a raid on an army twenty times its size. We dealt a blow to an evil and deceitful enemy that he will not soon forget. I have never been so proud of any army in my entire life!" Malik said, his eyes welling up with tears.

The soldiers, now for the first time completely aware of their victory, began to hoot and holler and hug one another. Several came up and hugged Malik, each feeling the complete honesty of these embraces.

There is perhaps nothing in the world that can compare to the feeling of warriors who have returned from battle. There is a bond and a camaraderie that cannot be experienced in any other way. They are more than friends or brothers—they are brothers-in-arms, willing to sacrifice their lives for one another.

The victory was not just a victory over the Caid; it was a moral and emotional victory. It showed each and every rebel warrior that the sacrifices and hardships they had suffered in their lives had been worth the price. It showed them that a better life was possible.

Further up valley, perhaps a day's ride away, the remainder of the camp rode and walked single file. Most were women and children, with a few men for protection.

Tariq, Aseem, Fez, and Margaret walked together. The sun was almost at noon, although walking in the canyon shadows provided some shade.

"Do you think the raid was a success?" Fez asked.

"Of course, Malik is a brilliant general. His plan was a very good one," Margaret answered. "Tariq, what do you think of the plan?"

Tariq was deep in thought. Something had been nagging at him all day; he just couldn't place his thumb on it.

"Tariq!" Margaret said.

"What?" Tariq answered with a startled look.

"Where has your head been all day? What do you think of the plan?"

"Oh, it's a very good one. I'm sure they will be successful. A sneak attack is always the best. With the information they have regarding the kasbah, the Caid won't know what hit him."

"Are you okay? You've been a bit off all day. Are you nervous about the raid?" Aseem asked.

"No, not that. Something else has been bothering me," Tariq said aloud.

"Well, what is it?" Margaret asked.

"Aren't we missing someone?"

"What? Who?"

Tariq couldn't quite put his finger on what was bothering him. It kept nagging at him but he just couldn't figure it out.

"Where is Jawad?" Fez asked.

All three looked at Fez.

"That's it! That's what has been bothering me," Tariq said.

"Wasn't he with the wounded? Let's check there first," Margaret said.

All four quickly made their way to the back of the caravan, where the wounded were being cared for. They went through four wagons, but Jawad was nowhere to be found. They searched throughout the remaining caravan, but nobody had seen him for some time.

"If he escaped, he knows all about the plan. He even knows our escape route and where the new camp will be set up," Tariq said, panic in his voice.

"We must tell the others!" Margaret said.

"Yes, we must let them know we are in danger," Fez agreed.

The four went to Sanaa, who had been put in charge of the caravan, and explained the situation to her.

"Do we know how long he has gone missing?" she asked.

"We last saw him at breakfast; he must have slipped out during the day," Margaret answered.

"We must assume he escaped just after breakfast. That would give him a seven-hour head start. On foot, it is at least thirty miles to the kasbah, depending upon how well he knows the landscape," she thought aloud.

"Can we send a tracker after him?" Tariq asked.

"We don't have any. All our trackers are with the raiding party."

"If he makes it back to the Caid, he can tell him about our camp location, the size of our tribe, how many weapons we have—everything!" Fez said.

Sanaa looked at the four of them. This was a predicament. She really didn't have any choice in the matter.

"We proceed as usual to the new rendezvous point. However, we won't be able to set up camp as we had hoped. We'll need to find a new location and hope the others reach us before the Caid's troops are informed. If not, they'll walk right into a massacre."

The four of them were silent. This wasn't what they were hoping to hear. It was because of them that Jawad was in their midst, and because of him, the entire raiding party might be walking into a slaughter.

Sanaa sensed their despair.

"Listen, it is not your fault. We tried to help Jawad, but some people are drunk with power. We will do as we always do—adapt and survive."

The pep talk helped a little, but they still felt responsible.

"I can't believe Jawad. We rescue him and we care for him and this is what he does to us?" Tariq said.

"You can't hate Jawad, he's just a boy. Remember, he helped you learn to ride a camel," Margaret tried to interject.

"No, I'm also just a boy and I know the difference between right and wrong. Whatever good he did is no excuse. He is my sworn enemy from this point on. I swear, if he turns traitor on us to the Caid, I will find him and destroy him," Tariq said, his anger growing more resolute with each passing moment.

The others could hear the anger in his voice. Nobody tried to console him because, mostly, the others felt the same way. Jawad had no right to put these people in danger after they had nursed him back to health.

Now, there was genuine reason to worry. Nobody knew if the raid was a success and nobody was sure if the Caid knew of their whereabouts. If a kasbah scout picked up Jawad, he could have told the Caid everything by now, and the Caid could be sending troops to meet them at this very moment.

The four walked nervously and silently, hoping that Malik and the others had escaped. They wondered where he was just now and if he indeed had fallen into a trap.

There was something else. Tariq felt down to his chest and his pendant was gone. It was the most sacred thing in the world to him and it was missing. He had looked everywhere, but it was nowhere to be found. Had Jawad stolen it?

The following morning, the sun rose, but no one had slept during the night. The Caid had posted triple guards outside the kasbah gates and walls. He also sealed off all known passages and tunnels. The previous day and night had been spent putting out fires, tending to the wounded, and burying the dead. In all, over thirty of the Caid's soldiers had been killed and six tents had been burned to the ground. The ammunition storage was severely damaged by fire and the rebels had stolen hundreds of rifles and thousands of rounds of ammunition.

The raid, by all accounts, had been a resounding success.

The Caid summoned all his generals back to the war room. Each sat, grimy with dirt and sweat, and tired from not sleeping for over a day. The Caid was dirty and sweaty as well. He walked to each and every one of his generals, looked them in the eye, and moved onto the next. He was looking for weakness.

"General Aqib, you were in charge of security, correct?" the Caid asked.

"Yes, Sire, but only for a couple of days after Zahir left..."

Before he could finish his sentence, the Caid had produced his sword and in one swipe decapitated the general. His head fell to the dirt floor.

The other generals gasped in surprise and fear.

Two guards quickly came and dragged both the head and body of General Aqib out of the room.

The Caid continued to walk and look each general in the eye. Finally, he finished and sat down.

"It is obvious I have been too soft on all of you. It is painfully obvious that all of you have become sloppy in your work. From this day forward, one hundred percent of your focus will be on your work and nothing else—not on concubines, or gambling, or hunting, or eating, or anything else. No distractions. Every one of you, including myself, will be focused on one thing—finding and killing every rebel within a thousand miles of this kasbah."

The generals sat paralyzed with fear. They had seen the Caid's temper, but never like this.

"None of you will be paid a penny. None of you will be allowed to attend festivities or races. None of you will be allowed to have any extracurricular activity of any kind until these rebels are found and dealt with."

The Caid's face was red, his eyes blazed with hatred, and purple veins bulged from his muscular neck.

Nobody dared say a word.

At that moment, the most inopportune moment, a guard presented himself. He stood there, not saying anything, terrified by the anger of the Caid.

The Caid, noticing the guard, turned and looked at him.

"What is it?" he shouted.

"Sire, we have—well, we're not sure what we have. He may be a prisoner, or he may be one of us," the guard stammered out.

"What are you talking about?"

"One of our scouts found a boy about five miles to the east. He was wandering alone. He said he had been captured by the rebels and knew their plans and whereabouts."

This bit of good fortune calmed the Caid considerably. He stared at the guard a moment, thought a moment, and then spoke.

"Bring him in."

Two guards brought in a dirty and scraped Jawad. A large bruise swelled over his right eye where a guard had hit him with a stick. His arms were shackled and his head hung low to the ground. He was nervous about being in the company of the Caid. He glanced around at the large tent and saw the serious, intent looks on the faces of the generals now staring at him. He didn't notice the stream of blood that led out of the room.

Jawad bowed low to the feet of the Caid.

"So who are you?" the Caid asked.

"My name is Jawad. I served as a camel jockey for Your Highness for many years. I was only one win away from being freed from being a slave and allowed to join Your Highness's royal cavalry," Jawad stammered out.

"Why were you with that rebel scum? You seem more like a spy to me."

"No, Your Highness. At my last race I was knocked to the ground. The rebels captured me and held me hostage."

This was mostly a lie, but Jawad thought, correctly, that it would sound better if he said he had been captured.

"So you escaped and ran back to me?" the Caid asked.

"Yes. The rebels are moving their camp. I slipped out of a wagon without being noticed and walked to the kasbah."

Even the Caid was amazed that a former slave would return to his services.

"So where are the rebels headed now?"

"To the eastern most mountain range, to a valley called Divinity's Playground. They are planning to rendezvous with the raiding party tomorrow."

The Caid listened to this information, as did the generals. It was a good bit of information, and the boy seemed sincere.

"What do you think of these rebels? How many are there? How equipped are they?"

"There are perhaps two hundred, half of them women and children. They are not well armed. A few rifles and bows and arrows. That is, until…" Jawad didn't finish.

"Until what?"

"Until yesterday's raid. A major objective was to get a good supply of rifles and ammunition."

The Caid thought this over. What the boy said was true. The rebels had made off with an ample supply of weaponry and ammunition.

"How did they come to know how to attack us? Only a few people have knowledge of our weaponry. They seemed to know everything about our kasbah, even the times we changed the guards. Do they have spies?" the Caid asked.

"I don't know if they have spies. They received the information from Zahir. They captured him just a few days ago, and he provided them with all the information."

This reply angered the Caid. His face turned an even brighter red. Zahir! One of his most trusted officers had turned against him. He would find that fat dog and cut him down.

The Caid studied the boy. He liked him. He looked strong. He was willing to escape capture and make his way back to the kasbah, which showed he was loyal.

"Jawad, you have shown much bravery and, even more importantly, much loyalty. You are welcomed back with open arms into the embrace of my kasbah. Only this time, as a senior cadet in the royal cavalry."

Jawad blushed with gratitude. This was beyond his wildest dreams. To be in the royal cavalry was an honor in itself. To be a senior cadet was unbelievable.

"Thank you, Your Highness. I am humbled by your generosity. You will not be disappointed," Jawad answered.

"General Barak. See to it that this young man is outfitted and joins the cavalry as a senior level cadet."

"Yes, Sire!" General Barak answered.

"Now, young Jawad, please sit with us and tell us everything you know about these rebels," the Caid said and had Jawad sit down at the circle.

Jawad felt very important. For the next hour, he discussed everything he knew about the rebel army—the leadership of Malik, their strengths and weaknesses, their camps. He was even treated to a nine-course meal of the most delicious Moroccan food he had ever tasted.

After his debriefing, he was taken to the cavalry headquarters and given a uniform, a horse, and a bed in the cavalry sleeping quarters. Jawad could not believe his good fortune. His life was set, and he could see his future before him. He would not disappoint the Caid. He would prove himself and move up in ranks and become a great man.

Never once did he think of the rebels and what might become of them because of the information he had provided to the Caid. Never once did he consider that the Caid would slaughter every man, woman, and child in the encampment.

Back at the war room, the Caid and his generals were deciding upon a strategy.

"There's a possibility the rebels know about his escape attempt. If they do, they will just move their camp," General Barak said.

The Caid had considered this.

"Do not worry. I have a plan for crushing this rebel scum. In a short amount of time, they will be wiped from this earth," the Caid said, his black eyes gleaming with hatred, his fists clenched with anger.

The generals all looked at each other. When the Caid had a plan, it was usually a good one. When he decided to crush an enemy, they were crushed. The mood in the room lightened and the generals even smiled. They could not wait to hear how the Caid was going to end this rebellion.

Adventures continue in:

Wrath of the Caid

ABOUT THE AUTHOR

The idea to write the *Red Hand Adventures* first came to Joe O'Neill while he was on safari in Sri Lanka. As he was driving along in an old jeep, under a full moon casting silhouettes of wild elephants against the jungle wall, the image of a rebel orphan in old Morocco popped into his head. While he wishes he could take full credit for coming up with the idea, it was, in reality, a story that was already out there, waiting to be told.

Joe O'Neill is the CEO and founder of Waquis Global, which gives him the opportunity for world travel and the experience of many different cultures.